NIGHT OF THE MOTHER

PRAISE FOR VICTORIA DOUGHERTY

What readers are saying about *Night of the Moon Witch*:

"Bravo on a spell binding read."

"Night Of The Moon Witch is intense and darkly spell-binding."

"Dark, deep and creepy, this book ticks all the boxes."

"If you enjoy reading horror and gothic romance with atmosphere thick enough to cut, I highly recommend this book."

"Dark, graphic, and filled with gore. Loved it!"

"The writing is absolutely beautiful. The prose isn't just functional; it's a core part of the experience."

NIGHT OF THE MOTHER

APPALACHIAN MOON WITCH CHRONICLES

VICTORIA DOUGHERTY

SPEAKEASY
EDITIONS

For mothers and daughters

A WARNING TO
THOSE WHO WANDER

"Did you hear your name whispered on the breeze? *It knows you now.*

Did you glimpse a figure between the trees? *It's already watching.*

The woods hold secrets between dusk and dawn—secrets that hunger. Tread there at your peril.

Never go searching for what dwells in shadow, for it has been searching for you far longer.

Beyond the veil of what you may or may not believe lurks the simple truth: the wilderness claims its tributes with cold indifference. One misstep, and you'll join those lost to creek and swamp.

Twilight isn't merely the dying of day—it's when the boundary thins. When your eyes can no longer distinguish between what is and what hungers.

Listen closely to that distant laughter from the brook. Is it merely water dancing over ancient stone? Or something mimicking sounds it knows will draw you closer?

And should you find yourself sinking into the

embrace of a swamp, miles from help, with no soul knowing your whereabouts...

...the forest will remember your name, even when no one else does."

—Silas Jasper Treadway

1

New Moon

I SHOOT up from my pillow, choking on air as thin as the veil between the living and the lost. The new moon's light is being smothered by a sheath of clouds, making it impossible to see much of anything. My hands scramble across our damp sheets. Everything smells wrong—not just of sweat, but fear, metallic and bloody.

Martin turns to me, his touch bringing me back from that cold, far away place. He lays me down, wiping the tiny pearls of sweat off my brow and kissing each of my cheeks with such tenderness his lips feel like a sprinkle of powdered sugar. Only I can also feel his decades of loneliness—all the years after the Gemini Covenant was made, when he believed I had abandoned him and our daughter. It's an open wound that's neither of our faults, but it's up to us to heal it anyway.

"What was it this time?" he asks.

This time was a lot like the last. And the time before that. The voice—the Bramwell witch's voice—reading my poetry aloud like scripture, hissing seductive taunts the way an old lover would. One who wants nothing more than your total destruction. About how weak I am inside, how unable I am to love, to live as a witch or anything else. That nothing will bring my memories back. She always says it like that's a good thing and I should be grateful for it.

"It's just a dream," Martin says. "You didn't go beyond the veil. I would know."

He would know. He's my anchor when I travel there. The human part of me that keeps the demons away. Literal demons. The evil kind that will devour you if you let them in just an inch.

"It feels so real," I whisper.

"What's real is you and I."

Martin kisses me again. Softly at first, then deeply. I'm still not used to love that feels like a thousand years. Or even a thousand seconds. Sometimes, when we're together like this, I dissolve into tears, shaking like I'm a newborn, learning the terrible weight of skin against skin. But most of the time, we move together in a way that's natural and perfect—honey settling into warm milk.

"Forget the voices," he says. "Listen to mine."

MORNING HAS me reluctant to wash away the night. I stare at my toothbrush like it's an adversary, but then Martin comes into our tiny bathroom and kisses my shoulder. Reminding me he's real and I don't have to hang onto him like a keepsake. As if he's going to disappear like almost everyone else has in my life.

Though sometimes I catch him doing the same—his hand

lingering on my wrist a beat too long when he hands me my coffee, his eyes tracking me across rooms like he's mapping my location. Fifty years of loss doesn't vanish in a few weeks, no matter how many mornings we wake up together.

He steps into the shower and I finish up my morning wash, slipping into one of the wonderful robes I apprehended—ok, stole—from The Montague Hotel. I make my way to the kitchen, putting the coffee on and baking a half dozen eggs with some left-over biscuits. I look forward to watching Martin demolish them with the gusto of someone who remembers hunger with his whole body. Even if he's been rich and fed for the better part of the last two centuries.

I peek out the window and see Colette coming out of her cottage. I wave to her as she picks up today's edition of *The Daily Lantern*, Sibyl Springs' version of the *New York Times*, from her leaf-strewn walkway. She flashes me one of her breasts, and I burst out laughing.

"I love that sound," Martin says, brushing by me. "It's almost wild." He pauses behind me, close enough that I can feel the heat from the shower still radiating off his skin. "I was starting to think I'd never hear it again."

He pours himself a cup of coffee and sits down at our cafe table, looking particularly big for it this morning. The Blacksburg Estate, where he'd been living with our daughter, Soma, until the horrible events of last summer was much more suitable to the way he moved through the world, but neither one of us can even stand to look at the place. And the boho-rustic cottage The Valemont School offers new teachers like me has been like a womb for us these past weeks. A place where Martin has been able to rediscover our love and I've experienced it for the first time.

There's a tentative knock at the door, and I think it's Colette at first, but she'd just walk in.

"You expecting someone?" I ask Martin.

He shakes his head and goes to the door, opening it to a man suited up in navy with French cuffs and a prominent signet ring from Washington and Lee. It sits where a wedding band should be.

"Shelby," Martin says.

"I'm sorry to come by like this, Martin, but it turns out I have to go to Richmond until the end of the week and I figured you'd want to get this squared away."

Martin glances at me and I shrug. "Would you like me to leave the two of you to your business?" I ask.

"Actually," Martin says. "This concerns you."

The man Martin calls Shelby steps inside and holds out his hand, introducing himself as Shelby Carter, from the law firm of Carter, Mullins & Tolliver. He lingers a little too long when shaking my hand, studying my face like I'm a specimen.

"Mr. Carter," I say. I don't quite feel like I want to be on a first name basis.

"Miss Stith, I have for you here some documents from the Blacksburg estate, a few of which I'll need you to sign. I emailed Martin some copies, of course, but we've always done business on the personal around here."

"I appreciate that," I say, although I don't. "But what documents from the Blacksburg estate would have anything to do with me?"

Shelby Carter shoots a glance at Martin, who takes up the conversation.

"Twila, Soma willed her entire estate to the two of us."

My hands flash cold all of a sudden, and I place them behind my back. I can feel them start to numb, spreading from my fingertips to my knuckles. I pull out the cafe chair clumsily and sit down, trying to seem like I did it just to have a few sips of Martin's coffee. "Since when?" I ask.

"It appears she amended her will last winter," Martin says.

"Winter!" Months before I came to Sibyl Springs. Before my job at Valemont even became available! I start picking at my cuticles. "How long have you known about this?"

Martin meets my eyes and reaches out, taking my fingertips and holding them tight. "Since just after we buried her. I wanted to give you time to adjust."

Shelby Carter takes in a long, deep breath that puffs his lips when he lets it out. "I'm very sorry for your loss," he says, but it sounds like congratulations.

My vision starts to tunnel, and I can't stop looking at Shelby Carter's signet ring. Can't stop my heart from pounding so hard I think it might wear out and stop. I try to suppress it, biting my cheeks, inhaling through my nose. I don't want to have an outright panic attack in front of some lawyer.

"Perhaps you can just leave the documents here," Martin says to Shelby Carter. "I'll make sure she signs them."

Shelby knows a thing or two about his client, and the goings on around here. He certainly knows enough to heed Martin's request at once and excuse himself. Even if he's dying to linger. The minute the door shuts, I stand up and go to the window, curling over myself. Martin comes up from behind and wraps his arms around me.

"Jesus, Martin," I say. "She was planning this for months—before I even got here. She knew all along what she was going to do."

"She'd had a lifetime of guilt and reflection about what had happened," he whispers.

"She was a child, for God's sake, when she made that covenant. She was lured into it by that—witch."

Martin turns me around to face him. He puts his forehead to mine and it's like medicine. As I breathe in his scent of clove and bergamot, my heart stops pounding quite so hard and I start to feel my fingers again. His thumbs press into the pulse points at my wrists—steady, rhythmic—like he's manually resetting my heartbeat to match his.

"It's unfair," he says. "I hate it every bit as much as you do. But we bear a responsibility to this world. And child or not, Soma's covenant with the Bramwell witch was a devastating event. One that could extend far beyond us."

"I know that," I say. "And I don't want you to be keeping all of this to yourself. You should have told me. Promise me you won't do that anymore."

"I promise," he says.

Martin starts to make good on that promise right away. He steels himself, then picks up the documents off the table, handing them to me. "You should take a look," he says.

"I don't care about her will," I tell him. "And if it's possible I would prefer never to see the Blacksburg estate again. It's like a haunted castle."

Martin nods, touching his hand to my face.

"I think you should take notice of the date Soma signed these documents," he says. His voice is always such a balm to me, only right now there's an underlying current of reluctance in his tone that makes me want to crawl back into bed and pretend this day never started.

But I'm not going to be a coward on top of everything else. I stare down the thick bundle of papers, then begin paging through them with a rough determination. Soma, not surprisingly, had a lot of assets. Not only had Martin set her up, her late husband, Elliot Blacksburg, who had jumped to his death from the bird tower of The Montague Hotel last summer on literally the day I arrived in Sibyl Springs, had been swimming in Blacksburg money. Despite their nearly ten years-long estrangement, he'd left Soma everything.

And everything was a lot

Apart from the estate itself and its surrounding grounds, it appears Soma and Elliot owned large swathes of land in West

Virginia, Virginia, and Kentucky. They owned mills and mines and held stocks that had been bought for pennies by earlier generations of Blacksburgs and are now worth a fortune. There are Xs marked with tabs every few pages, where it's indicated I should sign. Martin has already done his part. Towards the end of this breathtaking inventory of her world, is Soma's signature, neat and perfect as a Catholic school girl's. Beneath that is the date she'd signed: January 9th of this year.

"Oh, my God," the words come out like a desperate prayer.

It's the day my dean at UVA discovered that I'd been sleeping with his son. Not my shining hour. I was fired shortly thereafter. Had that day never happened, I wouldn't have taken the job at Valemont. I probably would have never come to Sibyl Springs.

I look back up at Martin and drink in his eyes, so full of concern for me I feel a swell of nausea. "I don't suppose there's a chance it's all a coincidence."

"I doubt it," he says. "You haven't yet looked carefully through her portfolio. What's clear to me is that she'd been following you throughout your life. Even the investments she and Elliot made together seemed to be made with you in mind.

"What do you mean? What sorts of investments?"

Martin smiles and takes my hand. "Things that you would like, that cater to your interests. Abandoned churches and monasteries across Appalachia. Some important libraries and an archaeological foundation that has been studying various manuscript collections, including one in particular—The Luna Selenography Collection at the Luna Archive."

"I think I need to sit down again," I say.

Martin guides me to the couch and we sink into its soft, overstuffed pillows, ones courtesy of Colette Montague Fillmore, God bless her.

"You know, after *Moon Child* was anointed by the literati, I tried to get in to see that collection, but got a hard no. The owners of it had been some big secret—at least until two minutes ago—and they wouldn't let anyone near it. I didn't take it personally at the time."

Martin chuckles softly under his breath. While he loves my laugh, I love his chuckle. It's sweet and world-weary all at once, with the soft tenor of a dog's whine running through it like an accent. Typical of a werewolf, I guess, although he's the only one of those I've ever met.

"I'm not even sure what's in the collection," I continue. "Only that it includes some handwritten journals and midwives almanacs, allegedly from a Moravian settlement in the 1800s. Lots of lunar observations and the like." I shrug, staring at the estate documents like they might burst into flame. "Honestly, at the time I just thought it might make good fodder for my poetry."

"Whatever the case," Martin says. "They acquired the collection on a rather auspicious date. June 16, 1997."

"The day I was born?"

Martin's eyes grow distant, as if tracing invisible patterns in the air. "Wish I could have followed you as she did. I didn't even know your full name and had no way of finding you."

"You thought I didn't want to be found."

I look down at our entwined fingers with an ache that borders on reverence—as if I'm holding something sacred that might dissolve if I breathe too hard.

"I still can't believe Soma never told you."

If she had told him about her role in the Gemini Covenant, which smeared my life across the hard concrete, destroying my memories and largely taking my birthright as a moon witch, Martin could've waited for me. He would have known I loved him but that I just couldn't remember him or what we'd been to each other. He could've helped our daughter mitigate the covenant's brutal destruction of our lives, and kept her from believing the only option left to her was slitting her wrists. And now, as I look at her portfolio of riches, backloaded with investments tailored just for me, all I can think about is how useless it all feels. Because I don't want her abandoned churches and collections. I want to know her—the way she sighs in her sleep when she's running a fever, and whether the moonlight cools her brow the way it does mine, or if she burns brighter.

I want my life back.

2

———

Martin's racing green '67 Jaguar announces us a mile before the road winds down to Valemont. I've been self-conscious about arriving with him these past weeks, basically broadcasting to the entire faculty that we're lovers. He's the headmaster, and a famous author besides, and I'm the newly installed chair of literature and poetry. Installed by him. My collection of poetry, *Moon Child*, may have won a handful of heavy-hitting prizes, but I'm still barely twenty-eight. And I was fired from University of Virginia for sexual transgressions, even if that isn't the official line. Word gets around. It always does.

Martin doesn't care one whit about what people think. After everything—the covenant, Soma, the vulture demon—he's done sneaking around. Plus, this is Sibyl Springs, and he's a Blacksburg. That pretty much makes him a pharaoh.

He keeps reminding me that last year's holdovers at Valemont—the teachers who weren't devoured by the vulture demon the Bramwell witch had summoned, and who were likely involved in torturing and trying to kill me—see me as a witch who came close to breaking a Gemini Covenant, and banished their dark mistress from our small place in the world, at least for the time being. I feel the need to point out to him that the new faculty, who Martin and I have brought in from places as variable as University of Chicago and University of Kentucky, might have a different way of looking at things.

"Petal's arriving this weekend," he says.

"I was just thinking about the University of Kentucky," I say. "But I thought she wasn't going to start until spring semester."

"She's not. But she's not a fan of most of her colleagues at U of K, either. Despite where they teach, most of them are coastals, and Petal really doesn't do well with people who are from outside our region."

"A hater? I'm liking her already."

We'd brought in Dr. Petal Whittaker as Valemont's new history department head. Martin used to lead both the literature and history departments, but we've split them up. An expert on Appalachian history and geology, Petal grew up in Abingdon, and her grandmother had known Martin's mother in the years before she died. In other words, she knows all about us. Is one of us. And we need all the allies we can get.

"I'll see you inside," I tell him, closing the heavy, metal door of the sedan. Despite her weight, the Jag is a delicate car that needs gentle handling.

Martin smiles, hesitating.

"Go on," I say. I hold up my hands. "No shaking, heart steady. But I won't be if you keep looking at me like that with those eyes of yours."

"We could go back home," he says. "It's early yet."

Except Clara Newberry is already trotting towards us from her car—a Monte Carlo yellow Saab 9-3 that's at least a decade and a half old, but looks brand new.

"Mr. Martin!" she calls, referring to Martin by his pen name, Langston Martin, the name he goes by at Valemont and when he travels outside Sibyl Springs. "Oh, hello, Miss Stith," she says, nodding at me. "I'm so sorry to interrupt. It's just that Mrs. Pembry arrived unannounced with her checkbook, and is demanding to see you immediately about something concerning her son and his ADHD."

Clara Newberry says "ADHD" like there's a fat period between each consonant, which I always find a little funny. But Martin isn't amused, and I watch his shoulders fall as he exhales. Mrs. Pembry is a major donor whose son is still in the lower school, so we have years yet of having to manage her.

"She's threatening to pull her donation this year," Miss Newberry says, "and is currently pacing in the commons, getting more agitated by the minute, I'm told."

Martin agrees to attend to the matter, however reluctantly.

"Lunch?" he mouths to me and I nod. He squeezes my hand before heading to the side entrance, knowing I don't like walking in together in the morning. It's become my habit to take a short walk along the hiking trails and sit at the edge of Hallow Lake for a few minutes, clearing my head, before I actually enter the building. It fools no one, but allows me the delusion of feeling we're being discreet.

The trail to Hallow Lake winds through stands of white birch that have turned a golden-yellow—almost glowing when backlit by the morning sun. The strange early snowfall last week has melted, bringing back the autumn like it never left. Mist clings to the hollows between roots, and my footsteps on the damp earth sound muffled, as if the forest has something to say, but is holding back. It makes me a little uneasy, but then the lake appears suddenly through the trees—a perfect black mirror. I settle onto the weathered log that's become my makeshift bench.

The silence here feels different from anywhere else, pregnant with secrets the trees have been keeping for centuries. I like to imagine them as secrets about my past that they might one day tell me. Even the birds seem to whisper rather than sing. All except one. Every morning, I look for the white dove that last visited me on the day Soma died—the day the Bramwell witch blew apart the windows at the Blacksburg Estate, nearly killing Martin in the process.

This morning, like the others, the dove is nowhere to be seen. I lean forward, studying my reflection in the lake's dark surface, searching for some sign of peace in my own face. A sign that I'm coming back together and my nightmares are just that and nothing more. Only right then, the birdsong stops entirely. A cluster of wildflowers at my right begin to wilt, turning dry and black, and the water before me ripples without wind. I freeze and watch my reflection begin to shift. My features disburse and reconfigure until what's looking back at me isn't mine. It's a woman, gray-white, ancient, with silver thread gleaming through her lips. They have been sewn shut. When she blinks, words spill from her eyes like tears.

"We've been saving your place," she says. "The others have been so patient."

"OH, MY GOD, MISS STITH!" Grace Goad, my new shadow at Valemont, chases me down as I'm hard-stepping it to Martin's office. Her busy charm bracelet tinkles as she waves her arms *in emergency.* "Your office hours are all booked up and I have to see you *today.*"

"Grace," I say. "Just email me and I'm sure I can get you in."

She looks me up and down, with her big violet eyes, round as a puppy's. "Are you alright?"

"I'm fine," I lie. "Just late."

"You don't look fine."

I'm not fine.

"I am fine. Just didn't sleep well," I say.

"Well, you look frightened, not tired."

Her mountain accent always becomes more pronounced

when she's emotional or excited about her work, so it sounds like "fahr-tened, not tarred," which she's normally self-conscious about.

"What is it you need?" I ask her.

Grace huffs and bites her bottom lip, practically swallowing it. Her dark, unruly hair, pulled back messily, frames her face, which bears the concentrated expression of someone always composing lines of poetry in her head.

"I think I've finished it," she says.

Grace was my very first student who qualified for my independent study in poetry—an independent study being the Holy Grail at The Valemont School. And not only did she qualify, she's been knocking it out of the park. Problem is, my disturbing vision at Hallow Lake feels like more of a priority than an adolescent's poetry project.

But Grace will not be deterred. In her Gillian Welch t-shirt and loosely knitted cardigan, her well-worn jeans that look like they'd once been her dad's, and her cowboy boots, she stands tall looking me straight in the eye.

"The old women in these hills
know things the college boys
in their pressed khakis cannot fathom—
how to pull fever from a child
with nothing but mint and moonlight.
How to pray a man sober
or curse him quiet.

GRANNY'S HANDS, *gnarled as oak roots,*
taught me to gather herbs
when the moon was fat and generous,
to whisper gratitude to the mountain
before taking what I needed.
She never called it magic,

just mountain sense.

BACK HOME THE *nights were sharp—*
coyote cries, the crack of rifles
echoing off ridges,
my boy kissing me hard enough
to leave fingerprints of heat
along my throat.

Now, *in this place of polished floors*
and careful pronunciations,
I hide my knowing like a bruise
beneath long sleeves. But sometimes,
when the moon climbs thin
above dormitory windows,
I feel that pull, that ancient tug
toward something older
than any book they'll hand me."

She closes her eyes and clamps her hands together, her bracelet sounding like one of Lyla's windchimes.

"It's better than anything in last year's *Hollows*, isn't it?" She bites down on her lip, embarrassed she said that, and shrugs. "I mean, it's not like *The Hollows* is *The Paris Review* or anything."

"Grace," I say, clearing my throat because something in that poem—the heat, the rifles, the quiet threat of curse work—caught me off guard. "That was spectacular. And raw."

She looks up, uncertain. "Raw?"

"You're not hiding anymore," I tell her. "At least not in your work."

She looks down at her toes. "Do you think I should read it at 'The Cave' next Wednesday night?"

"The Cave" is Martin's historical fiction club, and he's

folding in some of the poetry and classical literature-minded students, too. He makes it enchanting and wonderful, and I've been looking forward to it like a wedding.

"I think you should," I say, grateful to be reminded of talent and beauty and art and potential despite the dark magic that's been circling around me. "You are a walking page of poetry."

"That's what Caleb says. Well, almost," Grace giggles. "He says that every time I talk it sounds like something that should be written down."

Caleb is Grace's nineteen year-old boyfriend who's in the Marine Corps. I'm sure he's a nice guy—I haven't met him—but I'm making it my mission to make sure she doesn't get pregnant before graduating from Valemont.

"What's that?" I ask.

There's a new charm hanging from her bracelet. An eagle, globe and anchor charm, attached to a compass.

Grace gasps and flushes orangey-pink. "That's a Marine Corps symbol representing freedom and protection," she says, dangling the charm in front of me. "And this," she says, holding up the compass, "means that I'm Caleb's true north."

"Well, that's great," I say. "Just make sure you're concentrating on your words and what you're writing down. You and Caleb have lots of time for the rest."

I know that's easier said than done. During high school, my boyfriend Beckett and I were definitely concentrating on other things. We'd done the wild thing in our school's art closet, on the soccer field, in his mother's dark room, his younger sister's playhouse, the backseat of his dad's car, the front seat, even on the hood. That was the car he died in—Jesus.

"You ok?" she asks.

I run my fingers through my hair and give her the most genuine smile I can muster. "I will be," I say.

She glances over at the door to Martin's office. "I'm sure you will."

Grace arches an eyebrow and turns, practically skipping down the hallway. One of her friends, a queen bee named Rosanna Kingston, pops out from the student salon and puts Grace in an affectionate headlock, blowing a raspberry on her cheek. The two walk arm in arm to class, stitching my heart back together just enough.

The only person who has the power to heal it is in the new headmaster's office, which is Martin's old office. He says he doesn't feel like moving his things, but it's more complicated than that. The old headmaster's office—Soma's office—remains untouched on the ground level of the main building. I like to go in there sometimes to feel like I'm sitting with her.

I'm about to enter Martin's office when Brooks Craven, of the Classical Languages Department, intercepts me. Brooks is part of the old guard at Valemont, which makes me weary of him. But to be fair, he's always been nice, and not every teacher that Martin and I haven't chosen personally is tainted by the Bramwell witch's cult.

"Miss Stith," he says, with a slight fidget. "Would you be so kind as to allow me a few moments of your time?"

Brooks Craven carries himself with the quiet authority of someone who's spent decades conjugating Latin verbs and can quote Ovid from memory. Even if the man isn't a day over forty. He also embodies everything that makes Valemont feel painted into a portrait of colonial America—his habit of carrying fountain pens that match the ones in century-old Valemont class photographs, his tendency to check an actual pocket watch, and the way he seems to know which books are missing from the library before anyone reports them gone.

"By all means," I say.

Brooks Craven takes my elbow and leads me gently away from Martin's office. For someone whose every movement whispers of ancient texts and careful scholarship, he seems almost trembling with academic fervor—like he's discovered a cipher that might unlock centuries of linguistic puzzles.

"I understand, Miss Stith," he says. "That you've secured for yourself a visit to the Luna Archive this evening."

I stop briefly in my tracks, not having expected that one at all. I make my feet start to move again, and do my best to be casual.

"And who would have told you that?"

Brooks puckers his lips. "A little birdy who happens to work for the car service employed by the archivists. Apparently you wish to shuttle yourself to your appointment and declined their offer to pick you up."

"It's hardly that big of a deal," I say.

"Not a big deal! The collection is virtually impossible to access. The owners, whoever they are, must be tremendously impressed with your poetry—and it is, of course, lunar in theme, so I understand the connection. I, myself, found *Moon Child* to be an exquisite work of verse, even if I'm not partial to works that don't follow a strict meter."

This is the first time I've ever actually said more than a few words to Brooks, and I have to admit, that despite his cultivated pomposity, I like him.

"I'm afraid that if you want me to take you with me to my appointment, I'm not going to be able to do that."

Brooks shakes his head. "I wouldn't expect such a thing, no, but I would jump at the chance." He drums his fingers against each other, and I catch a glimpse of genuine scholarly hunger in his eyes—the kind that makes me wonder what else he's been researching. "You see, it appears some of the midwives spoke a Moravian dialect that had long been extinct even in the nineteenth century when they were writing their observations. They were from a remote area in the Jeseníky Mountains, where few people were literate at all, so the prospect of seeing the dialect in its original and written form is a rare, perhaps singular opportunity."

I tell him I really can't promise anything, but will see what I can do.

"Of course," Brooks says, and for a moment his expression grows distant, like he's listening to something I can't hear. Then he blinks and is back, that eagerness returning to his eyes. "The dialect, you understand, has a particular rhythm. Once you've heard it spoken aloud, it stays with you."

He pauses, tilting his head slightly. "Rather like a lullaby you remember from childhood, though you can't recall who sang it to you."

"I thought you said the dialect was extinct," I say.

Brooks smiles, but there's something absent in it, like his mind has already moved on. "Well, extinct things have a way of lingering in the oddest places, don't they?"

He gives a little wave and heads down the corridor, leaving me standing there with the distinct impression that we've been talking about two entirely different things.

3

"You need to tell Martin," Lyla says, lowering herself onto the picnic bench across from me. She's rubbing the little triangle tattoo behind her ear so hard I think she might just erase it. "I can't stand this anymore."

We're under a white oak tree at the little barn store that sells our favorite sandwiches. Martin and I usually eat lunch together in his office, but Lyla called with a tremor in her voice only minutes before the mid-day bell rang.

"I will tell him," I say. "Look. Ly—"

"He's going to find out anyway, and I'd just as well get this over with and throw myself at his mercy."

My head falls like a cabbage into my hands, and I try to take at least a couple of clean, deep breaths. "Please, Lyla. The past few months have been awful enough without the prospect of—"

"Of losing my head. After what I did." Her voice has gone small and hollow. "And I wasn't some baby like Soma. I was eighteen-years-old when I tore that page out of the registry."

A faded pink lock of Lyla's hair falls across her face as her tears begin to stream down.

I reach out and take her hand. "Before we do anything rash, we need to find out more about what exactly is happening and how or if the page is having the disastrous effects that you and Nox and Colette seem to fear. We don't know that. We don't know anything. All we know is that there's a witch out there who not only wants me dead, but wants to get her hands on that old Montague Hotel registry so that she can do God knows what—change history, change time, rule the worlds of the living and the dead." I reach over with my napkin and dab at Lyla's smudged mascara. "For all we know, you ripping that page out may have saved us all, or at least bought us some time."

Lyla takes the napkin from my hand and blows her nose. "You really think so?"

I don't, not for sure, but I nod anyway. The thought of losing Lyla and making Martin have to cast judgement on her makes me sick to my stomach.

"And we've got other things to worry about right now."

Lyla takes a sip of her root beer, her hands still trembling as she lifts the bottle. She smiles down at the owner's toy poodle, who's begging like a champion, and feeds him a piece of salty ham. Anything to keep her fingers busy. "Like what?"

"Soma has left me a virtual treasure map of moon witch archives and various abandoned structures in the region— monasteries, things like that. Feels significant somehow."

"You think she might've known who this Bramwell witch really is, and where my grandmother might have hidden the registry?"

"I wouldn't go that far," I say. "But she knew something, and she had to be careful how she communicated it to me."

"I wish she'd just appear to you and tell you right out like she did after...you know."

"I wish she would, too," I say. "And I don't know why she

doesn't. It's the only way she and I can communicate directly without risking the Bramwell witch eavesdropping."

Lyla takes a huffy breath and shakes her head. "With the way your abilities have been stuttering lately—even under moonlight—it's not surprising that the two of you are having a hard time communicating."

Lyla's right. As much as I want to attribute my general weakness of late to grief, the lump in my throat and cold current in my blood tells me otherwise. Martin keeps telling me not to try so hard, but the fact is, I haven't felt so decidedly human since before I came to Sibyl Springs.

"And something happened today, Lyla."

Lyla's eyes bulge as I tell her about the ancient witch's reflection in Hallow Lake. The awful way her mouth was sewn together and what she said about how the others were waiting for me.

"What did Martin say about that?" she whispers.

"I haven't told him yet. I was going to tell him at lunch, but then you called. Now I'm not so sure. He's got enough on his mind."

"I think he needs to know. In fact, I think all of us should go see Nox before the next moon phase. The man has a preternatural sense for these things and they sure have a way of progressing quickly." Lyla stuffs a biscuit in her mouth and chews slowly, like she's buying more time to steady herself. "And tell Colette I was able to cultivate that mandrake that was giving her trouble. All it needed was some deep, well-drained soil for the love of God. She should come and get it."

"I'll tell her," I say. "But you know, you could've brought it to her yourself. We're five minutes out of town." Lyla curls her lip and promptly ignores what I said. She made a solemn vow when she left Sibyl Springs all those years ago that she'd never return, so it's up to any of us to come see her. Or we have to meet at Nox's, which we haven't done since just before Soma took her life.

"Twila," she says, looking as forlorn as a child who's lost her mother in a crowd. The whole of her mouth droops, as she leans in across the table. "There are some wounds that bleed backward through time."

Part of me wishes we could curl up on a couch all afternoon and watch *The Great British Baking Show* together, like we used to. "I know Sibyl Springs is haunted, Lyla, especially for you."

"I'm not talking about me," she says. "I think yours might be one of those wounds, and I'm scared for you."

THE MARIGOLD HOUSE emerges from the Virginia countryside like a faded daguerreotype, its pale yellow façade glowing against massive oaks. Their branches arch into a cathedral above the slate roof, casting shade in a way that scoffs at the need for air conditioning. As we pull up in Martin's car, the wheels grumble against a gravel drive that's taken visitors for well over a century.

It's the kind of place Lyla would sniff at, but secretly love. The mansion's Greek Revival columns have mellowed from white to cream. Black shutters frame tall windows that catch the late morning light, and ivy climbs the eastern wall in spirals. The wraparound porch sags gently, its floorboards worn smooth by countless footsteps.

"I bet important women once took tea and planned revolutions here," I murmur.

Martin smiles, studying the building with the appreciation of someone who understands old things. "According to the deed transfer, it was built in 1847 by a tobacco heiress who never married. She left it to her niece, who left it to her daughter, who left it to hers. A monstrous regimen of women for nearly two hundred years."

I break into laughter and Martin takes my hand, kissing it. "Come with me, monster," he says, as he performs the semi-complex ritual of powering off his vintage Jag. He swears I picked it out straight off the assembly line the year it was assembled, but I have my doubts about that. "Next you're going to tell me that I used to love handcuffs," I'd told him. His eyes had gone dark at that, mouth curving into something that wasn't quite a smile. "Among other things," he'd said, and left it at that.

We walk to the entrance, where a brass plaque beside the front door reads "The Luna Archive - By Appointment Only," but what strikes me most is the tranquility of the place. Despite being just a few miles from Charlottesville, it feels removed from the world, concealed in its hollow like a citadel where heroes retreat to learn the truths that can save or damn them.

The door whispers open. "Good Afternoon, Mr. and Mrs. Blacksburg!"

A pear-shaped blonde, with lips so thin they look like a faint crack in a porcelain doll's face, introduces herself as Mrs. Honey MacDonald. She's at the deep end of middle age, and appears to know us. At least know the "us" who we were before July 14, 1976, when the Gemini Covenant ripped Martin and me away from each other. Before that time, we had been known as a couple in the region for a few centuries.

"Honey," Martin says, as if he's surprised to see her.

I peer up at him and he gives me an *I'll tell you later* look.

As the owners of the collection, we're welcomed with an esteem that borders on worship, and that feels awkward—at least to me. Martin's used to this treatment, and he and Honey seem to go way back.

"It's so good to see you again," Honey says to me, although to my knowledge, this is our first meeting. "You haven't changed at all."

Martin puts his arm around me and pulls me close. "Mrs.

Blacksburg has been away for a while and we're happy to have her home."

"Well, we've been waiting for you to come and couldn't be more delighted," Honey MacDonald says. "Mrs. Blacksburg—Mrs. Soma Blacksburg—said last winter that it wouldn't be long now. I'm terribly sorry about your loss, I must say. It's one we feel deeply here."

She means it, unlike Shelby Carter, and I appreciate that. "Thank you," I say.

"Mrs. Blacksburg—Mrs. Soma Blacksburg—was eager for you to see the collection. Would you like to do that now, or would you prefer to have some tea first?"

"Right away, please," I say, and Honey MacDonald seems mildly disappointed.

Nevertheless, she ushers us into the parlor, which is decorated exactly as it might have been in the nineteenth century, and has us sit down on a burgundy velvet settee that holds the impressions of every woman who has ever lowered herself onto it with a secret folded into her skirts.

"Wickham," she calls out, and a man appears from behind a door papered to match the wall in the same faded botanical print. He's a dwarf, dressed all in black like a funeral director, and seems irritated by our hostess. But he perks up when she widens her eyes in our direction.

With a new spring in his step, he goes back into the room he came from, and reappears pushing a brass cart loaded with old, leather journals wrapped carefully in waxy paper.

"Mrs. Blacksburg spent decades acquiring these documents," Honey explains. "Moravian midwife journals, property records, genealogies. At first I thought she was simply preserving regional history, but over time I realized she was searching for something specific."

"The registry," I say, the words slipping out.

Honey's expression shifts—relief mixed with caution. "Yes.

The original Montague Hotel registry from 1821. Not the guest book they kept at the front desk, but the other one. The one Beulah Corbin tended until her death."

Martin's grip on my hand tightens.

"I never saw it myself," Honey continues. "But Mrs. Blacksburg was convinced it was hidden somewhere in the region, and hoped these documents—" she gestures at the archives, "—contained clues to its location. She said once that historical documents are like breadcrumbs. Follow enough trails, and you find what's hidden at the end."

Honey stands there, her hands folded at her waist. Wickham's eyes flicker from me to Martin.

"Thank you, Honey, Wickham," Martin says, dismissing them.

Honey purses her tiny lips and nods. Then the two of them leave us alone with the collection, backing away like practiced assistants to a once iconic celebrity.

"How do you know Honey?" I ask Martin.

He plucks a thick, leather-bound journal off the cart and begins unwrapping it carefully. The paper is as fragile as onion skin, and tears even in the care of Martin's graceful fingers. "Her family has known ours for generations."

"You mean, served ours for generations?"

"Yes," he says. "I had no idea about any of this, however. Soma orchestrated it all on her own."

I take the journal from his hands, and it's heavier than it looks. The leather is worn smooth in places, as if someone held it often, fingers tracing the same paths over and over.

"What should we be looking for?" I say. "Apart from what our long dead Moravian friends observed in moon cycles and the like."

Martin unwraps another journal, this one bound in midnight blue leather with silver clasps. "I'd say anything that suggests why Soma believed these documents were crucial enough to acquire."

I open the first journal, its pages releasing the scent of old parchment and something floral and familiar I can't quite place. The Moravian script is dense and precise, filled with lunar observations and what appear to be midwifery notes. But as I run my finger along the margins, the pages feel warm beneath my touch, like the head of a feverish child.

"Martin," I whisper. "This doesn't feel right."

He looks up from his own journal, eyebrows raised.

"The paper. It's..." I pause, studying a page more closely.

Along the margin of a page documenting a difficult birth in 1836, there are faint impressions—as if someone has pressed their fingers repeatedly into the paper. But these aren't the impressions of the original writer. They're more recent, and almost seemed to glow faintly under the archive's soft lighting.

Martin sets down his journal and leans over my shoulder. His proximity, normally so comforting, can't keep the hair on my arms from rising. "Someone's been handling these documents repeatedly," he says quietly. "and within the past few hours, I'd say."

"Not just somebody," I say. "Whoever was handling them was a witch."

I flip to another page, this one containing genealogical charts of local families. The Bramwell name appears several times, traced in a delicate script that notes births, deaths, marriages. But here too, spectral fingerprints have worn certain entries nearly transparent—particularly the ones relating to my branch of the family tree.

"Martin, look at this." My voice comes out strangled. There aren't only old eighteenth and early nineteenth century entries from the midwives. Bramwells, whether by human hand or not, have been documented all the way until the last of our bloodline. Someone has been tracing over my mother's name, over and over, until the paper is fine as tissue. Lavinia Bramwell, born 1977. Below it, connected by a careful line, is my own name: Twila Bramwell Stith, born 1997.

But it's what appears in the margin that makes my blood turn cold and thin. Burned into the paper, so faint it's barely visible, are tiny words scrawled in a persistent script that most definitely doesn't belong to any of the Moravians. They're fragmented, lyrical, strange: *the night carries me in her black skirts. Your name is a stone/your name is a thorn/your name is a wound in my mouth.*

"Sweet St. Romedio," I breathe.

"Sounds vaguely like your poetry," Martin says. "But it's not."

Martin reaches for another journal, this one covered in faded green linen, and lays it on his lap. On instinct, I place my palm on it like I'm swearing on a Bible. As soon as my fingers touch the fabric, images flood my mind—not memories of my own, but impressions left by someone else. A woman, her face obscured by a thick curtain of her hair, sitting in this very room, night after night in the dark, studying these same documents. Weeping over them. Not tears of sorrow, but of rage that seemed to burn the pages where they fell.

"She's been coming here for months," I say. "Maybe years. The Bramwell witch—it must be."

I turn the page of the journal on my lap and find a catalogue of my personal landmarks, like recorded entries for a diary. None of them are written in Soma's hand—of that I'm sure. My first words and first steps, my part-time jobs and later, poetry awards. But also, our summer trips to Smith Mountain Lake, noting the summers when Beckett started joining us, my graduation from William and Mary, my job at UVA, and my firing. Some are mundane details written with an unsettling precision: a night when I awoke screaming at the age of seven, the dress I wore at Dad's funeral, the hour I first kissed Beckett, down to the minute. Things I didn't even remember from the one life I did have a memory of. Then, there was a last, cryptic line that put a prickly lump in my throat. *He will question the shape of her shadow when the leaves turn.*

My mouth goes dry as bone dust. "She knows everything about me, Martin."

His breathing changes, deepens. It's the kind of breath you take before a fight. The tendons in his wrist stand out like cords under tension, and when he speaks, his voice is carefully neutral in a way that makes it all seem even worse. "Every moment of the life you do remember. The one life the covenant left you."

The air in the parlor suddenly feels heavy, oppressive. The early evening light streams through the windows dimmed, as if clouds are gathering outside. But when I look out, the sky is clear.

Martin touches my cheek and stands up. He goes to the wallpapered door, pushing it open. I can hear him talking to Honey and Wickham, the two of them expressing shock and disbelief that feels genuine. Swearing that the items hadn't been disturbed in years—not since Soma Blacksburg studied them when she first bought the collection.

"The waxy paper is specially made and keeps the contents in remarkable preservation," Wickham explains. "But it's fragile. It binds to the book covers and tears easily in any attempt to remove it. We would certainly know if the items had been wrapped and rewrapped."

When Martin returns to the parlor, Honey MacDonald follows. Her skin is ashen, her lips red and raw as a fresh papercut.

"We've taken every precaution," she says. "We bless in morning and night. Nobody gets to see the archive. Not even the most illustrious inquisitors have crossed our threshold. We even denied Stephen Hawking!"

"It's not an accusation, Honey," Martin says. "I was stating a fact. And one you should be mindful of for your own safety, as much as the integrity of the archive."

Honey swallows and takes in a jagged breath. Her eyes fall on the stack of journals and stay there, like she's afraid of ever losing sight of them again.

"Mrs. MacDonald," I say, and her attention snaps to me. "If she comes back—"

"We won't let her—"

"When she comes back," I correct, and watch understanding settle into her face. "Don't try to stop her. Just... stay alive. Call Martin immediately."

Honey's throat works. She nods once, sharp and horror-struck.

But something tells me that no matter how vigilant she and her cohort, Wickham, plan to be in guarding the Luna Selenography, they won't be able to keep it away from the witch who's been studying it, studying me. And it's probably too late, anyway.

4

I wait until Martin is deep asleep until I sneak outside onto the porch. The rocking chair creaks against the weathered floorboards as I lower myself into it. The mountain air carries the faintest hint of woodsmoke drifting down from someone else's sleepless vigil.

"Sometimes the best thing you can do is sit still and let the world sort itself out around you," I whisper. It's something Dad used to say, and I decide, at least tonight, to take his advice.

The darkness beyond the porch stretches thick as velvet. The taste of approaching autumn—that metallic edge that promises frost—coats my tongue as a waft of Colette's night-blooming cereus hits my nostrils with narcotic sweetness. One that reminds me of the heavy perfumes that rich old women like to wear.

I brought with me the hand-bound field notebook Martin gave me as a gift late in the summer, after he'd returned from roaming the mountains to grieve Soma. I run my hand along its sun-faded indigo cover and open it to where I left off. At a poem I wrote for Martin on the night he came home to me and stayed.

You came back smelling of stone,
of pine,
as if the mountains had worn you—

AND *I,*
    still bleeding from the root of her absence,
    remembered—

HOW YOUR HAND *was once*
    the fire at my throat,
    the balm at my wrists,
    the only thing that steadied the river in me.

I HAVE *no daughter now*
    but I have you—
    your body bent by grief
    your eyes carrying storms.

W*HEN* I *TOUCHED YOU,*
    memory struck like lightening:
    love,
    feral and endless,
    rising through the ruin
    to claim me whole.

I close the notebook and let it rest against my chest, the poem's words still echoing in the night air around me. For a moment, everything feels suspended—even my own breathing—and I feel Martin's love as something older than the trees, something in the very soil of this place.

Then the air changes.

The sweetness of Colette's night-blooming cereus turns cloying and rotting, as if the coming winter has claimed them in seconds. Even the woodsmoke that had been drifting down from the distant cabin now carries the acrid bite of something that shouldn't burn.

I feel it before I hear it—a presence settling into the space beside me.

The empty rocking chair begins to move.

Not a gentle sway from a night wind, but a deliberate, measured rhythm. Back and forth. The weathered wood creaks in perfect time, as if someone has been waiting all along for me to finish reading, waiting for that precise moment when the last words of love fade into the night.

Never leave a rocking chair rocking, or you'll invite spirits.

Lyla's warning crawls up my spine like a hairy spider, and I can't do anything but watch that empty chair rock with the predation of something that has all the time in the world.

The notebook slips from my fingers and hits the porch boards with a sound like a gunshot, and I jump up from my seat.

"Stars above, Twila!"

I hadn't even heard Colette coming up the porch stairs. She's looking at me the way everyone's been looking at me these past few weeks, only more so.

"What are you doing up?" she says.

"I could say the same thing."

"You could. Only I don't have anyone tall and handsome to snuggle up with on my queen-sized." She takes a cigarette out of the pocket in her robe, lighting it with a match bent out of a pack she took from Buzzy's. She offers me the first drag and I take it. Lyla, Colette, and I all started smoking again after the events of last summer, and none of us feels the least bit sorry about it.

"What's on your mind," she says, easing into the now still and steady rocker.

I remain standing, looking out into the dense rampart of trees. It's hard to get the words out. "I have been having trouble seeing."

"You need glasses?"

"Stop it," I say. "You know exactly what I mean."

I glance over and watch Colette fold her arms under her breasts. They somehow manage to look twice as big in her worn cotton robe the color of a sugared violet.

"Maybe even the spirits are giving you some space," she says. "You know Lyla called me today."

"That was fast," I say.

"An ancient witch with her mouth sewn shut?"

I nod.

"Damn these old mountains," she whispers.

I sit down next to Colette, making sure I keep the rocker still. An occupied rocker doesn't have any superstition attached to it, but I'm not taking any chances.

"Lately, Colette, it's not just that I've been feeling drained and listless. Something's following me. Only it's been following me for a long time, so I don't know why I'm just feeling it now."

"Her?"

"Can't think of anyone else it would be, can you?"

Colette shakes her head. "As for this seeming to have suddenly come on...we both know time doesn't work like that. Especially for someone like you."

I close my eyes, cinching my lips together. Wanting to cry, but not going there. "I thought after finding out about who I am, and all that I was able to do, that I would get stronger. Isn't that how it's supposed to work?"

Colette takes a deep drag off her smoke, then hands it to me again. I pull hard, wet-lipping the filter.

"Twila," she says. "Just because you've got a knack for rhythm doesn't mean you know the dance steps."

Only Colette knows how to make me laugh in the depths of my misery.

"I'm not trying to be funny," she says. "Well, maybe a little. What I mean is, moon witches may have a different nature than regular folks, but we're still a part of nature. Our abilities have to be cultivated, and are subject to our emotions. If you're not feeling right, your talents will manifest differently. And there's really not a thing you can do about it, so you may as well say a prayer and have a little faith."

Colette pushes herself up from the rocker and leans over me, kissing the top of my head. "Now, go back inside and get some sleep. Don't you have school tomorrow?"

I shake my head. "Fall break. Four glorious days of nothing."

"Well get some sleep anyway," Colette says.

I watch her walk back toward her cottage, hips swaying, cigarette perched between her peace fingers. As her silhouette melts into the dark, the night-blooming cereus releases another wave of sweetness—but underneath it now, I catch something else. Something even deeper. It smells like old graves and patience.

5

It takes longer than the usual hour to reach the road that takes us to Widdershins Hollow. City dwellers looking to take in the fall colors have already begun their incursion and are clogging up the highway, even if the colors won't be at their peak for at least another week.

The breeze catches the early autumn leaves as we turn onto what could generously be called a road—more accurately, it's two tire ruts separated by a stubborn ridge of wild grass and Queen Anne's lace gone to seed.

"First gear still sticks," Martin says, making Selene comply whether she wants to or not. He isn't a fan of my Jeep, nor of any car made after nineteen-seventy.

But with four-wheel drive, we can pull all the way up to Nox's place and I resist the urge to point that out.

Martin rolls down his window and takes in the air, contentment softening the edges of his mouth. He doesn't just have a love of the outdoors, he prefers them, and looks as natural within their confines here as a true wolf.

The leaves dance in spirals around the car windows— yellow birch and scarlet maple spinning past like confetti from some woodland celebration. Where last night's darkness felt heavy with secrets, this dappled light reveals everything and nothing at once.

When we pull up next to Nox's cabin, the place seems deserted. One of the old Virginia license plates that Nox uses as roof shingles is conspicuously crooked, as if it might fall off any moment, and the grass is long and dotted with dandelions well past their prime. The only thing that's been given attention is his blessing-in ritual. Little hanging thuribles dangle from tree branches, gutters, and anything that will have them, full and smoking with black salt ash as a stern warning to the dark forces that lurk at the edges of the spirit realm.

"Looks like he may have had a rough night," Martin says.

It isn't until we get out of the car that I finally spot Nox, sitting in his window at the little cafe table near his kitchen. His eyes land on me like a slap on the face. Martin swivels his head, and that's when Nox's expression mellows. He gets up from the table and a moment later, the door opens and he beckons us inside.

There, the vibe of general neglect continues. A crocheted blanket, tattered all over, lays in a colorful pile on top of his fully reclined recliner. It's clear he's been sleeping there and not his bedroom. Cups and glasses are strewn about, and when I glance into his galley kitchen, I can see a pile of dirty dishes. The place smells like a witch's nursing home, where a potpourri of herbs for warding off bad juju might be deployed as much to keep the old conjurers safe from spiritual harm, as to cover up the stink of their failing bodies.

"How are you doing, Nox?" I ask him. "Have you been sick?"

The man is bleary-eyed and looks like he's downed five cups of coffee just to stay standing.

"Yeah," he says. "I've been sick."

. . .

MARTIN and I clean the place up while Nox watches us with only the vaguest interest.

"Do you think we should call a doctor?" I whisper to Martin, but he shakes his head. Maybe he's seen him like this before.

Outside in Nox's garden, I pluck and pull my way to some collards and turnip greens, plus two sweet potatoes the size of small loaves of bread. I light a fire in Nox's living room to chase away the chill, which is still lingering despite it being mid-afternoon. Then I get to cooking while Martin does his best to tidy up the outside. I peel and grate the potatoes, throwing them into a bowl with some flour and a couple of eggs. I know Nox keeps a bounty of herbs in his pantry, some still hanging to dry and others stored in sachets—unlabeled, since he knows how to tell herb from herb by smell alone. The sachets are piled up in a woven basket that sits just under the sign Nox hung there, as if to remind himself of his mission in life. Its burnished wood is carved with the Latin phrase "*Custos Noctis,*" Guardian of the Night. I start rifling through the basket, looking for the basics: sage, thyme, and rosemary.

At the bottom, my finger catches on a twine of some sort, soft like it's made of leather. I pull it up from the basket, staring in disbelief. Hanging from the leather cord like it's no big deal, is my wooden pendant. The exact triangle carved with Lyla's careful hands, the stick figure with its crossed pick-axes, the same tiny imperfection where her knife slipped on the left edge.

It's the pendant I lost when Sam Ralls drove us into Hallow Lake last summer. I can still feel the sharp tug against my throat as the leather cord snapped during impact, the emptiness against my chest as I fought my way to the surface through the dark summer water.

The pendant stayed behind in those depths, sinking with

the wreckage of Sam's Range Rover and everything I thought I understood about my life.

Yet here it is, bone dry and unharmed. The leather shows no water damage, or signs of having spent time at the bottom of Hallow Lake. The wood bears no warping or discoloration from submersion. It looks exactly as it did the day Lyla pressed it into my palm, uttering blessings and desperate prayers for my safety.

My first instinct is to call for Martin—to show him this impossible thing and let him make sense of it. But something stops me. A prickling at the back of my neck. The sudden awareness of being watched.

"Sss-mor-sheth, sss-mor-sheth."

The susurrous whispers come from behind me and I still.

"Sss-mor-sheth, sss-mor-sheth, true face hiding, true face death..."

"Nox," I say.

I can feel his eyes on me, like they're boring into my skull. With a slow, careful turn on my heel, I start to pivot, but before I can move even a quarter, the red-hot tip of an iron poker—the one I left in Nox's potbelly stove—rises up next to my face. It's so close I can hear it sizzle.

"Sss-mor-sheth, sss-mor-sheth," Nox whispers, his lip curling in disgust.

6

"Nox," Martin's voice comes from outside, drifting through the cracked kitchen window. "If you don't put that down this instant, you'll find it shoved down your throat before your heart can drum another beat."

Martin doesn't wait for that beat. A blur of him shoots through the window, smashing the glass, his shoulders splintering the frame. He doesn't shove the poker down Nox's throat as he threatened but he does knock it out of his hand, the red hot tip landing against the basket of dried herbs. That bursts into flame, and I rush to put it out with two pitchers of sweet tea I made for our early dinner. By the time I turn around, Martin has dragged Nox outside, where he's shaking him by the shoulders, upbraiding him in a low growl that even makes my skin burst into goosepimples.

Nox won't look him in the eye, but he does cast a glance at me in a way I don't like at all. I see fear, confusion...and shame.

"Martin," I say from behind the screen door. "I think we all need to sit down and talk."

. . .

I MAKE another pitcher of sweet tea and pour us each a glass. I'm not going to lie, I put a splash or two of bourbon in mine. Martin hardly drinks, and I want Nox to be sober as a judge. We sit down at the cafe table next to the kitchen, giving Nox the window seat.

His hands tremble as he reaches for his cigarette case. He lights a smoke and takes a long drag, the ember etching dusk-lines across his weathered features. "I was young and stupid and lonely as hell out here in the woods," he begins. "And she was fragile. Not beautiful exactly, but pretty in a way that felt like she was made for me." Nox's eyes find mine. "I didn't know she'd come from beyond the veil at first."

Martin's jaw tightens. "You had an affair with a corrupted witch."

"I didn't know she was corrupted. Not right away. Sweet as an elderflower cordial, she was. And don't look at me like that, Martin. You lived with a witch from beyond the veil for coming on six-hundred-years."

"What happened?" I ask.

"I wish I could say I suspected something. But I didn't. Not even a little feeling like the scratch at the back of your throat right before you get the flu." Nox takes a sip of his sweet tea and I feel a tinge of regret about withholding the bourbon. He looks like he can use it.

"You remember back in—I don't know seventy-seven or eight, when that little boy went missing out here for over a week?" He glances up at Martin, as he rubs the back of his neck.

Martin nods.

"Yeah...the Jeffers boy," Nox continues. "Fishin' at Blue Hole, summer sun on his hair, laughing...gone in a blink when his pa turned around to pick a grape Nehi out of the cooler. I was out there, down by the creek, lookin' for him. Part of the search party. I thought maybe he'd slipped, maybe the water took him. But no, it wasn't the water."

Nox crosses his arms and looks out the window like it's a portal to another time. A time when he was young and the rhododendrons near the walking path had just begun to grow wild. It would've been when he was still driving the sky blue mid-seventies Ford F150 that I've seen in a couple of his old photographs. A car I'd probably driven in when it was new, assuming he got it before July 14, 1976.

"I actually took some time out to gather some beechnuts that day, and pick the wild blackberries that were growing near the treeline. Thought she'd like those." Nox's voice trails off. His hand drops down onto the table making our glasses rattle. "That's when I seen her," he whispers. "On the damp, leafy ground bent over the Jeffers boy. His legs were bare and I could see the red and white Puma runners he was still wearing. The ones in the picture they handed out to help us find him."

Nox rolls his cigarette between his fingertips and licks at his chapped lips. It's like he isn't talking to me and Martin anymore, but to some invisible confessor.

"Only it weren't her," Nox says. "Not the woman I'd killed myself for, the one I wanted in every damn way, and followed like a fool. And she knew...she'd always known exactly how I wanted to see her. That tilt of her head, that little smile with lips like a babydoll's...made my stomach burn, my chest hot and cold. Turned my lungs to stone, so as I couldn't breathe."

Nox is shaking his head slowly with his eyes half-closed. He looks torn up, like a man recounting a war story he's never before put to words. One that tells of a stain on his conscience made of blood and guts and broken promises. The kind of sin that seals your fate in hell no matter what good deeds you try to paper over it. I meet Martin's eyes and take a deep swallow of my bourbon tea. That's when Nox opens his eyes wide and looks right at me—right through me.

"No matter what it was she wanted me to see, that day I saw the other, too," he says. "Skin pale like nacre with an icy luster. Hands too long, fingers curling like claws...eyes black and shiny, like deep water at night under a wisp of moon. Goddamn nearly died right there. And then you know what she did?"

"No," I mouth.

"She bent over the boy, a smile paintin' her face. Her tongue darted at his lips, and she put her whole mouth over his. But it wasn't a kiss, or not what you would think of as a kiss. She was taking something from him, or maybe putting something in him, too. When she lifted her head back up, silver strings, tiny and wet, pulled from his mouth to hers. Thin as hair, slick, sticky...shining like dew on a spidersweb. And then...oh, God... something slid out of him. Pale and wriggling. A slug that she held in her hand like a pearl. She glanced over at me, her eyes temptin' and mockin' at the same time. I wanted to say something, but I didn't. Then she lifted him up. Easy, like he was nothing more than a rag doll. Didn't rush. Just walked off with him. I should've done something. But my feet weren't havin' it."

Nox leans in closer to me. So close I can smell his breath of tea and smoke.

"Later, they found him. Whole. Talking. Laughing. Like nothing had happened. And everyone said he was fine. Me? I burned everything she touched. Every scrap, every feather, every shard of glass. Every damn day since, I've put black salt in the trees, in the burners. Holy water, blessings, curses. And still... I feel her. In the smoke, in the umbras, in the wind. I guess I always knew it wasn't ever gonna be enough."

"And the boy?" I ask. "Does he still live around here?"

Martin's voice, soft and low, breaks through the sad and dirty spell Nox's story has cast.

"Years later," he says. "I was living in Abingdon, but it was on the news. The Jeffers boy, grown by then, burned down the orphanage at Parson's Draft. Every child. Every crib. Every toy.

He just did it one day. No warning. He'd been working at the Montague as a bookkeeper, and called his wife to tell her he wouldn't be home for dinner. If I remember correctly, his wife was expecting a child."

Nox is nodding as he blows smoke out of his lips. "They gave him the lethal injection in '98," Nox says. "I'm told he didn't ask for a minister or nothing. No last meal. Went to his death as cool as a cucumber."

Outside, the wind picks up, rattling the bone chimes that hang from Nox's eaves. The sound is like skeletal fingers tapping against glass.

I look down at the pendant still clutched in my palm, the wood warm from my grip. Then I down the rest of my bourbon. "Nox," I say quietly. "How did you get this?"

His eyes, still haunted by the memory he's just exhumed, shift to the pendant. Something flickers across his face—recognition mixed with a weariness that seems to age him another decade right before us.

"Found it," he says, but the word comes out wrong. Too quick. Too rehearsed.

Martin leans forward, his voice dropping to that dangerous register that bends the room around his words. "Found it where, exactly?"

Nox stubs out his cigarette with more force than necessary, grinding it into the ashtray until nothing remains but shredded paper and scattered tobacco. He reaches for another, his fingers fumbling with the case. When he finally gets it lit, he doesn't take a drag right away. Just holds it there, watching the smoke curl upward like a serpent charmed from a basket.

"She left it for me," he whispers. "Three nights ago. Right over there."

He points out the window, past his shed, to the wooded area just outside the blessing. The pendant suddenly feels heavier in my hand.

"Why would she do that?" I ask.

Nox stands up slow and stiff, and walks to the front door. He leans on the frame and stares out the screen door. "I don't really know," he says. "I heard her voice, and I took a can of kerosene and a lighter with me. Some herbs that make her kind choke. I was gonna burn her, but by the time I got there, she was gone."

"And you thought I was her?" I ask.

"Doesn't matter what I thought," Nox says, then pushes open the door, letting it slam behind him.

The silence he leaves behind feels heavier than his words. I look down at the pendant in my palm—this impossible thing pulled from Hallow Lake, delivered by a corrupted witch. The wood is warm from my grip, or maybe from something else. My thumb traces the familiar grooves Lyla carved—the crossed pick-axes, the tiny imperfection where her knife slipped. It feels right in my hand. Feels like it belongs there, like it always has.

I slip it into my pocket. My hand stays there for a moment, fingers curved around the wood. Martin's gathering our things, his movements efficient and tense. Outside, I can hear Nox pacing on his porch, the boards creaking under his weight.

"We should go," Martin says quietly.

I nod, feeling the pendant's warmth through the fabric. Mine again. Safe again. The thought settles into me like a sigh of relief. A secret that wants to be kept.

7

Waxing Crescent

WE WALK IN SILENCE, Martin and I, leaving Nox's cabin behind like one of my bad dreams—one we promise not to speak of. A thurible dangles from Martin's finger, swinging on a chain. Smoldering blessed ash puffs from its seams, creating a faint cloud around us. The afternoon has begun to change into its evening attire, the light taking on that quality peculiar to October in the mountains—as if the sun is filtering through honey and smoke before it reaches us.

Martin moves ahead on the narrow path, his body remembering the way without thinking. I watch the set of his shoulders, the sure-footed placement of his feet on uncertain ground, and something in my chest pulls taut as a bowstring. He glances back once to check on me.

"Are you sure we should be leaving him alone?" I ask him.

"Nox has lived most of his life alone," he says.

The path winds upward through a forest that has just begun its transformation. Sourwood trees stand in their wine-dark glory, their leaves the color of old blood against the fading green of late-blooming asters. Here and there, witch hazel has started to unfurl those strange, spidery yellow flowers that bloom when everything else is dying.

I breathe it in—the smell of decomposing leaves and pine resin, cold stone and the weight of time itself beneath it all. Something that makes my body hum with recognition even as my mind fumbles in the dark.

We climb steadily, my thighs beginning to burn with the exertion, and Martin slows his pace without comment. Somewhere above us, a crow calls out—three sharp cries that make my shoulders tense. Martin turns around.

"Nothing will hurt us where we're going," he says.

The path narrows further as we climb, forcing me to walk directly behind him. I find myself watching the way his body moves through the landscape, how he seems to be *of* it rather than merely *in* it. Every so often, his hand reaches back without looking, palm open, waiting for mine. And every time, my fingers find his before my mind can question the gesture.

We round a bend, and the trees suddenly give way.

The rock outcropping emerges from the mountainside like an altar, a broad shelf of stone beneath a natural overhang that creates a shelter exposed on three sides. The view opens onto the valley below—where the tiny cluster of lights that is Sibyl Springs comes into view.

But it's the evidence of old fires that stops me cold. Blackened rings in the stone, char marks against the overhang's ceiling, the kind of marks that come from years—decades—centuries—of fires built and tended in the same place. My fingers itch to trace them.

Martin hangs the thurible from a blade of rock and goes to the edge, standing with his back to me, looking out over the valley as the wind picks up and brings with it the scent of coming rain.

"We used to come here," I say.

Martin doesn't turn around, but he nods. "Before there was a town. Before there were roads or names for any of it."

I move closer to him, feeling strangely, unreasonably shy. The stone beneath my feet feels warm despite the cooling air, as if it holds heat from some long-ago sun. I see carved marks in the rock face—symbols and patterns that my conscious mind doesn't recognize but my fingers trace anyway, following lines I know are etched somewhere in the memories that have been stolen from me. Ones Martin relives every day.

"How long?" I whisper.

Martin finally turns to face me. The failing light catches in his eyes, making them seem to glow from within. "Long enough that these mountains were sharper then. Long enough that the stars looked different."

A shiver runs through me that has nothing to do with the October chill. Behind us, deeper in the shelter, I can make out a natural depression in the stone—a place where two bodies might fit together, protected from wind and rain and the watching eyes of the world.

This is where we had been. Where we had loved and fought and told each other our truest fears. Where we had weathered storms together.

And I feel not even a trace of deja vu.

The wind gusts again, stronger this time, and somewhere in the distance—too far to matter, too close to ignore—something moves through the trees with deliberate care. Martin hears it, too. I watch the wolf rise to the surface of him, just for a moment, his head tilting to catch a scent I can't perceive, his body coiling with a vigilance he tries to hide.

Then he forces it down, turns back to me, and holds out his hand.

"Come here," he says. "Let me show you."

And despite the approaching dark, despite the watching trees and the stirring wind, despite every instinct that whispers of danger at the edges of this perfect moment—I go to him.

MARTIN'S SMILE is never sweet. It's honest. It can be beautiful. Tender. But it's almost sweet tonight—perhaps because we're here, where we've been so much to each other for so long. Above us, a waxing crescent hangs in the deepening blue— barely born, but sharp enough to draw blood from the sky. We will be nowhere near our strongest under it, he and I. The full moon is another two weeks away. The heavens are clear as a mountain stream, however, and for the first time in weeks I feel its power surge through me unfettered. My skin glows like a pearl, my bones visible beneath the surface. When I take in a breath, I feel as if I can take the world with it.

Martin watches me. To him this isn't some outlandish new creature, but the woman he's known for over half a millennium. As familiar as the mountains that stand brooding around us. He picks up my hand and brings my palm to his lips, the blue-white gleam of it illuminating his face as he kisses me there. Then he lets go of my hand and steps back, standing in the scant light of our great mistress.

My eyes stay trained on his and I watch his pupils dilate until there is almost no iris left, just a burning gold-grey at its edges. I can tell the difference in his breathing without looking away from them. His chest rises and falls deeper, faster, more like an animal's, and his scent changes. A salted, feral smell mixes with his soap of clove and bergamot, overwhelming it until it's only a subtle note that lingers. I watch his jaw set differently, his teeth visible when he parts his lips.

I can't help it, I start to shake. I'm not afraid of him, but I am afraid. I've only seen glimpses of his wolfen self. During the weeks we've been together at the cottage, even with the moon shining through our curtains as he holds me at night, he's remained a man. What frightens me is that he'll feel like a stranger.

"I want to see all of it," I whisper. He steps closer and I try to lighten the mood with a smile. "It's not like I haven't seen it before."

Martin leans over me and kisses my cheek. After, his change isn't the slow shift I saw with his eyes and his breathing. This is sudden, like a strong, cold wind. His muscles shift with a tremor, not quite grotesquely, but with a brutal efficiency. He turns his head employing the fluid grace of water, but there's a power in his movements that's barely contained and speaks of instinct over emotion. I think of the way he caught my Jeep as she flipped in the air last summer. The way Abner Chitwood's head smacked hard against the cocoon of horrors the vulture demon wrapped me in, then fell to the ground like a coconut.

I look down at Martin's hands. They tore Abner's head clean off with the ease of opening a pickle jar. They're still human hands, but the fingers curve differently—bent toward some violent purpose. The tendons are more visible, drawn taut beneath his skin, and the joints seem more flexible. Capable of movements that shouldn't quite be possible. And there's a ready tension in them, fingers shaped around an invisible throat, testing the air for something living to close upon.

This is who I lived with for days that turned into weeks and months and years and centuries. We moved through the world wearing careful faces, saving our true forms for the stolen hours when no one else could see. I realize now how all these weeks he's been constantly gentling himself in my presence.

And now he comes even closer. His hands—unchanged, still curved for violence—come to rest on either side of my face. The touch is firm and exacting. Not gentle. But mine.

I look up at him—at the truth of what we've been together

—and something in me that's been holding its breath finally exhales. I thread my fingers through his hair, tilting my face to the moon above him. When my eyes find his face again, I know they're different. I can see them reflected in his eyes. Bright and terrible. If Beckett had ever seen them, he would've gasped, maybe screamed. He might have run. But to Martin, they're home.

"What are you waiting for?" he says.

I don't wait. I crush my mouth to his in a way that would crush another man's skull.

8

"**M**iss Stith?" Grace's voice comes soft through the half-open door.

I look up from Soma's desk—her expensive Mont Blanc in my hand—and see her taking in the scene. Me in Soma's chair. Whatever expression is on my face.

She starts to back away. "I can come back—"

"No," I say. The word comes out rougher than I mean it. "Come in."

Grace stands in the doorway wearing dark jeans and a rust-colored cardigan over a white thermal, her hair caught up in a hasty bun. She has the look of someone who's been shelving books all afternoon—a canvas tote bag slung over one shoulder, ink smudges on her fingertips.

"I'm sorry to intrude," she says. "But Miss Newberry said Miss Blacksburg kept a collection of the bound volumes of *The Hollows* in here."

I take in a breath and Soma's scent comes with it, still haunting this place—Fracas and old paper, that white floral sharpness of tuberose that never quite faded.

"What are you up to?" I ask. "Fall break's got another two days left and I thought you'd have gone to see Caleb."

Grace gives a disappointed huff. "Caleb's on duty, and I need the money anyway."

I'd forgotten that she works for Clara Newberry in her spare time.

"I didn't expect to see you here, either," she says, a sly smile blooming across her face. "Miss Newberry said you wouldn't be working over the break, and come to think of it I haven't seen Mr. Martin around."

"Just spent a couple of days in the mountains," I say. "Visiting a friend."

I swivel in Soma's chair and reach for the low ebony credenza against the wall. The key is still in the small drawer of her desk where she'd kept it—organized even in absence. The lock turns with a quiet click, and I pull open the door to reveal the bound volumes of the student literary magazines she's looking for, stacked in chronological order, their spines facing out. "You got a year in mind?"

Grace nods as she reconfigures her bun. "Nineteen-eighty-six."

I pluck the volume from its place, grazing over the cover—a pen and ink drawing of a hollow with bare trees and a simple serif font at the top. "It's good," I say.

"Miss Blacksburg drew it!" Grace blurts out, then covers her mouth.

I stare down at the volume in my hand. It's a view looking down into a hollow from above, creating depth and perspective. The bare trees are rendered with obsessive detail—each branch mapped precisely. I realize Grace is waiting for me to hand her the journal, but I can't make it leave my hands.

"I'm sorry," Grace whispers. "I know you're new here and everything, but it seems you liked Miss Blacksburg a lot. Everyone did."

"She was devoted to Valemont," I say.

"Do you know what?"

I shake my head.

"Miss Blacksburg even wrote a poem in that edition."

"A poem?"

Grace nods. "Miss Newberry is putting together a permanent display in the commons to honor Miss Blacksburg and wanted to include some of her work as a student here."

"That's very thoughtful," I say.

I open the volume with more urgency than I intend, paging through its slightly yellowed pages. In the index I find her name, listed as Soma Bramwell. I turn to page nine, where the poem sits on the page like a pressed black moth, wings pinned open, delicate and ruined. The title leaves me breathless: Mother, I Ate You

> Mother, I ate you.
> Not pomegranate seeds— your name,
> your light, your memory of my face.
> I swallowed you whole and you became nothing.

> MY HANDS WET with chalk and milk.
> I thought I was binding shadows,
> but it was you I locked away.

> NOW YOU ARE ONLY the outline
> of an outline.
> A silence I carry in my throat.

> I SAW YOU VANISH.
> The sky split.
> The twin stars burned

eyes that did not know me.

IF YOU ARE EVER BORN,
  you will not come from me.
  You will come through the crack
  in the trickster's mouth,
  through the covenant's iron teeth.

I run my fingers over the Garamond script, its bookish, literary style so earnest. They begin to tremble. I want to tear out the page and eat it, for God's sake. The way my memory of her, the ghost of her with her bloody wrists eats at me night and day. Soma's title, her premise, is prescient in that way.

"Twila," Grace says. I'd almost forgotten she was here. "I mean, Miss Stith."

She sits down next to me, close but not intrusive, and reads the poem over my shoulder.

"That's really good," she says. "I think she was trying to write like Louise Glück."

Grace is right. I'd known immediately what Soma had been reaching for—the paired-down chill, the myth stripped bare. Vintage Glück. Fifteen, and already Soma knew how to put her mouth to the gods. A tear runs down my cheek and I wipe it with my sleeve. "It's almost as good as yours."

Grace reaches into her tote bag and hands me a travel-sized packet of tissues.

"You know what?" she says. "I think I could tell Miss Newberry that this volume wasn't in Miss Blacksburg's office. Like maybe she took it home as a keepsake."

I turn to Grace and smile, tucking a lock of her unruly hair into her scrunchie. "Thank you, but you don't have to do that. I think Miss Blacksburg's poem, and this beautiful cover she drew belong in the display."

I hand the magazine to Grace, who takes it with the care of

an archivist handling an old manuscript that can disintegrate if touched improperly.

"I'll see you in class next week," Grace says from the doorway. "And Miss Stith, I'll make sure this edition gets pride of place in the display."

After she leaves, I sit in Soma's chair for a long time, breathing in the faint scent of Fracas, thinking about mothers and daughters and the things we inherit whether we want them or not.

THE COTTAGE FEELS barren with Martin away. He stayed on the mountain to hunt, while I'm staring into a full refrigerator, not wanting a single thing. Not an omelet, or the Brunswick stew I made, or Colette's buttermilk pie. After grading a stack of essays on *Wuthering Heights*, I take a cup of hibiscus tea infused with a finger (or two) of bourbon to our bedroom, meaning to watch *Gaslight*.

Only I fall asleep during the opening credits, drifting into a dream that I know I can neither stop nor wake from until it's done with me. In it, I'm sitting by Hallow Lake again, on the weathered log that always seems damp, even if it hasn't rained in days. The woman in the water is watching me—gray-white, with silver thread sewn through her lips.

My breath withers to a wisp. She tilts her head, and I find myself helplessly mirroring the gesture, as if she holds invisible strings to my skeleton. The silver threads through her lips catch what little light filters through the canopy, and when she smiles —or tries to—the metal cuts deeper into her pale gray flesh.

I want to look away but can't. Lyla's always said the lake is old, older than the mountains themselves, but she never mentioned what lives beneath its surface. The woman's eyes hold mine with the patience of something that's been waiting a very long time.

The blackened flowers beside me crumble without sound, their ash settles on my hands like an Ash Wednesday blessing from the devil himself. When I try to brush it away, my fingers come back streaked with something that isn't quite dirt—and smells of copper and burnt hair.

The silence is pressing against my eardrums, making them ache, and when I try to remember how I even got here, the memory barely holds. Like I simply found myself sitting on this rotting log next to Hallow Lake as if I've always been here.

The woman in the water raises one translucent hand, and the silver threads begin to shift and tighten. Her smile widens impossibly, stretching the corners of her mouth until something dark leaks from the wounds.

From somewhere far beneath the surface comes a sound that makes my stomach clench and my fingers curl inward like talons. Wings beating against glass, desperate and rhythmic. The woman's reflection wavers, and for just a moment I glimpse pale shapes moving in the depths below her, propelling against the underside of the surface.

One of them has my eyes.

The woman nods once, slowly, and mouths a single word around the silver threads. I can't hear it, but I feel it settle into my chest. Then she begins to sink, her image dissolving back into the black water grain by grain, until only her eyes remain —two points of light watching me from below.

The lake's surface stills to perfect glass again, reflecting nothing but gray sky.

But when I look down at my hands, they're wet to the wrists with water I never touched.

Twila. That was the single word. She said my name.

I turn around, and she's there. Coming to me as if floating. Her face comes close, her eyes flickering over mine as if I'm a dear love. Then she pulls open her mouth, stretching the metal threads, black blood weeping from her wounds, and flickers her tongue over my lips before enveloping them in hers.

I wake up with a gasp that tears through my chest like something clawing its way out. I reach for Martin, but his side is cool and empty, almost like he's never been here and I made him up. Rolling over, burrowing further under the blankets, I look out at the crescent moon peeking in through my curtains. The moon can make me feel as strong as a gale wind—but tonight it only makes me feel alone. I try to think of all the good things in my life. Martin, at the top of that list. The way we'd come together in the mountains, two monsters finding their way to each other. I think of Lyla, but the burden of her having torn a page from the registry and the implications of that are too much to bear. So I think of Grace. Her bubbly laugh and her accent, which gets deeper with each minute I spend with her. Her free-hearted poetry and its deep thread of morality— the way she honors her grandmother, her traditions, and never once feels sorry for herself at a school filled with kids who've never wanted for anything in their lives.

I start remembering a story Grace told me at the start of the year. It's about the granny women in her family, healers of the body and spirit going generations back. How her own granny is one of these women, even if most people just go to the doctor now. But her granny keeps the traditions and never even lets Grace have an ibuprofen when she has cramps. She makes her a black cohosh root tea and tells her to go for a brisk walk.

Although I'm fighting sleep with a vengeance, afraid of it, wanting to keep the white lady with the stitched-up lips from coming again, sleep comes for me anyway. So does another dream. In it, I see Grace walking, leaning forward, her arms swinging at her sides, just like her granny told her to do. Then she stops and spins around, as if I've been with her all along.

"Miss Stith," she says, and her eyes reflect moonlight that isn't there. "I'm worried for your soul."

9

The dream of the woman with silver-sewn lips follows me into waking, and I spend the pre-dawn hours watching the cottage walls for movement that isn't there. Finally, I get up and drag myself, along with my blood-shot eyes, to the only coffee shop in town—where I have to swallow paying seven bucks for a flat white I can make better at home, if only I can stand being alone in my kitchen.

Hallow Grounds occupies a narrow brick building on Main Street that looks like it was three different things before someone got the idea to serve coffee there. The facade still has the ghost of painted lettering near the roofline—something about dry goods, the words worn to wraiths of paint. Like every-thing in Sibyl Springs, the building has a history it won't quite let go of.

Inside, the smell is all roasted beans and cinnamon and old wood, which I have to admit is one of my favorite bouquets. The space runs long and thin, and as I make my way to the counter in the back, past mismatched tables of tourists and locals, I feel the weight of eyes following me. Or maybe I'm just paranoid. Grace's voice from the dream still echoes: *I'm worried for your soul.*

A gentle tap on my shoulder makes me flinch. I spin around to see Brooks Craven standing behind me, looking like he's just eaten something that's still moving.

"Sweet St. Romedio, Brooks," I say.

"Forgive me, Miss Stith."

"Twila."

"Of course, Twila," he says.

It's my turn at the counter, but Brooks signals the barista with a twenty dollar bill and asks for my order. I try to object, but he isn't having it.

"It's the least I can do given your generosity."

I'd taken photocopies of a few pages in one of the Moravian journals—ones that showcased the dialect Brooks had been salivating over. Technically, that was *verboten* according to Honey MacDonald, but as the new owner of the selenography, I decided to exercise my privilege.

"It's nothing," I say. "I hope it was of value. The writing was pretty dense and specific, so I figured you'd have a nice sample."

"Yes," he says, a rather pensive look on his face. "The lunar eclipse they described, the one on March 9, 1830. It was quite illuminating. I would love the chance to talk to you about it. I think you'd find what I have to say most interesting."

"I'm afraid I don't know much about Moravian dialects." Nor have I ever wanted to, but I don't mention that part.

"Yes, but I do," he says.

The barista hands me my flat white and I take a sip. Too bitter.

"Are you free this afternoon?" he asks. "Could you perhaps meet me at The Montague Hotel at four-thirty for tea?"

School is starting back up tomorrow, and I'm expecting Martin back in the early evening, thank God.

"Sure," I say.

Brooks Craven takes his black drip coffee off the counter, along with a deep breath. He checks his pocket watch, clutching it in his hand like a talisman. "I'll see you then."

THE HALLWAYS of Valemont feel different in the late afternoon light—darker moods pooling in corners, the mahogany paneling drinking in what little sun filters through the stained glass. I left Hallow Grounds feeling slightly unsettled, and that feeling grew stronger throughout the day, making it hard for me to concentrate on preparing for the rest of the semester. There's something about Brooks' urgency over the lunar eclipse that isn't sitting right with me.

As I climb the stairs to my office after a late lunch, I notice my door is ajar. Just slightly. I know I locked it.

I push it open slowly and a waft of cologne attacks my nasal passages, its pineapple-birch-musk notes announcing power and money as surely as a platinum card on a marble bar.

Skelton Stanler, media mogul, Valemont board member, and likely one of the people who tried to murder me last summer stands with his back to me, examining the Oriental tapestry Clara Newberry had hung—the one with the dragon woven into silk. He's running his fingers along the threads as if reading braille.

"I could have sworn I locked the door," I say.

He turns, those pale blue eyes finding mine, that black freckle on his iris like a period at the end of a sentence. "Was it? Miss Newberry let me in before she left for the day. I hope you don't mind—I told her I'd wait."

He hadn't told her anything. Clara Newberry wouldn't have left, she would have hovered anxiously, at the very least left me a note. I step inside and close the door behind me, keeping my hand on the knob.

"What can I do for you, Mr. Stanler?"

"Skelton, please." He moves away from the tapestry, his hands sliding into his pockets. Casual. Relaxed. "I wanted to check in. After everything that's happened—Soma's death, and the other tragedies—the board felt it was important to make sure our faculty felt supported."

"How thoughtful." I walk past him to my desk, claiming my territory. I don't sit. Neither does he. "I appreciate the concern, but I'm fine."

"Are you?" He tilts his head, studying me. "Those first few weeks here must have been quite an adjustment. Sibyl Springs can be... overwhelming for newcomers. It gets so dark at night, doesn't it? No light to guide you at all."

There it is. The knife wound he'd stomped on gives a phantom ache in my abdomen.

"I found my way," I say.

"Yes, you did." Something flickers across his face—a hint of admiration, maybe. And something else. "That business at the hot springs with poor Amelia Jacoby." He shakes his head and I almost swear he's going to say *tisk-tisk*. "There is something of a history with animal attacks here. The daughter of one of our headmasters succumbed to one, as a matter of fact. But that was years ago. Long before you were born."

I lean against my desk, arms crossed. "Is that what you came here to discuss? Local wildlife?"

"Something like that," he whispers.

A silence stretches between us, and he moves toward the window.

"You know," he says. "Valemont has always attracted a particular type of student. Gifted, yes, but more than that. Students who understand that certain kinds of knowledge come with... responsibilities."

"Is that from the admissions brochure?"

He smiles. "You're witty. Soma mentioned that about you." He turns from the window. "She was quite fond of you. In her way."

When he says Soma's name, something in me goes very still. My daughter, though I can barely hold that truth in my mind. The grief is there—huge and ancient and mine—even if the memories aren't, and I want to reach down his throat and pull her name back out, unsaid.

"I loved her," I say carefully.

"Did you?" His eyes search my face. "That's gracious of you, given how brief your acquaintance was." He pauses. "Although I suppose intensity can create intimacy faster than time. Shared experiences. Shared... ordeals."

My pulse quickens but I keep my expression neutral.

"These old buildings," he continues, walking along the perimeter of my office. "They have a way of holding onto things. Echoes." He runs his hand along the wall, over the wainscoting. "Have you ever noticed how some rooms feel heavier than others? Like the air itself remembers?"

"I hadn't noticed."

"You will." He stops at my bookshelf, scanning the spines. "Ah, you've already started making this space your own. Sharon Olds. Hilda Doolittle. Langston Hughes. Excellent taste." His finger traces the edge of the Doolittle volume and I tense, knowing what's inside. It's the copy of the missing registry page —but then Skelton Stanler couldn't read it anyway. Soma had made sure it was only visible to me, and under moonlight.

"Poetry has always been good at saying what can't be said directly," Stanler muses. "Metaphor. Symbol. The thing behind the thing."

"Mr. Stanler—"

"Skelton."

"—I have work to do."

"Of course." But he doesn't move toward the door. Instead, he turns and looks at me with a furrowed brow. "I heard you had car trouble a few weeks back. A young man gave you a ride from a filling station, then drove his car off the road and into Hallow Lake."

My temples begin to throb.

"Terrible thing, that." He shakes his head. "The roads around here can be treacherous. Especially at night, especially near water. Easy to lose control. Easy to go under." His eyes lock with mine. "Lucky," he says softly. "Very lucky."

The word hangs in the air between us like a noose.

He moves toward the door finally, and relief floods through me. But then he pauses, his hand on the frame, and looks back at the Oriental tapestry.

"That dragon," he says. "Beautiful work. Do you know much about Eastern symbolism?"

"Not particularly."

"Dragons are fascinating creatures. Powerful. They can swoop down and destroy a city with a few deep breaths." He meets my eyes. "And yet, all that's left of them are images such as the one on this tapestry. Assuming they ever existed at all."

"I'll keep that in mind."

"Please do." His smile returns, pleasant and cold. "Oh, and Miss Stith? About the car accident. If you remember anything else about that night—anything at all that might help the authorities understand what happened—I hope you'll share it. With the appropriate people, of course."

"Of course."

"We take care of our own at Valemont," he says. "As long as our own understand where they belong."

Then he's gone, pulling the door closed behind him with a soft click.

I stand frozen until I hear his footsteps fade completely. Then I lock the door, test it twice, and sit down at my desk.

The chair presses against the base of my neck, right where the hook had been tearing into my muscle, keeping me tacked to the wood virtually immoble. I wonder if the hook had been Stanler's idea. Seems like a flourish he'd come up with somehow.

Outside, the valley is filling with shadow. My palms are damp, and my fingers shaking. I pull Martin's field notebook from my bag and hold it until they're still.

Then I take a deep breath, close my eyes, and try to put the rest of my day into some kind of order.

Brooks will be waiting at four-thirty. Something about the lunar eclipse in 1830 that he's eager to share with me.

I need to leave. But I stay in my chair, watching twilight begin its reach across the valley toward Valemont, and think about the way Skelton Stanler smiled when he said *we take care of our own.*

Brooks didn't show at four-thirty. Nor did he come at five. I texted Clara Newberry, and she claimed he'd left at four-fifteen. She'd returned to her office and passed him as he walked in the direction of town. The man didn't carry a cell phone, so there was no way to reach him.

When I arrive home, Martin is already there, rereading *Blood Meridian* in front of the fire.

"What kept you?" he asks.

It's nearly a quarter to eight and I'd been meaning to be home before six. "I was supposed to meet our esteemed classical languages instructor for tea at The Montague, but he stood me up. Luckily, I'd brought the beautiful journal you gave me and got lost in a poem I started writing."

"I missed you," Martin says. "You should have stayed on the mountain. Or I should have come with you."

He gestures for me to sit next to him and I do, snuggling at his shoulder like some damned kid. To top it off, tears flood my eyes, dampening his shirt.

"What's wrong?" he asks. "Did something happen?"

I hold him tighter, burrowing my face into his shoulder. "I don't know how to be what I'm supposed to be."

"It's in your blood, your bones," Martin whispers. "Even if your memories never return."

10

I'm still not myself when I get to Buzzy's after class. It's a full day later and Skelton Stanler's smile remains burned onto my brain like the bright ghost of a camera flash. My classical literature students crowd through the door behind me, Grace leading them like she owns the place, and I force myself to breathe. To pretend everything's normal. To play professor while my world splinters.

I order the early dinner of fried everything I promised: sausage gravy fries, fried green tomatoes, fried chicken. We claim the back booth, right next to the corkboard where all the nineteen seventies photos used to hang. July 14, 1976. The night that forever changed my life, though I hadn't even been born yet.

They ogle the old, yellowed Polaroids while I try to keep them on track, pondering Euripides' *The Bacchae*. You'd think a story about Dionysus driving women into a mountain frenzy—tearing a man apart with their bare hands—would hold their attention, but gold chains and bell bottoms are winning the day. I give up and head to the bar for more sweet tea and Dr Pepper.

"My lip is still sore," a man's voice says behind me. Deep and deliberate, like he's savoring the words.

My stomach hollows out as I look over my shoulder. There, I find a tall man in his late-thirties, the worked-out type who looks like he's just gotten off the trails. "Excuse me?" I say.

He leans in close, his tongue running over a small, red wound on his bottom lip. "Where you bit it," he whispers.

I turn all the way around, taking a step backward—my hand unfolding to slap his face. Only he lights up, like he's here for it.

"I didn't mean to fall asleep, but you wore me out. And then you were gone."

"What are you talking about?"

He glances over at the group of students. Grace is already looking over here, her eyes narrowed.

"That's right," he says. "You told me you were a teacher." He drops his voice to a whisper again. "But listen, Stella. My wife doesn't arrive until tomorrow, and I've got a big empty bed in room 756." His eyes travel down the length of body, slow and certain, as if retracing familiar territory. "And the shower at The Montague—big enough for two... maybe three."

"You need some help with those?" Grace appears at my side, nodding toward the ready pitchers. I know my mouth is hanging open. I can't speak. Can't do anything.

"Are you lost?" she says to the man, looking him up and down like he's something stuck to the bottom of her shoe.

"I was just leaving," he says.

"Well go on, then."

And he does, Grace's eyes training on him like a rifle laser until she watches him walk out the door.

I throw some money down on the counter and touch my jaw, which aches from clenching. I pick up the pitchers and hand one to Grace.

"Who was that?" she asks.

"Just some creep." A creep who somehow knew the fake name I used to give guys in bars back in my more self-destructive days—Stella.

MARTIN IS SETTING up a circle of polished wood folding chairs when I arrive at the entrance chamber, his back to me. I press my palm against the cool limestone of the cave, willing my pulse to slow. My throat feels tight and dry, like it's lined with cotton.

"You're late," he says without turning around.

"Students wouldn't stop talking." My voice comes out normal. Almost normal.

He turns then, and his eyes find mine. Holds them a beat too long.

"Long day?" he asks.

I nod, not trusting more words. The back of my neck prickles—not from fear this time, but from being seen. Martin can always tell when something is wrong. And plenty is already wrong without throwing what happened at Buzzy's into the mix. I feel guilty at the concern in his eyes, even though I have nothing to feel guilty about.

Martin cocks his head to the side, ever so slightly, and I can see him take the air in through his nose. He looks past me then meets my eyes again. "Did you see Stanler again?"

He can always smell when I'm frightened. And Skelton Stanler's five hundred dollar cologne was no doubt still lingering in my office like an evil spirit. "No," I say. "I'm just being paranoid, I think."

"It's not paranoia if you really are in danger."

I nod, untying the grey wool sweater from around my waist and pulling it on.

He steps toward me and I lean back, then realize what I've

done and try to right myself. I'd never seen that man at Buzzy's before, damn it, and I'd never do that to Martin.

"I'm sorry," I say. "I'm out of sorts."

Martin's brow knits together. "I should have paid a visit to Stanler before school started."

"No!" The word comes out like a jump scare. But it does ground me back in my body again. "Martin, I feel more strongly than ever that he could be the key to finding the Bramwell witch. You should have seen him. He talked about Theo and Amelia Jacoby like it was nothing—like he wanted me to know he wasn't the slightest bit afraid that you could do to him what you did to them."

"There are other ways to get to the Bramwell witch," he says.

I shake my head and come closer, taking his hand. Touching him feels good and right. It reminds me not to let some demonic fakery get between us.

"I think he not only knows the Bramwell witch's identity, but has been acting as her agent. He'd certainly seemed in charge when the members of her cult hooked me onto a cross and tortured me. Left me to be consumed by that thing she'd summoned."

Martin takes a deep breath. The memory of that night is both a physical and emotional horror. Soma slit her wrists the next day and Martin nearly died in my arms.

"If he comes by again," he says. "I won't be asking for your counsel."

"If he comes by again," I say, walking straight into his arms this time, "I won't try to talk you out of ripping him to pieces."

Voices are coming from outside, echoing into the chamber. I hear Rosanna Kingston's voice of supreme authority, informing her friends that her grandfather had been a close friend of Hemingway's until they came to blows over a woman. Grace's laugh comes on its heels, a little sharp. I can picture her eye-roll at the gratuitous name-drop. Then the shuffle of the boys' feet and a shiver-voiced *"mwah-ah-ah-ah"* worthy of a scythe-toting phantom from a haunted house. Martin and I unwind from each other and I gather a few more lanterns. Although the sun is still coming in from the entrance, it's already getting low.

I look up as the kids file in, followed by a woman who has to be Dr. Petal Whitaker. She looks one part academic, another part backcountry guide—dressed in well-fitted dark jeans, a corduroy jacket, and a messy, gray-streaked bun that reads like a beloved gardening hat. She gives off an aura of confidence that makes me not dread getting older. Without even looking I can tell she has calluses on her hands that suggest she spends as much time with rocks as with people. Martin told me she has an encyclopedic knowledge of karst geology and the region as a whole, including the real stories you'll never find in the history books.

She doesn't even pause—just beelines past me and straight to Martin, pulling him into a quick hug that he returns with obvious affection.

"Look at you," she says, leaning back to give him a once-over. "Haven't aged a day, you old dog." She kisses him on the nose, then softens. "I'm so sorry about Soma."

Martin only nods.

Then she turns, taking me in head-to-toe. "And you! Lordy, your hair's shorter. You used to look like a mermaid—now you look like one of them Charlie's Angels." She notices the baffled students watching her. "That was a TV show," she stage-whispers to them, "about pretty girls who solved crimes with not a single brassiere to wear between them."

She sticks out her hand and I return the gesture. "Petal," she says.

"Nice to meet you—again, I guess."

She throws her head back and laughs, exposing a row of

strong, white teeth that look like they could chew through barbed wire.

The students are getting seated in the round, and Petal retrieves a large flashlight from her backpack. She shines it above on the stalactites dripping down from the vaulted ceiling, then holds it high above her head, training it on the blackness of the inner chambers. "Oh, hello," she says, then starts toward the back.

"Aren't you staying for the readings?" I ask.

Petal snorts. "I ain't here for poetry, bright eyes."

Petal steps further into the cave and stops, closing her eyes. She draws in a long, slow breath through her nose.

"Mmm," she says. "Ordovician limestone, maybe 450 million years old. You can smell the calcium carbonate—clean, alkaline. There's iron staining on the walls, probably from surface water percolating through. Active seep coming from..." She turns her head slightly. "Northwest. Spring-fed, not just runoff." She pauses, breathing deeper. "And wood smoke, old—maybe a hundred, hundred and fifty years? Cherokee, most likely, before they were pushed out." Another pause, longer this time. "Something else, too. Blood on the stones. Not recent, but it's there. And..." Her eyes open, finding Martin's. "Bone ash in the soil at the back. Old protection work—older than granny magic, older than what the Indians knew, or the savages that came before them. Your mother's hand, I'd wager. Whatever she was keeping out, it's stayed out." Then, flashlight beaming ahead, she ventures into the throat of the cave.

The students by then are settling into the circle of chairs, their voices dropping to reverent murmurs as the cave swallows the last of the daylight. Martin lights the remaining lanterns, placing them strategically around the chamber so that firelight flickers across the limestone walls, making the stone seem to breathe.

"Welcome to The Cave," he says. Martin stands at the center

of the circle in a pale shirt and dark wool coat that falls almost to his knees. The lamplight catches on the edges of the fabric, making him look less dressed than draped in a dark mantle. "Plato believed we spend our lives watching shadows on a wall, mistaking them for reality. But here—" he gestures to the darkness beyond the lantern's reach "—we'll do the opposite. We're going to turn away from our comfortable illusions and look directly at what's true."

Grace leans forward in her chair, rapt. The other students shift, some eager, some uncertain.

"Tonight's theme is transformation," Martin continues. "Not the kind you choose—the kind that chooses you. The moments when you realize you're not who you thought you were. When the person you were becomes impossible to return to." His eyes find mine briefly, then move on. "I want you to read something you've written that unsettles you. Tell us about an emotion or revelation you almost didn't see through to the end."

A hush falls over the circle. This is different from my classroom discussions of Dionysian frenzy—this is asking them to bleed onto the page and then read the wound aloud.

Rosanna Kingston speaks first, her normally strong, high voice just a notch above a whisper. She reads about her grandfather's funeral, about lifting the veil on his casket and seeing a stranger's face, realizing she never really knew him at all. The poem is naked, unfinished, and when she stops, she doesn't look up.

"Thank you," Martin says simply, and somehow those two words hold more weight than any critique.

One by one, the students read. Grace's poem about her grandmother's hands, how they'd known things about healing and hurting that Grace is only beginning to understand. A boy named Chen reads about watching his parents speak Mandarin to each other—a language he's refused to learn—and realizing he's made himself an outsider in his own family.

While they read, Petal drifts toward the back of the chamber. She tucks her flashlight into her belt and clicks it off, but puts on a headlamp that frees her hands but isn't nearly as powerful. I can barely see her outline as she dabs her fingers along the limestone walls. I watch her disappear into the darkness beyond the lanterns, hear the soft scrape of her boots on stone.

Martin catches my eye and I tilt my head. He shrugs. Petal's a geologist. This is exactly what she's come for.

Grace is halfway through a second poem—tracing the slow insistence of roots splitting concrete—when Petal's voice echoes from the darkness.

"Martin."

Not loud or alarmed, exactly. But something in her tone makes us all take notice.

The reading stops. Martin is already on his feet, grabbing one of the lanterns.

"Stay here," he tells the students.

I follow him anyway, and Grace is right behind me, moving so quietly I don't notice until we're already in the narrow passage leading deeper into the cave.

Petal stands in a small chamber. Her headlamp is illuminating something on the ground. She looks up as we approach, her face unreadable.

"I found something," she says quietly.

She kneels down, and we crowd around her. At first, I can't make sense of what I'm seeing—just pale stone and ashen marks. Then Petal's finger traces the outline, and my stomach drops.

It's an arm. What looks to be a human arm, fossilized into the limestone. The bone is delicate, the fingers slightly curled. And pressed into the stone beside the hand—or maybe clutched in it, impossible to tell—is the clear impression of a pocket watch. I can see the circular shape, the chain, even the faint outline of Roman numerals on the face.

"This limestone," Petal says, her voice academic and steady in a way that somehow makes everything worse, "is nearly half a billion years old." She looks up at us.

I stare at the bone. At the watch. At the impossible juxtaposition of deep time and human artifacts.

Petal touches the bone, traces the watch impression. "Radius and ulna. Fossilized the same age as the stone around it—which means it's been here just as long." She looks up at us. "But humans didn't exist back then. Nothing even close to anything human existed."

I stare at the bone. At the pocket watch pressed into rock that formed before anything walked on land. It's like seeing a cell phone in a dinosaur skeleton.

"Seems someone was sent back," Petal says simply. "And they died there. What the hell kind of evil would do that?"

Martin crouches down, bringing his lantern closer to the watch impression. He's very still, in that way he gets when something is deeply wrong.

"Brooks Craven didn't come to work today," he says quietly.

The cave suddenly feels much smaller. Much darker.

Grace finds my shoulder, gripping it tight. She's staring at the bone, her face bloodless in the lamplight. "How long would it take to die there?" she whispers. "Alone. That far back."

The early light filters into my Jeep and I glance at my phone, which tells me straight up that it's six. The mountain roads have been empty of traffic, but full of fog and mist, so the hour it should have taken me to get to *Our Lady of the Angels* has turned into two.

The monastery sits on the ridge like a broken tooth, its stone walls softened by two centuries of weather and neglect. I chose it from the list of sites Soma acquired with me in mind, mostly because it's closest. I drove here alone before dawn, needing to be somewhere Soma had touched, somewhere holy, somewhere that might offer protection from whatever is happening to me. Somewhere that isn't near Martin.

My latest dream is still clinging to me like wet wool. It's a montage of horrors, some of them as clear and linear as a scene from a movie, others more like impressions. Vacation photos that curdle as you flip through them.

I was at The Montague waiting for Brooks, staring at a page in the journal Martin gave me. In my dream, it wasn't filled with the poem I'd written, but was empty. The man from Buzzy's walked in, and I looked up, catching his gaze. Next he was sitting beside me. Had bought me a bourbon. Said his wife wasn't coming for a couple of days. I smiled. Then we were in his suite, on his bed, and I was on top. Gritting my teeth and scratching at his chest. His wrists were tied to the bedpost and I could see the glint of his wedding ring in the evening light. The whole time I was wishing his wife could walk in and see us— maybe his kids, if he had any—and imagining that made it feel even better.

I didn't wake up gasping like I did from my other dreams. Just opened my eyes to the steady sound of Martin's breathing. I felt hollow, like something had come to scoop out my insides— everything that made me human—leaving me as lonesome and abandoned as the arm bone in the cave. Slowly, as I laid there, I came back to myself, but even once I was whole again I couldn't stand the thought of drinking coffee with Martin. Looking into his eyes while he ate his breakfast. I snuck out into the dark, leaving a note on the counter, along with some sweet potato muffins and the coffee maker ready to go.

The path up to the monastery is overgrown, but the dry grasses have been flattened by wind and rain. I turn off the torch on my phone, and squint up at round, gray stones that make up both the chimney and the turret. They look formidable here in the early morning, the sun barely peeking above the horizon. But the rest of the structure, which is made largely of once white-painted wood, is weathered hard and looks like it will blow over if the big, bad wolf happens to come by. That reference, irreverent and unbidden, makes me think of Martin and I shake it off, climbing the stairs to the entrance. Next to the arched double doors is a plaque that reads, *Our Lady of the Angels Monastery*, founded 1829.

Inside, it's quiet, with only a whistle from a breeze that blows through some of the cracks in the walls. The same round, gray stones from outside make up the floor and rise up into a sanctuary and altar at the front of the church. In the nave are rows of sturdy wooden pews, that despite their functionality aren't artless. Their backs are curved, almost like shells, and fleur de lys are carved onto each side, making me wonder if the building had been built by French Catholics. Seems strange, given the location. Catholic churches and monasteries are rare enough in Appalachian Virginia today, let alone in the early parts of the nineteenth century. But stranger things have happened.

I walk up to the altar, running my fingers along the stone, trying to imagine Soma here. But I can't. The place is empty of her, of ghosts, even critters. I hope God is still present.

"Dad, I wish you could hear me," I say. "Because I really need you."

Despite the peace of my surroundings, the persistent beauty of this forgotten place, I feel defeated. My dream keeps rising up, cruel as hell, insistent. As a kind of exorcism, I close my eyes and recite the short poem I wrote for Martin as I sat at The Montague waiting for Brooks.

Your hands—
I have memorized their weight.
Even the ghost of them
presses the air into shape.

WHEN I WAKE and you are not beside me,
the bed is a tide gone out,
and I lie in the salt of it—
drenched, still calling your name.

IF THERE IS ANOTHER LIFE,
I will find you there too—
by scent, by wound,
by the sound of your heart

breaking open for me again.

My voice was soft as I spoke the words. And now my heart feels kindled, if barely. I open my eyes to the sound of flapping wings. Above me, the white dove lands upon the altar, its head turns, its tiny, black eye trains on mine. In it, I can see my father's house, the one that I grew up in, that became Lyla's house. It's burning.

12

I find Petal near Valemont's greenhouse just before eight. She's squatting barefoot on the grass strip at the tree line, her boots neatly paired beside her field bag. Her eyes are closed, palms pressed flat to the ground like she's listening for something through the earth itself.

When I approach, she keeps her eyes shut. "My grand-mother used to do this," she says quietly. "After someone died. She'd go out before sunrise and press her hands to the ground, see if she could feel where they'd gone."

I nod, half-listening. I'd spent the drive back to Sibyl Springs blowing up Lyla's phone—four calls before she finally picked up from her friend Brunie's place in Scottsville. She was hung-over and wondering what in the amber waves of grain I wanted from her at seven in the morning. She was safe, she said. Everything was fine. I didn't tell her about the dove, or watching the house burn in its eye, just that I'd had a funny feeling and wanted to make sure she was okay. She said she loved me too, in that way she has of understanding what I'm not saying.

Petal finally opens her eyes. They're red-rimmed. "Nobody's

seen Brooks since he left campus. Not even that snoopy land-
lady of his, according to Miss Clara Newberry."

She stands, brushing the dirt from her palms.

"I keep thinking about what it must've been like. Arriving in
a world that hasn't invented language yet. No moon to call to.
No one who could hear you scream." She wipes her face with
the back of her hand. "My grandmother always said the worst
thing that could happen to our kind wasn't dying. It was dying
alone, outside of time, where even the earth couldn't remember
you properly."

"But the cave remembered him," I say. "That's something, I
guess."

"I guess." Petal's sigh feels as heavy as an incoming storm.

"Four-hundred-fifty-million-years," I say, trying to ground
myself back in the conversation. "It doesn't seem possible."

"Why not?" Petal asks me. "Is there really a difference
between four years and four-hundred-million. Bending time is
bending time."

"I suppose," I say. "But when traveling beyond the veil, a
witch follows her own historical arc, right? At least that's what
Colette and Lyla told me. That's what I seemed to do."

Petal lifts an eyebrow and flips her braid from one shoulder
to the other. "That's assuming a lot. That Brooks is a witch who
can travel beyond the veil, for one thing. And that he actually
did travel beyond the veil rather than being thrown into the
nethers. Being flung back in time isn't the same as traveling
beyond the veil, Twila. One is done by a rare and powerful
witch to herself, and the other by a powerful witch to someone
else."

"What's the difference?"

"A witch has power beyond the veil, and can manipulate
her time arc if she's strong enough. Because she's part of the
veil. Whether it was a witch who threw Brooks Craven back in
time, or he stumbled through some sort of portal—which he'd

still need a witch for—he arrived helpless and human. And he died that way."

I'm about to ask what happens to someone who dies in the past—does their body return?—when Petal's gaze shifts over my shoulder, her expression changes. I turn to see Grace running toward us across the lawn, her face pale, her hand clutching her phone.

"Twila, Miss Stith!" She calls out. "Your house is on fire!"

CLARA NEWBERRY GOT the call just a few minutes after I arrived at Valemont. Lyla had turned off her phone and gone back to sleep after we talked. The Charlottesville police were looking for me because my name was still on the title, as Dad had technically left the house to both of us, even though I'd long considered it Lyla's place alone.

Martin wants to come with me to make the drive to Charlottesville, but I still can't bear ninety minutes in a car with him. I feel like I'd have to tell him about what happened at Buzzy's and my dream, and I'm just not ready for that. I reassure him Colette will join me and that somebody has to stay behind at the school. I also tell him to keep trying Lyla to let her know what happened.

Colette, bless her heart, seems out of sorts from the get-go. She climbs into Selene with too much energy for a night owl who'd probably been up until three. But news of a house fire will do that to you.

"Mind if I turn this down?" she asks, already lowering the Jeep's heat down to nothing.

I don't mention that she might be more comfortable if she takes off the thick Peruvian sweater she's wearing, especially since she's being so generous with her cigarettes.

We're quiet for the first thirty minutes. Everything since the monastery—the dove, the vision, Grace running across the lawn—has the texture of an art film that's leading to a bad end.

"You got insurance?" she asks.

"Yeah." Not that insurance would give us back our old photos with dad, or the doorframe in the hallway where he'd marked my height every birthday until I was twelve. And there were Lyla's recipe books and oh, my God—my poetry journals from when I was a kid! They'd been stacked in my closet and I kept meaning to get them.

"They give you any idea what could've done it?"

I shake my head. "I saw the fire in the eye of a white dove," I say.

Colette takes a breast-swelling breath that she quickly huffs out. "Is that why you went running out of the house before four in the morning?"

"Are you watching me?"

"Yes."

I crack the window and light another smoke. "I didn't see the dove then. It was at an old monastery in the Blue Ridge. One of the abandoned places Soma left me."

"You just up and decided to go to that old place all by your lonesome before the crack of dawn?"

"I needed somewhere safe. Somewhere Soma touched."

"Safe from what? Martin? I thought he was the one keeping you safe."

I blow some smoke rings and Colette fans them away.

"You drive over to Lyla's after?" she asks.

"No."

"You couldn't have been more than thirty minutes away."

The red light turns green and the car behind me honks. I crank Selene hard into first gear. "I called Lyla and she said everything was fine. What exactly are you asking me, Colette?"

"It's just you get up and go sit in some empty church for hours on end while Lyla's house is burning down."

"It's not some empty church, Colette. Soma wanted me to have it! You think that doesn't mean anything?"

"Alone in the dark, only a sliver of moon, and with bad magic looking for you?"

"It wasn't dark anymore," I say.

"That hardly makes it better."

"And I was in a church. That's about as blessed-in as you can get."

"Depends on whose church!"

We don't say another word until we pull up at the Charlottesville police station. We just smoke as we watch the Blue Ridge Mountains come closer, Colette fiddling with her moonstone necklace the whole time—click, click—driving me half mad. I park up close and stare at the building feeling a little sick. Last time I'd been here, I'd come with Abner Chitwood. Or at least what I thought was Abner.

Inside, we're greeted by a young cop who introduces himself as Officer Berry. He's clean-shaven except for a tuft of black hair under his bottom lip and leads us through a fluorescent-lit hallway to a perfect square of a room filled with cubicles. The place looks like a maze. We sit down across from him on a pair of low-backed chairs as he signals a curly redhead. He starts asking the usual questions: the name, rank, and serial numbers ones that he already knows the answers to. Then he starts getting specific about the where's and what's—namely mine.

"So, you drove up from Sibyl Springs around four in the mornin' and would've arrived at this abandoned monastery, The Lady With the Angels—"

"Our Lady of the Angels," I say. "A close relative recently died and left the place to me."

Officer Berry nods. "You arrived there at five?"

"No," I say, for the second time now. "It was six. The fog

made driving in the mountains a little unforgiving, so I went slow."

The young cop nods and glances over at Colette. "And you weren't with her?"

"No," Colette tells him, also for the second time.

The redhead returns with some surprisingly good-smelling coffee and Officer Berry thanks her with a crisp, warm smile. Then, he pivots and points his pen at me.

"And you called Ms. Corbin four times roughly between six-thirty and six-forty-five."

"That's correct," I say. "Lyla and I are very close. We have a sixth sense with each other." Not that I needed to justify calling family.

Officer Berry leans back in his chair and drops his pen on his desk. He folds his arms.

"Ms. Stith," he says. "I want you to think very carefully before you answer this next question. Where were you at roughly five-thirty this morning?"

"I've already answered that."

Officer Berry reaches into his top drawer and pulls out a tin of mints, offering one to me and Colette. We both decline.

"Ms. Stith, a neighbor of Ms. Corbin said she saw a silver Jeep driving away from the premises right about that time. Which was also the time the fire was set."

"Set?"

"That's correct, Ms. Stith. We're investigating this as a probable case of arson."

13

First Quarter

THE MORAVIAN JOURNALS won't give up their secrets.

I've been staring at the astronomical symbols until they pixelate into abstraction, my laptop screen glowing in Soma's darkened office. March 9, 1830. The lunar eclipse. Brooks's research. They're all connected—I know it—but the thread keeps slipping through my fingers.

"Hy-dee-who." Grace pops her head in, a metal thermos wrapped in a sunflower-print kitchen towel clutched to her chest.

"You haven't been gone ten minutes," I say.

She'd followed me here after office hours, full of questions about Brooks and Petal and inter-dimensional time-travel. It took an hour to convince her to go eat dinner with her friends. All I wanted was to understand the Moravian journals—every faded page, every marginal scrawl, to wrap my head around what Soma was trying to do with all of her acquisitions. Not the ones that had made her ungodly rich, but the ones that spoke my name as loudly as my poetry. Places like *Our Lady of the Angels*.

"You looked like you needed this more than I needed dinner," she tells me.

Soma's desk is a battlefield of paper: printouts from the Luna Archive, photographs I'd snapped with my phone, notes I'd scribbled on whatever paper I could find. Grace carefully pushes some of them aside and plants the thermos right in front of me. She unscrews the cap and steam rises up like a genie.

I smell chamomile and valerian, something woodsy underneath. Something that reminds me of sleep and home.

"My granny's recipe," Grace says, pouring into the thermos cap. "For when the world gets too loud in your head." She hands it to me. "You're supposed to steep it under moonlight first—and I did my best. I mean, there's no window in the caf's kitchen, but I figure if the moon is strong enough to affect the tides, it can make its way through some stone and insulation."

She blows softly into the steam and mouths a blessing. "You have to seal it in," she says.

I take it, and the warmth spreads through my palms. The first sip tastes exactly like the tea Lyla used to make for me when I was down. In the first few months after my mom left, when I couldn't sleep. After Dad died, then Beckett. There were years when it felt like this tea was all that was getting me from day to day.

"Your granny taught you this?" I whisper.

Grace tucks a strand of hair behind her ear, and nods with an impish smile. Her smile is contagious enough that I almost return it.

"She said some teas you gotta make with intention, or they're just hot leaf water."

"She sounds wise," I say.

Grace looks at me then—really looks—the way you look at someone who matters. A sense of recognition passes between us, like when you spot your own kind in a crowd of strangers. In our case, I guess we're two natural outliers with a love of poems. Ones who were lucky enough to be loved well by women who stepped up when our mothers didn't.

Grace sits down and fiddles with her charm bracelet, the eagle, globe and anchor charm with the compass fused to it, and a little acorn. She watches my eyes get drawn to it.

"My granny gave it to me—the acorn. Said that even when an acorn drops from a tree, it just grows another tree."

"That's a lovely sentiment," I say. "You should write a poem about it."

Grace lifts her shoulders up and giggles. It's clear she's already started one.

"You know, she had me promise something before I came here," Grace says. "Made me write it in my Bible and say it out loud. I think she was scared I'd forget."

"Forget what?"

Grace glances toward the door, where I see Martin's shadow looming.

"How to come home maybe," she says, then stands and starts backing up to the door. *I think it's time for me to go have dinner,* she mouths.

"And you can keep the thermos. Just bring it back whenever." She pauses at the threshold, making room for Martin to enter. "Mr. Martin," she says, and slips away, sunflower towel swinging at her side.

Martin fills the doorway, bringing with him a quieter, heavier gravity. He's still in his teaching clothes from that afternoon. His jacket is gone, and his shirt sleeves are rolled to his elbows. I realize I have no idea what time it is.

"You missed dinner," he says.

"I wasn't hungry." I glance at Soma's desk. "I keep thinking if I stare at them long enough, they'll rearrange themselves into sense."

He comes in all the way, closing the door behind him. Then he pulls up the chair across from Soma's desk and sits down like he has all the time in the world. Like he isn't exhausted from the aura of suspicion that has fallen around me since the fire yesterday—the calls from the Charlottesville police, my prickly defensiveness, my own inability to let him close.

"What are you looking for?" he asks.

I gesture at the chaos. "The registry. Or where it might be. Or—" I stop, press my palms against my eyes. "I don't know anymore."

"Twila—"

"I'm broken, Martin." The words come out hard. I don't even mean to say them, but once spoken they bruise the air between us. "And the longer I stay this way, the more vulnerable I am to the Bramwell witch. To whatever she's doing to me."

He doesn't say anything. Just waits.

"All these places Soma left me." I drop my hands on the desk. "The monastery. The properties. The longer I sit with them, the more I don't think they're just things she knew I'd love. They're investigations. She was looking for the registry, too, and she left me her research. I just have this feeling...she was so close, Martin. She was right on the edge of finding it."

Martin picks up a photocopy of one of the Moravian journal pages. "Then why would she kill herself?"

"I don't know." I look at the photo on my screen, the dense Moravian script and the astronomical chart—both incomprehensible. "I keep thinking—if I can just finish what she started. If I can find it. The registry would make me whole. That's what she told me. That's what it's supposed to do."

Martin leans forward, elbows on his knees. "What do you need?"

I sit back into Soma's chair, feeling myself shrink. "Help me," I say. "Help me search the properties. Look through everything Soma acquired, what she thought might be illuminating somehow."

"When do we start?"

"Now."

He stands, and comes around the desk, holding out his hand with a careful tenderness. "You could use some sleep."

I smile up at him, fragile, and it feels like the first smile I've given him in eons. "I'm not going to be able to sleep. And you and I are at our best in the night. Tomorrow's Saturday anyway —we can nap in the afternoon."

Outside, the campus has gone quiet, the old trees shuddering against the windows like something listening. I follow Martin to Selene. My mind is still tangled in Moravian symbols and Soma's unspoken secrets.

Martin is searching his memory, trying to understand bits of the rare dialect in the journals, so he takes the passenger seat. While he reads in the dark, the archaic language seems to twist against him.

"We'd see them at the trading post sometimes," he says. "They were easy to spot as they'd retained their habit of donning their traditional dress. The kroj was elaborate—bright colors, a lot of embroidery, puffy sleeves. Our clothes were plain by comparison."

It's strange talking about our life together in the 1800s in this way. Like I'm reading about characters in a historical novel.

"That was a long time ago," I say. "And how often did we really talk to them?"

"It was a fairly social occasion," he explains. "Depending on where you were coming from, it could take days to reach the trading post. Not for us obviously. We were fast and could travel at night."

"Faster than Selene?"

Martin chuckles.

"I wish I'd understood their significance then. I would have paid closer attention. Apart from their foreign ways, it wasn't unusual to follow lunar cycles. Most people did."

Selene's tires crunch over scattered branches as we reach the building. The trading post sits at a crossroads rarely traveled anymore. My headlights catch the sagging porch first, then the faded paint on the clapboard siding. SHENANDOAH MERCANTILE, the sign whispers, half its letters eroded like a name forgotten mid-prayer.

"This was called Mackey's Post then," Martin says quietly.

I kill the engine and we sit there for a moment. Something tugs at the edges of memory, a pull I can't name. The weight of a wool cloak heavy with rain, the smell of lamp oil and unwashed bodies pressed close, someone's laugh cutting through foreign syllables. A hand—Martin's hand—guiding me through the crowd.

I blink and it's gone.

"You remember something," Martin says, watching my face.

"It's almost familiar," I say. "Or maybe I just want it to be."

Inside, it smells like rot and old wood and something else musty. Probably mice. The shelves are still there, empty except for a thick coat of dust and a few glass jars that have somehow survived. The counter where people would have bartered and traded runs along one wall.

"It was loud at night," Martin says, moving carefully. "Lamp-light, fire, drink flowing. Three different languages at once—English, German, and the Moravians' distinctive chatter. Sometimes Cherokee. Mackey used to keep a jug under the counter for special customers."

"Were we special customers?"

"We were strange customers. We showed up after dark. No one ever saw our wagon." He pauses near what would have been the fireplace. "You liked it here."

I try to imagine it—myself in homespun or whatever women wore then, bartering for salt or powder, our basic needs. Martin beside me, pretending to be human.

He crouches over the hearth to brush away the soot that has collected over nearly two centuries. His sleeve comes away black.

"Here," he says softly.

I go to him. The mantel is cracked, streaked with ash, but beneath it, carved shallow into the soapstone, there are uneven scratches cut into the face. Martin leans closer. In the flicker of my flashlight, the words take shape, faint but legible, like something whispered through centuries of ash.

Still as water under the moon.

"You used to write that in your journals," he says. "You carved it here one winter night."

For a moment I don't breathe. That was the repeating stanza I'd used in the title poem of *Moon Child*.

"*Still as water under the moon—*" Martin began.
"*the night breathes through the reeds,*
and I listen for what the wind forgets:
a name carried in the hush between heartbeats."

Even in the dark, I can see the soft, whiskey-lit glow of his eyes. The trace of his lips as they move to the words of my poem.

"*My father is there, I think—*" he continues.
"*in the hush before the heron lifts,*
in the small gold sound the stars make
when they fall into reflection.

STILL AS WATER under the moon—
I feel his breath at my shoulder,
warm as the earth before rain,
and the river trembles with recognition.

. . .

MOON CHILD, *he calls me,*
 and the night folds around the sound—
 soft, infinite, forgiving—
 still as water under the moon."

The word *forgiving* comes softer, like it cost him something. I look down at my hand, pearl blue in the poor light. As much as I want to, I can't make it take his.

That Martin had memorized my poem—didn't even need to summon the words. They simply came. That he'd read my verses over and over decades after he thought I'd abandoned him. He must have known the poem by heart the first time he saw me after I returned to Sibyl Springs. The night of Soma's party—when she was welcoming me home but I didn't know it.

Sometimes it all hurts so much I think my heart might stop.

"You know," Martin says. "There is beauty in loss and recovery."

"So you tell me," I say. "And speaking of, there is a back room." I'm determined to force my mind on the present, not on ghosts of a marriage I can't touch. Not yet, anyway.

We search methodically. Martin pulls up loose floorboards that had probably been replaced half a dozen times since the 1830s. I run my hands along walls and shelves seeking hidden spaces. The back room yields nothing but more emptiness. A cellar accessible through a trapdoor gives us dirt and darkness and the scurrying of mice.

Twenty minutes and we've covered everything.

"I guess I'm not surprised," I say.

Martin stands in the center of the empty room. For a moment I think he might share another memory—maybe about us sitting by the hearth, something he wishes I could remember with him. But instead he tips his head up like he's catching a scent, his gaze sliding along an invisible thread to the back corner. There, just discernible in the dim light, fresh scratches mark the floorboards. Not words, like the ones I carved into the mantle, but oblique lines and symbols. The marks are shallow and recent. The wood around them darkened, like acid burn.

"She's been here," Martin says quietly. Not weeks ago, or months. Maybe days, hours, even minutes. The char patterns are still distinct, not at all weathered by time.

I crouch beside the markings and my stomach clenches like I've swallowed a stew of nails and broken glass. They're positioned directly under the window, where someone would stand to look out—to watch the road leading here. To watch for us coming.

Martin guides me up, unsteady, to a standing position.

"The mill, then," he says.

THE DRIVE TAKES two hours through empty mountain roads, even with Selene flying twenty miles over the speed limit. When we arrive, the mill sits waiting in the dark. This structure is darker, damper, older. Or at least looks that way. Built of fieldstone with a wooden water wheel that has long since stopped turning, though I can hear water running through the sluice below. The sound fills the night—constant, rhythmic, like the building still has a heartbeat even as it's decomposing.

"Careful," Martin says, catching my elbow as I step over the threshold. The wooden floor is rotted in places, holes yawning into the cellar below.

Inside, the grinding stones sit massive and silent as the centerpiece of the room. They'd be impossible to move without machinery, and look far too rooted in their place to have been dislodged—at least during the time Soma owned the mill. Nothing would have been hidden beneath them.

I circle the room while Martin examines the walls, looking

for loose stones, hidden compartments. The upper floor is accessible by a ladder missing half its rungs. Martin climbs it easily, disappearing into the loft above. I hear him moving around, the creak of old boards.

"Hollow as a ribcage," he calls down.

The cellar entrance is a stone stairway at the back, steep and narrow. I take the stairs carefully, my phone's flashlight cutting through the dark. Down there the air is cold and smells of standing water. The walls weep in streams and wooden beams overhead look ready to give way.

I stand near a small rectangular window and close my eyes, reaching for the moonlight outside. For that connection that should make searching easier, that should let me feel if something magical has touched this place.

And the power comes.

But wrong.

It surges through me like nausea, violent and sudden. I drop to my knees in the dirt.

The flamingo—Dad's gift, pink and foolish and beloved—crumples in the blaze, its beak folding like paper.

I'm not watching anymore. I'm there, and in the moment.

The smoke alarm is shrieking, underneath it all—that sick, electric satisfaction singing through my veins.

Something unspools inside me—a scene I've refused to watch. My stomach lurches. I press my palms into the dirt floor, trying to ground myself, digging my nails into the grit. I can feel a couple of them break.

Moonfire is dancing between my fingers. Spite slicks my tongue as Brooks stumbles backward, his hand reaching for me in confusion, betrayal. On his face—a flash of terror, then nothing. He's gone.

I watch him fall, then disappear. And the worst part—the part that makes bile rise in my throat—is how good it felt. Like scratching an itch I didn't know I had.

"No." The word comes out strangled.

But the vision doesn't stop. It keeps playing frame by frame, showing me exactly what I am. Not just what I'm capable of, but what I've already done.

"Twila."

Martin's voice sounds far away. I hear his footsteps on the stairs.

I force myself up—hands shaking, vision swimming. Brush the dirt from my jeans with fingers that won't work right, hands that are all scraped up. The blood on my palms smears into the denim.

"There's nothing here," I say.

He takes the last step and starts toward me, but I move past him. "We should go."

I need out of this dark hole in the ground, and away from what I've just seen. Martin catches my arm—gently, but firm enough to stop me.

"It doesn't matter." I pull free, climb the stairs too fast, stumbling on the third step and catching myself.

In the main room, I head straight for the door. The night air hits my face but it doesn't help. Nothing helps. The running water below sounds almost human—whisper or breath or accusation.

Martin follows but doesn't speak. Just stands beside me in the doorway, looking out at the way the mill sits in relation to the peaks beyond.

"What is it?" I ask him. I'm trying to sound normal, engaged in what we're doing.

Martin shakes his head. "Elliot always built with intention. The estate sits the same way—positioned for these exact sight lines to the ridge. Soma must have noticed—maybe that's why she was drawn to this place. "

I stare at the Hallowmist Mountains, black shapes against a sky just paler than coal. "We should search the estate," I say.

He turns to look at me then. Really look. I wish more than anything that I could let him hold me.

"If I wanted to hide something," I say, "I'd put it someplace personal."

I can feel Martin watching me, reading something in my posture, my breathing, the way I hold myself. What he sees, I don't know.

"All right," he says. His voice is so low, I can hardly hear him.

We walk back to Selene, our phones dark in our pockets. Behind us, the mill's water wheel stays frozen in place, but the water keeps running underneath. Relentless and unforgiving.

And I can't stop seeing Brooks's face. Can't stop feeling the ghost of moonfire between my fingers. The devouring fire taking Lyla's house in one big gulp.

Martin opens my door. I slide in, pull my seatbelt across with hands that don't quite feel like my own. In the driver's seat, he doesn't start the engine right away.

"Twila, please," he says softly.

I stare straight ahead at the dark trees, the rutted road, anywhere but at him.

"I'm fine now," I lie.

He waits for a long moment, then turns the engine over, headlights cutting through the dark. As we pull away, I catch a glimpse of the mill in the side mirror. Just for a second, I think I see something in the upper window—a pale shape, too still to be alive.

But when I blink, it's gone.

14

The sky above the Blacksburg Estate is just starting to go from onyx to deep purple as dawn starts her creep up the horizon. We turn onto Soma's long and winding driveway—our long and winding driveway, Martin reminds me. The stables fit for kings. The landscaped grounds —artfully wild, shaped by a small army of gardeners. From what I read in Soma's will, the land itself has been in the Blacksburg family since the early eighteenth century. I must have known it, walked it, lived on it. Maybe even loved it once. But now, I can't forgive it.

We pull up in front of the house just as we had last summer, right before all hell broke loose.

"This is the last place you saw her," Martin says. "Soma loved it here."

The modern monstrosity—black glass and stone, undeniably beautiful—has been repaired. Its massive windows, all of them shattered by the Bramwell witch, are gleaming and new. Colette had blessed the place with ash and smoke, spinning and howling through the rooms like a Cherokee stomp dancer, but I still feel uneasy. Something about the way the house sits on the ridge, the way the mountains frame it—

"She wanted this place from the time she was little."

"You didn't raise her here?"

Martin shakes his head. "Elliot built it and lived here with a string of women until he married Soma. I think she was happier about moving in than marrying him."

"You weren't a fan of their marriage?"

In all of our grief over her death the past few months, we've talked precious little about our daughter's actual life.

Martin sighs. "Elliot was twenty years older, with a difficult personality. But he had a talent for investing money, and he did love her deeply."

"But—"

"But Soma wanted to be a Blacksburg. And despite our being her guardians, this town would never let her forget that while she was a Bramwell by blood, she was also the result of a tedious scandal. One few people had an appetite for acknowledging let alone forgiving. Marrying Elliot changed everything for her."

I look up at the house again. The black glass is catching the first light, which the stone seems to drink in rather than reflect back. A monument to ambition, to transformation, to becoming someone new.

"She must have been lonely," I say.

Martin's silence is answer enough.

I open the door and step out onto the gravel. The air still smells of the incense Colette had used, only now it's infused with witch hazel, sassafras, and rotting leaves, making it sweeter, sadder.

The front door isn't locked. Martin walks in almost like he's never left.

"I guess a Blacksburg has nothing to fear except the supernatural," I say. "I mean, really, what could a meth-head or thief hope to gain by breaking in."

Martin turns, giving me a wry smile.

"I know. You hate the word supernatural," I say. "We're not outside of nature, but part of it. No different than a leopard or an angler fish."

Inside, the foyer opens into the cavernous living room I remember. The shattered glass has been completely vanquished and everything is almost exactly as it was. The only thing missing is the enormous antique Tabriz rug—I'm willing to wager it was Martin's only contribution to the place. It had suffered a lot of damage from flying glass and blood stains and was out for repair. In the corner, that onyx Masterson sculpture still twists its figures into impossible positions.

Nothing soft. Nothing that suggests a family with children in mind. Just Soma's deliberate transformation of herself into a Blacksburg, into someone who belonged in a house like this.

"I'll start in the library." Martin's voice echoes slightly in the rugless, high-ceilinged space.

I take a few moments to take in what's left of Soma, before heading toward the stairs. Those are curved up along a glass wall that overlooks the grounds. I keep my eyes forward, not wanting to see my reflection in all that dark glass. Not wanting to see what might be looking back.

The hallway upstairs is narrower, more intimate. Doors on either side, all closed. I go to the last one on the right—Soma's bedroom—and push the door open.

Heavy curtains are drawn against the coming dawn, the room caught in half-darkness. The bed is severe, modern, covered in chocolate velvet. But on the nightstand, is a small lamp shaped like a crescent moon—the kind a child might love.

I find the light switch.

Soma's nightstand also has a single framed photograph of

her and Martin when she was about twelve years old. The age I'd lost my dad. In it, she's seated on a stunning gray Arabian, her long, blonde hair gushing from under her helmet. Martin is standing next to her. It occurs to me that there are no family photographs in the common rooms of the house, which make sense for a place that's used for entertaining. Especially since a certain member of the family doesn't appear to be aging. I pick up the photograph and tuck it into my purse.

Her drawers hold silk and cashmere, her closet a fortune in designer pieces. Soma, unlike Martin, used her money in a none-too-subtle way of wielding power. She did it tastefully, but she did it. She wanted the rich Valemont board members—people like Skelton Stanler—to know that she could not only keep up, but had the freedom to pick and choose whose patronage she was willing to accept.

I wonder how Stanler made his way into her inner circle. Why she'd gone out of her way to introduce me to him at her party last summer and made sure we did more than exchange pleasantries. She wanted me to remember him, get a flavor for him. And him to get a flavor for me. He'd gotten his taste the night he'd tried to kill me.

On her wall, across from her bed is another contemporary art abomination. This one is all hard angles and negative space —black lines intersecting across a canvas the size of a door, with points of gold leaf scattered like careless coins. The only soft edges come from an irregular oval illustration that floats in the distance. Its addition somehow makes the painting look even more severe.

I turn away from it, moving to Soma's bookshelves. They line one wall, floor to ceiling, packed tight. There's a lot of poetry. Dickinson, Plath, Olds, Bishop. Collections I recognize, some I don't. A few highly selective journals that had featured my work, their spines cracked from reading. Then I see another copy of *Moon Child*. I pull it out and it falls open to the title poem, the page dog-eared.

Still as water under the moon.

My eyes drift back to the painting, taking it in as a whole, stopping at the points of gold leaf.

I step closer. The black lines cut across white canvas in sharp diagonals, meeting at unexpected points. The illustration is in the center of those points. And the gold—not scattered carelessly after all. They mark something. Intersections. Positions.

I think of the mill. The way Martin stood in the doorway looking out at how it sat in relation to the peaks beyond. *Elliot always built with intention.*

I go to the large picture window and draw open the curtains, looking out upon Soma's view of the Blacksburg grounds. Now that I can see it, it's unmistakeable—like a formation in a cloud.

The painting isn't abstract. It's a map.

The lines are sight lines. The gold points mark where structures sit—the mill, the trading post, this house. The illustration is Hallow Lake. All positioned deliberately, all aligned to specific points on the ridge. And in the center, barely noticeable unless you know what you're looking for, a cluster of gold points form a pattern I've been staring at all night on my phone.

The constellation from the astronomical chart in the Luna Archive. The one from the page I'd given Brooks. The configuration of stars during the 1830 eclipse.

"Martin," I call, my voice not quite steady.

I hear his footsteps on the stairs, quick and certain. He appears in the doorway.

"Look at this," I say, pointing at the painting. "It's not just art. It's—"

"A survey," he finishes, coming to stand beside me. His face has lost expression.

I SNAP a photo of the painting and its position in the room. Then of the view. Martin suggests we take it with us, but I don't want to move it. I want to be able to return here and sit with it.

The painting is relatively new, according to Martin. He'd only gotten a few glimpses of it before today. Unlike some of her other purchases, Soma hadn't made much of it. Its inclusion of Hallow Lake, disproportionately prominent, makes me uncomfortable in my skin.

"Martin," I say, as we step outside. "There's something you need to know."

I tell him about Hallow Lake first—the woman, the demon's kiss, how it mirrored what happened to the Jeffers boy. Then, harder, I tell him about the mill. The vision of fire and spite. The only thing I keep back is Buzzy's. The man. What I'd dreamed of doing to him.

"Martin," I whisper. "I saw it. I felt it."

This time I do reach for his hand, and he takes it, then brings me in close. His soft breath warms the top of my head, his palm cradles my skull. Over his shoulder, the line of trees is starting to become visible in the early morning light. While it is still dark, I can see a mist that curls between them. And something else. A shape that almost looks like a man. I step away from Martin and walk toward it. I can hear him behind me, following. As I draw closer, the figure becomes clear. It comes out from the trees and walks in our direction.

"Sweet St. Romedio," I say.

It's a man. Naked and covered in blood. His head is all but gone, with only a jagged stump for a neck, the top of his spinal column sticking out. It's Elliot Blacksburg.

The mangled ghost—Elliot, who'd jumped from The Montague Hotel's bird tower—gestures for me to follow. He begins walking back towards the trees, his step a determined march. I can hardly breathe, but I do follow. I do it unthinking, without choosing.

Martin comes up behind me. We stride past Soma's garden and into the dense tuft of trees that sits in the hollow of Nightvale Mountain. Elliot's bare feet step carefully over their roots. On the other side of the trees, we come to a soft swell of rolling hills that lead into the mountain range. At the top of the hill closest to Nightvale Mountain is a crumbling stack of stones that look like they could've been something once. The ruins of a chimney, or just the bones of something the mountain had reclaimed. The three of us stand looking down upon it.

"This was my mother's altar." Martin crouches down, looking at the stones. I don't know much about his mother, only that she'd been a powerful moon witch who'd been murdered over a century ago. Martin doesn't like to talk about her death, and I don't want to push.

He tips his face up at the lightening sky. The brightest stars are still shining, the crescent moon is still aglow.

"The configuration of stars is correct," he continues. "But her altar wasn't identified on the canvas."

"The painting didn't lead me here, Martin," I say. "Elliot did."

But by this time, Elliot is gone.

15

It's almost three in the afternoon by the time I wake up. Martin left a note on the nightstand, telling me he should be back in time for a late dinner. I shower quickly, just to get the smell of shame and foreboding off my skin, and drive straight to the cave where we found Brooks Craven's fossilized remains.

Petal Whitaker is there, which I half expected. I'd wanted the place to myself—to think, to untangle how much of what I'm seeing is memory and how much is dark magic working its way into me.

The cave exhales a chill that smells of old rain and even older rock. Drops fall with the patience of centuries. My phone light catches on the wet innards of the place, turning every curve into a living shadow.

"Find anything else?" I ask.

Petal shakes her head. "No modern junk, thank God. Just trilobites and brachiopods—Ordovician era. The stone's a graveyard for sea creatures, not people." She crouches and brushes the rock where Brooks's arm had been embedded. "See this little guy?" A trilobite, perfect as the day it died, its shell and multiple eyes gleaming. "He belongs here. Brooks Craven didn't."

A shuffle sounds at the mouth of the cave. Colette appears, wrapped in a long, wool cardigan, her skunk-stripe hair loose over her shoulders. Even in hiking boots, she looks like she's wandered straight out of a tarot reading.

"Fillmore," Petal says, referring to Colette by her last name.

"Came to pay my respects," Colette says with a nod. Her eyes meet mine, then dart away.

"You knew Brooks?"

Colette nods. "A little. He was local—well, nearby."

"I'd had Brooks pegged for a Boston transplant," I say. "Harvard man, according to his résumé."

She runs her hand along the cave wall, sniffing the damp air. "You think mountain folk can't get into Harvard?"

Since our drive to Charlottesville, Colette has been challenging everything I say.

"I think they can," I tell her. "But most don't want to."

Petal snorts. Colette drifts deeper into the cavern, her boots echoing.

"Hey," I say quietly to Petal. "You said something the night we discovered the arm bone." I still couldn't bring myself to say that it belonged to Brooks.

Petal widens her eyes. "I said a lot of things that night. Most unfit for polite company."

"You said you saw evidence of Martin's mother's work."

Petal mm-hmm's.

"Is that because she'd been here for so long that you'd find traces of her all over the mountains or something more specific?"

"There's the general residue of a person's long-time presence in an area," Petal says. "And there are artifacts from more complex behavior patterns—cooking in a kitchen or around a fire, for instance, certain religious rituals and other witchcraft."

"Was that what his mother was doing here?"

Petal shrugs her shoulders. "Hard to say. Sure looked to me like she was working hard to keep something out."

"I guess she didn't succeed."

Petal raises an eyebrow at me. "Oh, she succeeded. This place is pure, clean. About the safest place you could be."

"Then how did Brooks end up dying here?"

Petal takes a deep breath. "I wouldn't say he died here, exactly," she says. "A lot has changed over half a billion years. This place was mostly underwater then, and there's a good chance Brooks just drowned. Or he washed up on land and slowly suffocated in air he couldn't breathe. Could've been a mile from here."

For his sake, I hope he drowned.

"Someone sent him," I say. My throat tightens.

"Someone eaten up by spite," Petal says. "Something done with pleasure, not purpose. You know the kind."

I do. "It would take a powerful witch in a powerful place."

"Only one that fits is The Montague Hotel."

From deeper in the cave, I hear Colette's footsteps stop. She's been listening.

"That's right," Petal says, looking at me steadily. "You were supposed to meet him there that day we found the bone."

"He never showed," I say.

The words feel hollow even as I speak them. My feet are already taking me out of the cave.

"Where you going?" Petal asks.

"I need out of this coffin, away from the stares of the trilobites."

OUTSIDE, the crisp October air feels like summer compared to the interior of the cave. I put my face to the sun and breathe in its rays—a perfectly human way of drawing strength that does nothing to make my skin glow or my legs run faster, but reminds me I still belong to God.

Behind me I hear the sound of hiking boots snapping twigs. "Petal?" I call back toward the cave mouth.

"She's staying," Colette says. "She's got work to do."

We're alone then, just the two of us and the changing woods —leaves gone yellow and rust, their scent bitter with autumn.

"Do you want to go grab a cup of coffee?" I say. "Or bourbon."

"I sure don't." Colette's voice is flat and wrong.

I turn to face her. "What's with you?"

Colette points at the necklace Lyla made for me. I'd forgotten I'd put it back on after Martin and I returned from Nox's place. "Look at that," she says. "It just sits there like it's nothing. Neither hot nor cold."

It occurs to me that was why I'd forgotten I was wearing it. Lyla's Rowan wood pendant, which grows cold when danger is near me, and hot as blazes when someone like Martin comes close, has been sitting against my collarbone, unchanged, for days.

"You think it's broken?"

"I think it's warning you," Colette says. Her eyes unsettle me. They remind me of Nox's—wary, pitying, afraid. Like I'm something to be watched and studied. Maybe stopped.

"You said Brooks never made it to The Montague?" she says.

"That's right."

"And you just sat there for a few hours writing poetry."

Not just any poetry. A poem for Martin, but I don't tell her that.

"It's funny because Page said Brooks did show. Walked in at 4:30 sharp and made a beeline for you. Page had a clear view from the concierge desk." Colette folds her arms like she's protecting herself. "He said you and Brooks went downstairs where the old disco used to be, but that you came back up alone. Then you stayed around for a few hours, but you weren't writing any poetry, that's for sure."

The forest lurches. The ground shifts beneath me like the deck of a boat.

"That's not—" My throat closes. "Colette, I didn't—"

"Room 756 at The Montague Hotel would have a lot to say about that evening, Twila. The people in the room next door sure did and made sure Page got an earful."

Room 756. The married man from Buzzy's. His gold wedding ring catching lamplight. The satisfaction of spite.

"I couldn't—"

A sound like glass breaking fills my ears, high and sharp and endless. The world goes white at the edges. My knees hit the dirt and dead leaves, a sharp rock catching my shin. I hardly feel it.

"Colette." I can barely form her name. "Please. Help me."

"Jesus, Lord Jesus." Colette's voice cracks. She covers her mouth with both hands. "Twila, I don't know if I'm strong enough for what you need."

But she's moving toward me. Pale, reluctant, but coming.

I reach for her shaking hand, pressing it to my forehead, then my lips. "Please."

Her fingers thread through my hair. When she speaks, her voice is weak, trembling:

"Lord of Mercy—
keep her name from the mouths of demons.
Wash her clean in the rivers of light,
where angels dip their wings at dusk."

HER VOICE STEADIES, grows stronger:

"BY SALT AND SMOKE, *I bind the dark.*

By ash and thorn, I break its mark.
Let no shadow feed on her sorrow,
no serpent whisper her worth away.

IN THE NAME *of the Son who bled,*
and the Mother who wept beside him,
let her heart be uncorrupted,
her soul unkissed by flame."

The wind stirs the leaves around us, then goes still. Finally, her voice rings out—loud, commanding, furious with conviction:

"So I speak it, and so it shall tremble,
until morning burns the lie from her skin!"

When I open my eyes, Colette's face is full of tears, dropping one by one onto my cheeks. Her hand rests on my head like a blessing or a goodbye. I don't feel cleansed. I don't feel saved. But I feel *seen*—and that's somehow worse. Because now someone else knows what's been happening to me.

The woods around us have gone too quiet. No birds. No wind moving through the branches. Just us and the cave behind us and the October sun that now feels cold as judgement.

"Did it work?" I whisper.

Colette's hand slips from my head. She wipes her face with her sleeve.

"I don't know," she says. "I honest to God don't know."

16

I fall against Selene, resting my head on her canvas top. I thought I'd put behind me my days when my Jeep felt like my only friend. I think about Lyla's house—Dad's house—now only a shell of blackened brick. All of those memories—gone. The tangible ones that we can see, smell, hold in our hands. What we had left of Dad. I've only talked to Lyla once since that early morning fire. All she did was cry. All I did was wonder how things would be different if she hadn't been drinking Apple Jack at Brunie's. If she'd gone home that night, she'd be ash just like our vacation pictures from Folly Beach. And I can't help thinking—thank God she didn't tell me.

If I did send Brooks into primordial oblivion, just for kicks. If I did go to room 756 with that creep instead of writing a poem for Martin, then I would have stopped at Lyla's on my way to the monastery and lit her house on fire.

I push away from Selene and peer into her window.

The poem. I wrote it into the field journal Martin gave me. It took me two hours to write. To distill what I wanted to say until there was nothing left on the page but what was in my heart, my soul.

I throw open Selene's door and grab my leather backpack from the driver's seat, rummaging through it like a fiend. The journal sits at the bottom, untouched since that evening at The Montague. I run my hand over its indigo cover, barely able to breathe. Slowly I open the journal to where I left off, a simple green ribbon keeping my place. There, on the thick, pressed paper... is nothing. Not a word, or a scratch. I flip through the pages, but the poem I wrote for Martin, the one I put to memory and recited at *Our Lady of the Angels*, is nowhere to be found.

I throw the backpack on the floor and collapse into the driver's seat, gripping the steering wheel, thumping my head against it harder and harder, until a smear of blood paints its light gray plastic. I want to bash my skull in and let my brains spill out all over the dash, along with whatever good sense I have left. To scream holy murder and beg God for forgiveness.

I let that ancient witch touch my lips. I've been rotted from the inside out and it's only a matter of time before it takes the rest of me. The parts that are horrified by what I've done. Until I become like her—the Bramwell witch responsible for unleashing the vulture demon, killing a fine man like Abner Chitwood, driving Soma and Elliot Blacksburg to their deaths. And right now, I actually feel sorry for her. Because maybe one day in the past, she was sitting somewhere just like I am. Horrified by what she was becoming and not able to do a damn thing about it.

"Miss Stith?"

Grace Goad's voice hits me like a perfume I used to love. I look up from the bloodied steering wheel to a pair of violet eyes, wide and worried, with a brow knitted so tight it seems to hold the world together.

"Oh, Miss Stith." She reaches out her hands and I swat at them.

"Stay away from me!"

"You're all bleeding," she says.

My voice is alien—the roar of a lion and the croak of a frog all jumbled together. "Don't you touch me, Grace," I shriek. "Get back! Get as far away from me as you can!"

"No," she says. Her voice starts to quiver. "I won't."

She takes my face in her hands and makes a cross on my forehead, then circles it. She leans in and kisses that mark, and when she steps back, my blood streaks her face. She wipes it away with her trembling forearm.

"You have to seal it in," she whispers. "The blessing. Or it just floats away and you're back where you started."

I hang my head and drops of my blood fall in a steady rhythm onto the empty page in the journal, where Martin's poem should be. I pick a pencil out of my backpack and tell Grace to hold tight. Then I scribble a note to Martin telling him everything I've done. How I killed Brooks and tried to kill Lyla. Burned everything from the only life I did remember to the ground. The way I drank with a married man and went up to room 756. I'd tied him to the four-poster bed, biting and scratching at him like a wild cat, giving him a hook-up he'll be thinking about for the rest of his natural life. And the whole time I wanted his wife to catch us, thrilled to it. I tear it out of the journal without even folding it once and hold it out to Grace.

"Get this to Mr. Blacks—I mean Mr. Martin right away, will you?"

Grace looks down at the bloodied page, then back at me.

"Twila, I think you need to go to the hospital," she says.

But I'm done talking. Outside the windshield, the trees at the edge of the parking stand sharpened, as if carved into my view. I can feel attention on me—patient, pleased attention. The way you'd watch a mouse realize the trap has already sprung. And somewhere, in a place I can't name or reach, I feel the ghost of a hand smoothing my hair. The way a woman might soothe a child. Or a puppeteer might gentle a string.

I flip the ignition and jam Selene into first gear. Pine needles blow out in gusts from underneath her tires as I speed past Grace. I can barely hear her calling after me.

SELENE and I bounce and thud our way up the crap road to Widdershins Hollow, four-wheeling it too fast, probably cracking her axel. Nox's cabin looks simple and righteous in twilight—the thuribles are still smoking with black salt, only now they feel like they're meant for me. Like I'm the thing those protections are designed to keep out.

I kill the engine but leave the keys at the ready. My head throbs where I split it open against the steering wheel, blood crusting in my hair. I can see Nox through his window, sitting at that same café table where he'd told us about the Jeffers boy, about the woman who stole children's souls with silver threads. Who'd wounded him in places that weren't meant for healing.

Nox comes out of the door before I can reach the ivy-captured gate of his chain-link fence. "You stay right there," he says.

"Nox," I say. "I'm not here to hurt you. I need some answers."

"Seems like you got all the answers," he says.

I look past his shoulder at the house that kept me safe when the vulture demon Vyrithra was after me. Behind it is where I watched Martin chopping wood and realized for the first time that he wasn't my enemy, but someone who'd loved me. Yet another person I destroyed without knowing it.

"You were the first to notice something," I say. "And you were different towards me from the moment Martin and I pulled up here last week. I need to know what changed. What you saw."

I watch Nox's shoulders rise and fall with his breath. He closes his eyes, and licks his lips, nodding slowly. Then he holds out his arms, palms up, and looks at the sky.

"Finally, my brethren, be strong in the Lord," Nox says.

"And in the power of His might.
Put on the whole armor of God,
that ye may be able to stand against the wiles of the devil.
For we wrestle not against flesh and blood,
but against principalities, against powers,
against the rulers of the darkness of this world,
against spiritual wickedness in high places."

Ephesians 6:10-18—The Armor of God. I remember it from Sunday School. Nox smacks his lips as if he can taste the words on his tongue, then he walks toward me, slow and steady. He glances at the smoking thuribles, and looks me right in the eyes, like he's steeling himself for a fight. Or for his end.

"Come on in," he says. "The herb and ash don't work on you anyway. Never did."

THE HOUSE IS in better condition than it had been when Martin and I had come. Like Nox has made an effort to keep up with what we'd done to set his place right again. The dishes are clean, the floor is swept. He's still sleeping on his recliner though.

I sit down on the windowsill bench, leaning back against the glass. Too worn out to sit up while he tells me the details of what happened. Nox stands in the galley kitchen door frame, his arms folded across his chest as he speaks.

"It was in the wild parts of the hollow, a few weeks back," he says. "I went feeling an itch in the soles of my feet. I'd felt that itch before, so I knew whatever was there was no good."

Nox pulls a handkerchief from his jeans pocket and wipes his nose. "The body was the first thing I saw—laid out like an offering. Young man, dressed like he had a job to go to. And not the kind that would get him dirty. Symbols were carved all over him—ones I recognized from that missing page in the registry you showed us in that poetry book last summer. His jaw been forced open and not a bug or scavenger would touch it. I knew even before it spoke that the veil had been torn."

I can imagine the scene all too well. The desecration of the body, the air thick with decay. It doesn't feel like a memory, thank the Lord, but I can make a strong and vivid picture of it. "The body spoke to you?" I say.

Nox nods. "It was her."

"The Bramwell witch?"

"Not a lot of living witches that powerful these days."

"What did she say?"

Nox shrugs, but not like he doesn't care. Like he cares too much.

"Nothing important to anyone but me," he says. "Few nights later, she started talking to me from the trees over there." He points beyond his shed.

"The blessing-in works on her, because she's fully corrupted. Every cell in her putrified soul gone blacker than outer space." He tips his head and narrows his eyes at me, like he's looking at the woman he knew last summer and not the thing he fears I've become. "She would call on me, taunting and seductive. I didn't go, but I wanted to."

"Then one night I had enough. I took a kerosene pitcher and a torch out there with me, blessed ash in my pockets, rubbed in my hair, all over my skin. Drank a yarrow tea down in one gulp. Coming up, though, I heard two voices. Women whispering together the way they do. Only the whispers were like the hisses of snakes."

Nox comes over to where I'm seated. He stays a few feet away, but it seems like he's trying to prove to me, to himself, that he isn't going to let evil get the best of him. Whatever needs to happen, he's here for it. "There, by the wisteria," he says. "You stood with that thing like you were at a garden party. And when you heard me, you looked up, all surprised. 'You been sick, Nox,' you asked. Just like you did when you came with Martin. This time I knew not to wait. I squirted the kerosene and threw the torch to the ground. The fire followed up to her, lighting her dress and back. And I ran. Ran all the way back to the house and shut the door. For a few minutes you called to me, asking me to let you in, saying you could explain. Told me how you'd see me on the weekend. That you and Martin were coming up. Next day, I found that necklace you used to wear—outside from where the voice came. Few days later, you and Martin came up just like you said you would and you pulled it from the herb basket, where I'd put it to keep it well blessed, so it couldn't do no harm."

I can't stop fingering Lyla's Rowan wood pendant. "It doesn't seem to work anymore," I say. Nox just huffs.

"Nox, I don't remember ever being here before I came with Martin."

"Well, there's a lot you don't remember, isn't there?"

"I don't know what's been going on, but I do know I'm scared. And I know that the Bramwell witch is powerful and knows how to manipulate people, places, even time."

"So do you."

I look down at my lap and fold my hands. I want to say a prayer, but it won't come.

"I wanted to believe that when you came back, you were the same woman I'd known. That Martin had known," he says. "I thought you were. I thought you come to save us. Only when I think about it, things only got worse since you showed up. And after last summer, when every one of us was doing a victory dance over how you were going to get your birthright and how you spanked that witch hard and would get her gone once and for all when you got your power back...well, things only got worse after that, didn't they? Makes me think maybe you didn't come to beat her, but to join her. Whether you knew it or not."

"Don't say that," I whisper. "Don't even say that."

Nox hands me one of his clean handkerchiefs so I can wipe my face of tears and dried blood. "If you're not too far gone," he says, "there may be a shot."

I look up, and for the first time, Nox isn't glaring at me like I might flay his skin the second he lets his guard down.

He walks to his kitchen and I hear him pulling things from the pantry—glass jars clinking, dried herbs rustling. When he comes back, his arms are full of roots and satchels and that same cast iron pot he uses to brew his teas.

"A revealing ritual," he says. "Called The Unbinding. It'll show glimpses of what's hidden, what's been taken, what's been changed." He sets everything on the table between us. "Like a dream that expresses your subconscious. It'll help us see whether there's anything left in you worth saving."

The crescent moon has risen and hangs outside his window —barely visible through the trees. A sliver of bone against the darkening sky.

"When?" I ask.

"Now," he says. "Before you lose what little light you got left."

Nox moves with the practiced efficiency of a man who's performed rituals in the dark too many times to count. He fills the cast iron pot with spring water from a mason jar, then begins adding ingredients one by one, naming them as he goes like he's reading me my last rites.

"Wormwood," he says, dropping in a twisted bundle of gray-green leaves. "For revealing what's been hidden and banishing what shouldn't be."

The water darkens immediately, turning the color of tarnished silver.

"Mugwort." A handful of softer leaves. "To open the inner eye and protect the vision."

"Bloodroot." He holds up a gnarled root, its cut end weeping red like a wound. "Three drops of its sap. For binding the vision to truth."

The crimson drops hit the water and spiral down like smoke.

"And jimsonweed," he says, his voice dropping lower. "Dangerous as hell, but it'll take you where you need to go. The dose has to be exact or you won't come back right."

He measures out the white trumpet-shaped flowers with care that borders on reverence, then sets the pot on his two-burner stove.

"This has to brew for twenty minutes," he says. "While it does, you're going to tell me everything you think you've done. Everything you believe makes you corrupted."

"I already know what I've done."

"Then saying it out loud won't hurt none."

I take a sip of the cold spring water he'd brought and pull my thick, wool cardigan closed—the plum-colored one Lyla knitted for me. Then I tell him. All of it. Even the ugliest.

Nox listens without interrupting, stirring the brew counterclockwise with a wooden spoon. The cabin fills with a smell that makes my eyes water—bitter and medicinal and old as rain water.

"That's what you remember," he says when I finish. "Or what you think you remember."

"What's the difference?"

"That's what we're about to find out."

He lifts the pot from the flame and pours the dark liquid through a piece of cheesecloth into a clay cup that looks like it was made for a high school art project. Steam rises from it like tiny ghosts.

"And take that off," he says, pointing to Lyla's pendant. "I don't trust it and neither should you."

I do as he says, pulling the necklace over my head and dropping it back into his basket of herbs.

"We do this outside," Nox says. "Just beyond the blessing line. Where she left that thing for me to find. Or one of you did."

My stomach drops. "Outside the protections?"

"The ritual only works if you're vulnerable to whatever's hunting you. Can't reveal truth if you're hiding from it."

He picks up the cup and a bundle of dried sage, then walks to the door. I follow, my legs unsteady.

Outside, the crescent moon watches us with its single, unblinking eye. The thuribles smoke and sputter, their black salt ash making the air taste like sulfur and grace all mixed together.

Nox leads me past the fence line, past the last of the blessed perimeter, to the edge of the trees where the wisteria grows wild and tangled. He uses the sage bundle to draw a circle in the dirt, the smoke leaving a visible trail.

"This is for witnessing," he says. "Not protection. Whatever truth wants to show itself, we let it."

I step into the circle, my heart drumming hard against my ribs. Nox stands just outside it, close enough to intervene but far enough to observe. He hands me the cup and I stare into its depths.

The liquid inside looks black in the moonlight, but when I tilt it, I can see swirls of red and silver moving through it like living things. I cinch my eyes shut and swallow. I think of Lyla and Colette, but most of all Martin. The way he looks at me with loving eyes and the thought of that changing makes me want to die.

"Nox," I say. "What if I'm too far gone? Will you—"

He reaches out and steps closer, touching me on purpose, which he hasn't done since last summer. He puts his hand on my shoulder and rubs it, meeting me eye to eye. "If it comes to that, I'll do it so Martin doesn't have to."

He may as well have cut me in two.

"Now drink it all," he says. "Every drop. No matter what you see, no matter what you feel, no matter who calls your name, you just keep watching like it's a movie. Watch until the end. You've got to see it whole or you might misinterpret what it's showing you."

I nod, bringing the cup to my lips. The smell alone makes me want to retch—bitter as penance, sharp as regret. But I tilt it back and drink.

It burns going down. Not like whiskey or hot tea, but something that digs in and eats at you.

I drink every drop, like Nox said.

The cup slips from my fingers and Nox catches it before it hits the ground. I wrap my arms around myself, feeling Lyla's love knitted into my sweater.

"Now we wait," Nox says, his voice already sounding far away.

The crescent moon sharpens overhead, and the trees begin to breathe—I can hear them, in and out, like lungs made of leaves and wood.

And somewhere deep inside me, something starts to fall.

17

It's like falling through time, water through fingers, each drop a memory I can't quite catch. A dimension where the moon is always full. Not silver but bone-white, carved from the skull of something old and watchful. Its light doesn't illuminate—it devours, pulling pieces of me toward its hungry face.

Twila Bramwell.

The voice comes from everywhere and nowhere, spoken in a language I understand in my marrow. It invites me into the vision until I'm part of it, but still able to watch what's happening, too. I can hear myself commenting on what I see. The way I'm begging God to keep my dad from dying, demanding to know why he took Beckett away from me. Tears stream down my face, burning my skin.

I'm lost, and I'm at home. The mountains fold and unfold before me like origami made of mist and memory. The Montague Hotel rises up, too, but its windows aren't windows. They're mirrors reflecting faces I should know: a woman with my eyes but harder, a child with blood on her hands, a man whose love spans centuries but whose face I cannot quite—

Martin.

His name tears from my throat. One part prayer, another part scream. I want to rip at his clothes, feel my hands on his skin, claw my way inside him and wrap myself around his beating heart. Protecting it, drinking the blood that pumps through it. But when I reach for him, my hands pass through smoke. He's there and not-there, solid as quartz one moment, scattered like ash the next.

"I've been waiting," he says, and his voice is the sound of wind through abandoned houses, "for you to realize you never left."

My toes feel slippery, like eels twisting between them. I look down and find the ground beneath my bare feet is poetry—literally. Words spiral up from the earth like vines, wrapping around my ankles: *blood-moon, covenant, betrayal.* They climb higher, these word-tendrils, seeking my heart, my spine, my tongue. *Forsaken, beloved, damned.* I say them out loud—an incantation.

And then, I grow cold, like winter has come on the heels of a hot summer day. The Bramwell witch appears—a stain spreading across the vision. She doesn't have a face, then she has too many faces, shifting too fast to hold. But I know her. In the parts of me that remember what my mind has forgotten, I know her.

She's standing at that split in the forest path. She's standing in Lyla's garden. She's standing between me and Martin in every century, every lifetime, casting a silhouette that looks exactly like mine.

"Moon child," I say. But I know she's not that, even if she wanted to be. And she knows it, too. "We could be the same," I tell her, feeling a pull so desperate and ruinous that it could destroy me—what's left of me. But even as I say it, I know we're not the same.

"You want to swallow my soul," I hear myself say, and I don't know if I'm speaking now or then, in the vision or outside it. "You would chew my heart and spit it out!" Into a turquoise lake of blue fire, that glows with burning sulfuric acids. I can see it. Feel its heat so close.

I fear it'll melt my skin to bone, but the scene fractures like glass.

Now I'm watching Soma as a child—small, terrified, standing in a room with symbols carved into the floorboards. The Bramwell witch is there, speaking to her in honeyed tones.

The vision shifts and I'm seeing through Soma's eyes now—watching as the covenant takes hold, watching as I split like a cell dividing.

"Mother!" she screams. I am torn limb from limb, my organs flung to the ground. Cut in two. Then I am sewn back together. The brides of Frankenstein.

One of us makes a pilgrimage to the past, living centuries with Martin, accumulating memories and belonging. Birthright intact, power surging with the strength of eight moons. The other wakes up in Charlottesville with a headache and no memory of travels. Only vague glimpses of the wilderness and a creature she follows there.

Both are real. Neither is whole. Neither is fully alive.

"You made a choice," says a woman who might be me in forty years, or four hundred. Her hair is white as winter morning, her eyes a gray made of mountain water.

I want to ask what choice but my mouth is full of moths. They flutter against my teeth, their wings dusty with starlight and sorrow. When I finally manage to speak, my voice is in their whispers: "I don't remember choosing anything."

"That was the choice," she says, and her smile is heartbreak given form.

The mountains around us begin to move, not earth-shifting, but time-shifting. I see flashes of myself in different centuries, always on the knife's edge of remembrance. And in every century, there is Martin. Always watching. Always waiting. Always losing me just when his fingers brush mine.

I call his name until my voice is but a scratch on a turntable.

Then I hear another voice. A distorted funhouse mirror of a voice that bends and expands until it nearly shatters. It's Lyla's voice, I'm sure of it. "Some stories can only be written in blood," she says. "Some truths can only be spoken by the dead. Some choices, once made, echo across lifetimes."

"I know what you want," I say. Not to Lyla, to the witch. The pages in the Moravian journals begin to flurry before me. The detailed chronicle of the eclipse of 1830 drifts away from the rest, hovering. "I know what I—"

The eclipsing moon bursts, and in the instant before the dark rushes in, I think I hear wings. Only it's me, gasping as the world comes into sense again. A world of trees and grass and the crisp fall air smelling of dried leaves and night flora. My body is mine again, and I can feel flickers of light from the moon casting over me through the canopy. It seems to speak to my bones, and I feel a surge where it touches me.

"Nox," I say. "I know."

But when I look up, I see him looming over me. His face is contorted in horror and pain, and he holds a thick branch in his hands. He brings it over his head and down onto mine.

IT DOESN'T FEEL like my body. The ground is frigid, digging into the points where my weight is concentrated—shoulder, hip, ankle. I'm lying on my side with my cheek stuck to the floor in a small pool of blood. Blood I can taste on my tongue. One by one, the sounds fill the air. A barred owl gives its eerie call, *who cooks for you*, and there's some clattering close by. Last comes the persistent sound of hitched breaths and sniffling. All of my senses are engaged and I'm awake. All except for sight. My head is throbbing and the thought of opening my eyes feels like raising a draw bridge by hand.

But I do it.

And I almost can't believe what I see, even if every other sense told me it was true. I'm surrounded by a circle of candles, lying on the stone floor in the nave of *Our Lady of the Angels*.

The wind moves through the Gothic arches of the windows. I can smell it—not just the damp and moss that's claimed the walls, but centuries of ash. The few remaining panes of stained glass are as dark as etchings.

I try to sit up but my body won't comply. I could use a direct stream of moonlight, but the ceiling is largely intact, with only one hole that offers a view of the starry night sky.

"Don't." Lyla's voice is close, trembling.

I turn my head, and it feels like my brain wants to burst through my skull. She's kneeling at the edge of the circle, her face blotchy and wet. Beyond her, Colette's standing there with her arms wrapped around herself, staring at the ground. And Nox—Nox is at the altar, his back to us, shoulders hunched like he's carrying something too heavy to name.

"Ly," I whisper. My tongue feels thick.

"Baby," she says.

"What—" But I already know. Its reek gives it away. Petrol. Splashed across the stones around me in dark, glistening arcs.

Colette finally looks at me. Her face is terrible—grief-stricken. Like she's not just mourning a loved one, but part of herself. All that she knew was right with the world.

"Nox heard what you said," she says quietly.

"I didn't—" My voice cracks.

Lyla makes a sound like something breaking. "Colette, we can't know for certain—"

"He's certain." Colette's voice is soft but immovable. "And he's seen more of this than any of us."

Nox turns around, his every movement a burden. His face

in the candlelight looks cut from something harder than flesh. As if he was sculpted by a failed and bitter artist.

"'We could be the same.'" He lowers his head, his voice barely a whisper. "That's what you said."

"She wears my face," I say. I can barely make the words and they come out slurred.

"You want to drink Martin's blood. Claw your way inside him." Nox's voice doesn't rise. Doesn't need to. "You know what she wants. You said it yourself. You said you know what you—" He stops. Swallows. "You didn't finish that sentence, but I know how it ends."

"You don't." As I try to push up onto my elbow again, Lyla moves to help me. Colette won't let her. She grabs her arm and jerks her back hard, like I might grow teeth and tear into her. "It's not what I meant."

The wind moves through the ruined monastery, and I watch the candles flicker as Lyla begins to sob. Her whole body is shaking.

"Nox, please," she says. "This is Twila."

He lifts a jerry can from the floor next to the altar—red plastic dulled by age. The liquid inside sloshes.

"No." Lyla's voice is barely sound. "You can't. I won't let you—"

"This place was consecrated for it," he says. "There was a time when moon witches brought their corrupted here. Gave them a chance to choose. Ask to burn and be saved before they're too far gone. Or burn anyway."

He walks toward me, and the petrol smell grows stronger. "For the sake of your soul, I hope you choose the former."

"I'm not corrupted," I say. But even as I speak, I still feel the doubt. I try to recall the visions during my Unbinding, but it hurts to think. All I can do is remember what I felt. I'm not like the witch. I'm something else. I don't want to scrape the good from the living, eat the world and make its people dance in my puppet theater like some hollow god. I want to help Grace and I want Lyla to be happy. I want to cook lasagna with Colette and watch old movies. I want to write poems for Martin, hold his hands when they're curled and monstrous, hear the way his chuckle rumbles up like a growl disguised as laughter. More than anything, I want to love him for the six centuries we lost, and another six after that.

Colette moves aside as Nox approaches. Lyla doesn't. She stays between us, her face upturned, crying out towards the heavens. It's the cry of an animal dying alone.

"Twila," he says. "It's time to make your choice."

"Please don't—"

He sets the jerry can down, and the petrol starts pooling around my feet. It soaks into my jeans, the chemical reek making my eyes water.

"For our God is a consuming fire," he says. Hebrews 12:29.

His hands are shaking as he pulls a matchbook from his pocket.

Lyla's body is so wracked with sobs, she collapses on the floor outside of the circle.

Colette touches Nox's arm. "Are you sure?" she asks. Just that. Just those three words said with a tremor.

And I realize—looking at his face, at the terrible certainty there—that he really is. That I'm too dangerous to let live, even if it kills him to do it.

A slight beam of moonlight falls through the hole in the roof. At least the moon is up there, watching over me. Maybe it will help guide me to Dad. Or maybe it can help me stay around Martin and Lyla, visiting them the way the dead visit me. I hold my breath, afraid that if I let the air in, it'll give me hope. Then I nod to Nox.

"Do it," I say. "Do it so Martin doesn't have to."

And Nox tears a match from the book

18

The match is struck and leaves Nox's fingers. It arcs through the air, growing brighter as it falls—like it knows it's about to be born again in fire. Before the match can land—before the flame can kiss petrol—I'm jerked off the floor. My head snaps back and I cry out in pain. But I'm not burning. Below me, the petrol ignites a fiery sun in the wreath of candles. The world is a blur of firelight and moonlight. Colorful shards of glass and night air rushing past—Martin's arms around me, his chest a wall against the cold.

He's running fast, and I can see the monastery erupt in flames behind us. Lyla and Colette are standing outside—Lyla screaming with joy—and Nox is calling Martin's name. Through the woods, the crescent moon tracks us. My head feels better under moonlight, and I can think more clearly. I must have had a brain bleed. The world streaks past—trees, darkness, the tang of petrol sharp and mean, the smell of smoke following us like a ghost. And all the time, Martin's heart is hammering against my cheek. I love the rhythm of it, the way I'm rocked in his arms to the beat of his soles hitting the ground.

"Rest," he says. "We'll be home soon."

MORNING LIGHT FILTERS through somewhere to my left, soft and gray, like the sun hasn't fully committed to the day yet. I roll from my side onto my back. The ceiling beams are rough-hewn, darkened with age, crossing one another like the ribs of an ark. I lie still, listening. No fire. No scripture. Only a hearth crackling somewhere. I'm alive.

I try to put the night into some sort of order. The monastery, Lyla, Colette, and Nox. The circle of candlelight, the petrol, the match. And Martin. He's holding me close and I'm growing so tired. It's not my body that needs the rest, it's my mind, my heart and soul. Somewhere in that haze of exhaustion is a deep drum of warm, soapy water and a roaring hearth that's not meant for my burning.

But now I can't remember how I got into this bed. One that's low to the floor and sturdy, much bigger than the queen size in my cottage. The sheets smell like fresh cut wood—dried grass, maybe, or just the scent of a house that's been closed up and waiting.

I touch my head where Nox hit me with the branch, and where I'd bashed it against Selene's steering wheel. There's a tenderness at my temples and behind my eyes, but it's not from being struck. It's from anguish—a claw of terror and desperation still dug into my skull. Moonlight can't heal the psyche as readily as the body.

The petrol smell is gone, replaced by lavender. My nightgown is soft cotton, faded from washing, the kind of thing you'd keep for decades because it fits just right. My skin is clean. My hair, no longer crusted with blood, falls soft and wavy beneath my hand.

More memories from last night bob to the surface, coming in fragments. Martin's hands, careful, but thorough. His voice, blessedly soft. The way he whispered the last few lines of *Litany*, a Langston Hughes poem we both love.

"*Gather up*
In the arms of your love—
Those who expect
No love from above."

I sit up. At least my body is feeling good as new. My eyes graze across my surroundings.

The bedroom I'm in is a reasonable size—neither lavish nor cozy. Windows on two walls—those floor-to-ceiling casement windows, currently closed but with simple linen curtains pulled back. Through one window I can see trees, endless trees. Through the other, more trees and what might be the edge of a terrace or patio. Everything is wood and simplicity. Built-in shelves along one wall, books crammed into them in that specific disorder that means someone actually reads them rather than decorates with them. I could live in this room alone.

On the nightstand beside me: a stack of poetry collections. I recognize some of the spines. H.D., Mary Oliver. A worn copy of Leaves of Grass. And underneath them, a fine journal with a ribbon bookmark, its leather faintly cracked. My hand reaches for it before my brain catches up.

"Sweet St. Romedio," I whisper.

It's my handwriting. Page after page of my handwriting. The letters are mine but looser, more confident. Poems I don't remember writing. Entries about our days going back years—decades. The very last reads July 13, 1976.

I can't stop my fingers from peeling back the pages.

This was our place. Mine and Martin's. Our home before I vanished into the chronosphere. Before the Gemini Covenant split me in two and I woke up in Charlottesville thinking I'd always been there, thinking my life started with Dad and ended with a teaching position I'd just lost.

I set the journal down carefully, like it might shatter, and swing my legs over the side of the bed. The floor is smooth wood, worn soft by decades of walking. As I put one foot in front of the other, I feel like I've done this here thousands of times.

I throw open our bedroom door, and enter a hallway. But it's more of a breezeway—one side leading to a central courtyard that I can only see in part. I follow the hall, trailing my fingers along the stone wall, noting its every imperfection. My feet know where to step, which boards creak, which don't. Muscle memory from a life I don't consciously remember living.

The hall opens into a great room, and I stop in the doorway, a swell of joy overtaking the residual horrors of last night. I actually gasp.

Books are everywhere. Floor-to-ceiling built-in shelves on every wall not made of windows. A massive fireplace, with a dying fire smoking up into the chimney. Furniture that looks hand-built—Craftsman style, easy lines, beautiful in their restraint.

And through the windows, through the open French doors on the far side—the whole courtyard.

A sycamore tree stands in its center like a pale ghost, its white bark catching the gray morning light, its orange leaves alive in contrast. The tree is huge, ancient, its branches spreading across the open space overhead. The house was built around it. For it. For me.

I walk toward it like it's an old friend. Through the great room, through those open doors, and into the courtyard itself. Flagstones underfoot, moss and wild thyme growing between them. The air smells green and alive.

I put my hand on the sycamore's trunk, petting its smooth bark the way I would a beloved pet.

You were standing under a sycamore the first time I saw you.

The courtyard opens on all sides into the house—the great

room behind me, what looks like a kitchen to my left, another wing to my right. And ahead—the back of the house falls away entirely. Wide doors accordion-folded open, and beyond them, a terrace that simply... ends. Becomes forest. No fence, no boundary.

And that's where I see Martin.

He's sitting on the edge of the terrace where stone meets soil. His back to me, head down. He's in fresh clothes—clean, light gray shirt, dark pants. Seems like he's been there for hours.

My feet are silent on the stone, but of course he hears me walking toward him. He probably heard my feet the moment they touched the floor in our bedroom. Caught the subtle change in my scent as I woke up.

His shoulders shift slightly.

"How long have you been up?" I say.

"A couple of hours." He turns around and holds out his hand, guiding me to sit next to him, but leaving a careful space between us. My legs dangle over the edge of the terrace and the forest spreads out beyond, all dense and green and indifferent to everything that's happened. Birds call somewhere in the canopy.

"You should have let yourself sleep. Especially after last night," I say. "It's Sunday."

It occurs to me that he might not have wanted to lie next to me, and I look away from him into the woods. I'm so sick of being such a cry baby.

"It's Monday morning," he says.

My head spins toward him like I'm a damned owl. "I've been asleep for a day and a half?"

He nods.

"The petrol—" he starts. "I burned your clothes. The smell wouldn't come out. But there are clothes here you can wear." His voice is flat and measured. Like he's afraid if he puts any emotion into it, something will break. "You were shaking. Even after you were clean, and after I got you into bed. You couldn't stop."

I look down at my hands. They're mostly steady now, but I remember the shaking. The way my teeth chattered even though I wasn't cold.

"They were going to burn me," I say, testing how it sounds in daylight.

"Yes."

I bite down on my lip and force myself to look at him. I owe him that. "I assume you got my note."

Martin's mouth hardens. Finally, he meets my eyes, fully. His are bloodshot, exhausted. "I got it."

And I can't hold it in anymore. My eyes brim with tears and my lip begins to quiver. Martin reaches over, but I shake my head. He hesitates, then takes my hand anyway. Squeezing it tight, pulling me toward him.

"You fool," he says. "Do you think I wouldn't have smelled him on you? You couldn't have scrubbed yourself clean enough with a month of scalding showers."

The words hang between us.

"Oh, God," I say.

"You didn't burn Lyla's house. You didn't kill Brooks. The Bramwell witch—she can wear your face, but only you can turn against yourself."

I want to deserve what I see in his eyes—the love, the concern, the quiet understanding. But all I can see is Lyla collapsing outside the circle, her body wracked with sobs. Colette's grief. Nox's face when he struck the match—certain he was saving me from myself. Martin, desperate to save me before I burned to nothing. I'd done that to them. I'd believed the witch's lies so completely I'd nearly destroyed not just myself, but everyone who loved me.

"How did you know where to find me?"

Martin's expression darkens. "I picked up your scent at Nox's house. Your fear and shame were hard to miss."

"Grace," I say. "Poor Grace, I must have scared her to death."

Martin nods. "Grace came by again yesterday. You know she read your letter—couldn't help herself. But she didn't believe a word of it. She sat in the courtyard under the sycamore and waited for you to wake up. I finally had to send her home."

"Good Lord, Martin," I say. "She's just a kid. What must she think?"

Martin smiles and pulls me closer. "She thought the poem you wrote was beautiful. So did I. She asked me if you were the moon child, and if that's why you named your book of poems that way. Her grandmother told her all about moon witches and the various prophecies and legends."

"Until yesterday she thought they were legends anyway."

"No," he says. "She always believed them. People from around here are different. They don't dismiss what isn't easily explained. They keep the stories from the past alive in their hearts."

We sit in silence for a while, the forest breathing around us. Somewhere above, the moon hangs there, slowly shaping from first quarter to waxing gibbous. Watching.

"You said Grace read my letter *and* poem?" I ask.

Martin reaches into his pocket and unfolds the crinkled paper I tore from my journal. It's splattered with my blood and my frantic confession. But beneath that is the neat, simple poem I'd written for Martin as I sat waiting for Brooks at The Montague Hotel.

"This was blank," I say. "I thought I never wrote it."

But of course the Bramwell witch could have easily concocted a spell to manipulate my perceptions. Especially if I was willing to believe. I handed the page back to Martin and he sat looking at it, reading the heartfelt words beneath the desperate ones. His mouth curved into a soft smile, his eyes falling over the page as if it were the face of a beloved. They lingered on the last few lines.

If there is another life,
I will find you there too—
by scent, by wound,
by the sound of your heart
breaking open for me again.

Slowly, he folds the page again and places it back in his pocket. He looks out into the forest seeming lighter, nourished somehow.

"This was our home," I finally say.

"Yes."

"You built it."

"In 1924. We had another house before that—next to the sycamore, not a part of it. But it was more typical of the region and a bit suffocating. We often slept on the porch." He looks towards the sycamore framed by the open doors behind us. "You said you wanted moonlight in every room. To be able to sleep under stars if we chose. We both wanted the forest to be part of the house, not apart from it."

"God, how you must hate the cottage."

Martin leans in and kisses me. His hand lingers on my face, holding me as though memory alone keeps me here. "I don't hate anywhere with you," he says. Then he gathers me against him. I let go of everything I've been holding balled up in my fist, heaving into his chest while he holds me, arms tight and sure, his hand in my hair.

"You're safe now," he murmurs. "You're home."

19

—————

"Are you hungry?" Martin asks.

We sit on the terrace edge, the forest at our backs. The morning sun is climbing higher, warming the flagstones, but neither of us moves.

The question is so ordinary after everything—after fire and petrol and Nox's certainty that I was a corrupted witch—that I almost laugh. But I am hungry. Starving, actually. I haven't eaten since before The Unbinding. Part of me wants to talk to Martin about what happened during that ritual—I know I need to—another part of me wants this time together to remain pure. At least for a little while longer.

The Bramwell witch is still out there wearing my face, rage and hatred like whiskey on her tongue. She'll rear her head again, but today I just want to sit in my house, in the company of a man I've called my husband since the time before Columbus.

Inside, the kitchen waits. Copper pots and dried wild-flowers hang in an oval above a huge farm table scarred with use. Martin moves through the space with an ease I've never seen in him—not the careful precision of the cottage, where everything seems small, or his formality at the Blacksburg Estate, where everything is cold and distant. Here, he knows where each implement lives: the cast iron pan dangling from its hook, the wooden spoon in the ceramic jar by the stove, the eggs in their bowl on the counter.

I lean against the stone countertop without thinking. My hip finds the exact spot. My hand rests on the worn edge as I watch him cook.

"You stood there every morning," Martin says without turning. "Just like that."

I trace the wood grain with my toes. "Were you the one who did the cooking then?"

"Sometimes," he says, cracking eggs into the pan. The sound and smell are achingly normal. "Coffee's second shelf, left side."

My hand reaches before I can think, opening the cupboard. The tin is exactly where he said, and beside it is a mug. Plain white ceramic, chipped at the rim, and gone slightly gray with age and use.

My fingers close around it and something in my chest cracks open. This mug has touched my lips an untold number of times. Has held coffee exactly the way I like it.

Martin glances over, sees me standing frozen with the mug in my hands.

"That one's yours," he says quietly. Then turns back to the stove.

We eat at the small table tucked into the corner of the kitchen. Morning light falls across the worn wood, and a warm, comfortable silence settles over us as if our only worry is whether the early frost has damaged our late beans. I can't stop thinking about my old journal in our bedroom.

Outside, the sun shines, but a cold drizzle begins tapping at the windows, fogging the glass at the corners.

"You used to write on the windows when the glass fogged

over. Poems sometimes, or just silly things for me to find. I'd wake up to your words frozen there."

I smile at him, picturing it. Not remembering any of it, though. "Can you remember something specific? Like a joke between us?"

Martin puts down his fork, then turns toward the window. He hesitates, then lifts his finger to the glass and writes, *If I lose my name, let yours stay in my mouth.*

"I wrote that?" I whisper.

Martin nods, mostly with his eyes. "It was the last thing you wrote to me." He rests his chin on his knuckles and looks at the window, the words. "I wouldn't clean the glass because I wanted the imprint of your fingertip to stay. Your turn of phrase, the sound of your voice, the way you moved throughout the house. I didn't want to forget anything."

"You wouldn't have forgotten," I say. "Fifty years is nothing to you."

"It's everything," he says. "When you've had centuries of mornings just like this one, and then suddenly—nothing. Just empty rooms and the ghost of your voice." He unfolds his hands and picks up his fork again, moving his eggs around on his plate.

"I used to do that at my dad's house all the time," I tell him. "Only the words were for me. I liked to think that when they disappeared, they would be absorbed into the house like spirits. My imprint on the place." That place was gone, burned to the ground, but here, in our house, it almost feels alright.

I look at my words in Martin's hand—slightly back-slanted and precise, even against a fogged window. Then I reach out and set my finger to the glass. *I don't remember my name yet*, I write, *but I remember you.*

Martin goes very still. His eyes track over my words, reading them once, twice. "Go read your journals," he says softly.

· · ·

THERE ARE DOZENS OF THEM. Not all of them are leather, like the one on our nightstand. Some of them are linen, a few strikingly similar to the one Martin gave me late in the summer. Those are my favorite, and I can tell they're well loved. The spines are cracked, the pages curled from being visited and re-visited. I start with those, even if they aren't the oldest, pulling them out of the box Martin had brought down from the attic.

They're filled almost exclusively with poems. There are a few notes in the margins on each page, and intermittent sketches capturing a moment, a feeling. I drew an oak, heavy with leaves, casting hushed light onto a grassy knoll on the left side of the house. The tree is no longer there. Martin, in leather work boots with a flat cap in his hand, bent over the buds of a small vineyard we'd planted, also now gone.

I fluff a couple of pillows and position them against our headboard, leaning back. Then I start at the beginning, inhaling each page. From the very first words, I'm struck by my choices of phrase, my observations, the emotions they're stirring in me—then and now.

I know my poems are filled with longing—I can feel it as I write them. Critics have said they "drip with a yearning they inspire." Only these poems, written by my moon witch self, seem not to long for what they don't have, but what they do. Every word is heavy with the fear of loss, as if I knew that at any time I could disappear and never wake up in this house, or see Martin again.

In these yellowed pages, I express myself in a way that is more raw than anything in *Moon Child*, or any poem I've knowingly written—even ones I've kept to myself. They are explicit in ways I would never publish. Not always in subject, although some of them are boldly, unapologetically sexual.

Most of the poems, however, are explicit in feeling, and the naked intimacy of it is startling.

One poem in particular stops me cold. It's about the sound

Martin makes in his throat when he's trying not to laugh. It's even funny at times, building to the point when he actually does laugh. No stanza breaks—just my heart spilling onto the page.

His laugh—it starts low, under his breath. Like the moon hums through him. He tries to press it down (he always tries) that almost-laugh, holding it back the way you hold secrets you want to be caught telling.

I feel it in my ribs first. The ripple before the wave.

Then it spills—ruins me every time. Something truer than joy. The moment his throat opens and the sound breaks free and I want to live there, in that breaking. His throat the keyhole. His laughter the door I keep trying to walk through.

The sound of him laughing still makes me shake like I've never heard music before.

I sit with that poem for a while, letting it sing through my blood. It starts to give me courage. Because I know what waits for me in a deep burgundy journal that looks like something I picked up in a stationary shop. It's not fancy, but well made, with a thread-sewn binding. Big enough for sketches, but portable enough to carry around. It's the journal I wrote in when we first brought Soma home to live with us as our daughter. I flip through it briefly, avoiding the words and their meanings, but catching the telltale signs of a busy mother. Coffee rings on several of the pages, smeared ink from a hurried hand.

"Soma," I say out loud, as if to make her real. Sometimes she feels like a figment of my imagination.

Finally, I open to the first page and begin to read.

Her eyes were still milky when we finally got her—the deep blue of an iris that hadn't yet decided what color it wanted to be. That was from the first page. The journal is written in notes to myself, sometimes whole paragraphs or pages. Basics about Soma's hair (white and downy, like a chicks), her skin (pink and pale like a rising strawberry moon). And there are fleeting moments, scenes sketched out in haste that I didn't want to forget. Nothing meant to be read by anyone other than me or Martin.

Like the way she almost never cried—not from hunger or chill or loneliness. Just watched us with those solemn, old eyes of hers. The pediatrician said some babies were just naturally calm, but I knew better. She was listening. Absorbing. Learning the rhythms of a house that existed half in the world and half beyond it.

She never startled when Martin moved too fast. She'd track him, as if she always knew what he was. Once, when a coyote howled in the distance, she turned her head toward Martin instead of the sound. Waiting for him to answer. And there was the way she'd go completely still when moonlight fell across her face. As if the moon was speaking to her in a language never meant for words. Martin would carry her to the window on full moon nights just to watch her watch it.

"There's a poem in that journal, about the night a murder of crows came. She was three, maybe a little older."

I look up to see Martin leaning against the doorframe, his hand running through his hair.

"Like the crows that came to Nox's last summer," I say. "When that thing—Vyrithra—was hunting me."

Martin nods.

"She was afraid, and you told her that the crows were guarding us."

I set the journal down and hold out my hand, inviting Martin to sit on the bed with me. He nestles close at my back, his chin resting on my shoulder.

"Maybe she was better aware of the danger than I was," I say. "The crows may have known who else was circling us."

"That's occurred to me, too."

I put the journal back into the box next to the bed and lay down on my back, Martin settling on his side next to me.

"You've read all of these," I say.

He runs his finger along my neck. "Yes."

I imagine him reading my thoughts over the years, looking for clues as to where I'd gone and why I left them.

"You once told me that she and I—that me and this me— are a lot alike. That I'm more sarcastic, though."

Martin emits that low, restrained laugh the other me had written about. It warms every part of my body.

"I recognize her, I do," I say. "She was less guarded, at least with you. I like her better than I like myself. But I can see how behind her words was this feeling that all of this was a mirage, and the rug could be ripped from under her at any time."

Martin brings me closer, lifting up his head and bringing his face over mine. "You only like her better because she's the other side of you. The one you only see glimpses of and can't quite hold for long."

"What if she and I never converge again? We could be stuck this way."

"There are worse things than happiness," Martin says, coming closer. His breath dances a slow waltz over my lips.

20

Waxing Gibbous

THE AIR SMELLS HEAVILY of sex, with notes of minerals, pine and woodsmoke at the edges. It's a scent that practically takes me by the hair and pulls me out of bed. I remember it from my dreams about following Martin through the wilderness, always feeling frightened and exhilarated, definitely aroused and confused when I woke up.

I roll over softly, so as to not wake him up, and tip-toe out of our bedroom and down the hall to the courtyard. There, I stand looking at the sycamore, its orange leaves dripping with the blue light of a half moon.

We'd spent the afternoon as a tangle of limbs, then read more of my journals together—the ones I'd written about him, about us, in ways that made us both forget the world outside existed. She—I—had written about him without apology, without hedging. About everything. The taste of his mouth, the weight of his body, what it felt like to fracture time itself in his arms. But not about the witch who came for Soma. Not about whatever she knew that made her warn a five-year-old to stay away, to keep it from Martin.

After the sun set, we put the journals down and turned back to each other. I knew my secret—the fear of corruption I'd hidden from him, the shame about the man from Buzzy's that connected to older shame, to my self-hating days, my grief-stricken days, when hurting myself was the only thing that kept me from killing myself.

My other self had her secret, too. And she'd loved him just as fiercely despite it.

The sycamore's leaves catch the moonlight. My skin is still warm from him, my body still carrying his shape. I don't know what she knew about that witch. I don't know why she kept it even from her journals. But I understand now that secrecy isn't something that happened to me when I fractured. It's some-thing I've always done.

"I've been waiting," Martin's voice said to me during The Unbinding ritual, "for you to realize you never left."

A puzzle of a statement that I'm now starting to get my head around. I'd been ripped away from him and in two. But I'd also started reconnecting with my moon witch birthright from almost the moment I arrived back in Sibyl Springs. Which shouldn't have been possible, according to the iron strictures of the Gemini Covenant. And the moment I began doubting myself again, entertaining my own corruption, I grew weak.

A light breeze blows through the sycamore's leaves, making them shiver. I walk to the ancient tree, the same one I was standing under when Martin first saw me, and let the moon-light claim my naked body.

I do it knowing who I am and that I'm not tainted by the Bramwell witch or any of the creatures with the sewn-up

mouths who called to me from Hallow Lake. Nor will I be. Not
if I have anything to say about it. And I have plenty.

"O Father of light—" I begin.

"You watched while they struck the match,
while the air filled with my own burning.

NOW YOUR FACE breaks through the smoke,
silver and scarred as I am,
and I remember what he told me once—
that the moon was the closest thing
to God's face I'd ever see.

SO, look at me now,
half-ash, half-girl, still trembling.
Hold me steady in your light.

LET your mercy breathe through me,
quiet the trembling in my chest,
the doubt that makes me flinch from love.

AND IF I AM YOURS—
as he said I was—
then make me whole again."

At once, the moonlight consumes me like silver fire, hot and
insistent, curling across my skin and pressing into my bones. I
breathe deep, and it isn't just air that fills my lungs, but the
pulse of the night, the hush of the forest, the weight of
centuries of light. My body trembles, quivering with a force that
can unmake me, but instead it weaves through me, wrapping
my marrow in quiet strength. My veins throb with its rhythm,

each heartbeat a wave it commands. My hair lifts in a wind I can't see, and I know I was never lost. I am luminous, unbroken, alive—the moon's daughter.

"Moon child," a tiny voice says. Sweet and full of wonder.

Out from behind the sycamore tree steps Soma. Only she isn't bleeding from her self-inflicted wounds. She isn't even grown. She is as I would have seen her just before I was banished by the Gemini Covenant. A beautiful white-haired girl who looks like she was made of the moon.

"I've been waiting here for you," she says.

She comes to me and wraps her small arms around me. Only now, instead of taking the world in a breath, I take her in and it feels like the universe. Like everything good and pure.

"You've been living here all this time, alone?" I ask.

She nods, and I know. When Soma made her own secret wish, her part of the covenant, she asked that I would somehow be returned to her and Martin. Part of her, the part who made that wish, had remained a child, her essence living here in our house, while the other grew up into a woman doomed by her mistake. Martin would have wanted to remain in this house, in the place where he'd last had both of us. But Soma—the Soma who grew up—she couldn't have lived here. Not with this child wandering rooms that should have been empty, a mirror she couldn't name and couldn't ignore.

"Are you alive," I ask her. Since I can perceive the spirit realm with the same clarity as the human realm, I can't tell.

"I'm not alive," another voice says.

I look over my shoulder to see Soma standing in her bloody bathrobe, just as I saw her on the day she did this to herself.

"But when you become whole, so will I."

It's then I feel the weight of his gaze like a firm hand. From the corner of my vision I can just make out Martin's silhouette —still as a monument, watching.

He can't see what I'm holding. The child-shaped moon in

my arms, or the woman bleeding silver behind the tree. He can only see me, naked and trembling under the sycamore, embracing the empty air and speaking to ghosts.

Martin steps out of the doorway, crossing the courtyard toward me. His bare feet make no sound on the stone.

Little Soma's face lights up. She lets go of me and moves toward him, her small hand reaching out. He walks through the space where she stands, and she turns to watch him pass, her bow lips turning up into a smile.

When he reaches me, he doesn't speak. Just looks at me with those wolf-gold eyes that have seen me in every lifetime, and waits.

"They're here," I tell him. "They've always been here."

BOTH SOMAS ARE FADING—CHILD and woman dissolving into moonlight. The courtyard feels emptier without them, and fuller somehow. Like something has been named that can finally rest.

Martin takes my hand and leads me to the base of the sycamore. We sit with our backs against its trunk, his shoulder warms against mine, both of us bare to the night air and each other.

I tell him about what I saw, and what Soma revealed. What her young self had first said when she saw me, "Moon child."

"In Nox's book," I say. "The one he wrote about Appalachian folklore. He says that the only witch who could truly harness the forces of the moon's light, forming a legion who could fight the demonic forces when they emerged was called the moon child."

Martin holds his face up to the moon, then meets my eyes again. "That is what they say. What my mother said. Although there hasn't been a moon child in a long time."

"Did I tell you my dad used to call me that?"

Martin shakes his head.

"I don't think my mother did. Not that I know of."

"You never talk about your mother," Martin says.

"Neither do you. I figured it was too painful a subject."

Martin brushes his fingers over my cheek and I nestle closer to him, resting my head on his shoulder.

"It is painful," he whispers into my hair. "But mostly I don't talk about her because you knew her so well. Sometimes I forget how much shared knowledge we've lost."

Even with the journals, and the revelation about Soma, there's still so much that remains hidden.

"For me it's not really painful," I say. "It's more like I actually have forgotten. But not the way I forgot our life together. Everything that happened before she left is so hazy. I was young, so that's part of it. Most people don't have a lot of strong memories from their childhood. But I don't really have any. Just vague notions."

I look up at him again, and he strokes my hair, letting his fingers ride the soft curls. It feels almost as good as the moonlight itself.

"The only vivid memory I have from that time is watching my candles melt into my birthday cake after we found out she'd gone," I tell him. "Lyla says that's a common reaction to childhood trauma. Like sweeping it away into a locked room."

"For some, I suppose."

I smile into his eyes. "Terms like *childhood trauma*—that's therapy speak. I know you hate that."

"I don't hate it," he says. "I don't like sweeping generalizations. Especially when it comes to the human psyche. Yours particularly."

"I thought we weren't human, exactly." I say.

"On an emotional level, we're nearly identical."

Unconsciously, my eyes trace the shape of him—down the long lines of his legs to the pull of his hip, up across his chest where the moonlight breaks like frost over open tundra. He looks otherworldly and heartbreakingly human all at once. I kiss his shoulder.

"And your mother?" I ask. "What did she think?"

"She loved you. She knew what you were when I first described seeing you, and asked me to lead you to us. She didn't need to ask twice."

I close my eyes and try to imagine Martin at age fourteen. "Is that why you had me chasing you all through the wilderness?"

"Partly," he says. "I also simply enjoyed it." Martin reaches behind us, placing his hand on the bark of the sycamore tree. "This tree. It'll live as long as we do. That's how I knew you were still alive after you disappeared. Had my mother been alive, she could have told me you were coming back."

"Would she have?"

Martin looked up into the massive expanse of the tree. "We'll never know."

"Did she think I was the moon child?"

"Yes, but she also knew that your travels beyond the veil weren't the travels of a healthy witch."

I thought of the vision Martin had in Soma's garden last summer—that of his mother's corpse. *They killed her*, he'd said.

"Do you think the Bramwell witch killed her? Because your mother could see so much. Maybe she saw her?"

Martin eyes land on the interior of our house, flickering over the rooms that open from the courtyard. He shakes his head. "My mother wasn't killed by the Bramwell witch," he says. "But by a court of witches who feared her predictions. It was easier for them to believe she'd been corrupted."

"But they didn't burn her."

"No," he says. "Theirs was a blood-letting ritual enacted in the hope that they could leech some of her power."

The thought of her being carved up bit by bit, drained of

her essence like that, seemed worse than burning. I thread my fingers through his and squeeze them. "What predictions of hers did they fear?"

Martin's lips turn up, but not into a genuine smile. One made of bitterness, irony, and the kind of grief that will simply never fade. "She told them that dark times were ahead and the moon child was near."

"Good God," I say.

"Don't," he tells me, bringing our entwined fingers to his heart. "She of all people knew what could happen if she spoke up."

"Do you think after everything, that the covenant took that from me as well? Being born the moon child, I mean. If that's even true." Part of me hopes so.

"The Gemini Covenant is designed for the total annihilation of a witch's birthright," Martin says. "And yet here you are. You drank in the moonlight. You weren't just using it—you became part of it. The soil, the leaves, the air. Just as I am."

My stomach drops, sharp as a fall, and my hands curl against my thighs on instinct.

"I thought celestial persistence was rare. A choice made by only the most powerful witches."

"It is." He puts his fingers under my chin, tips my face up. "And you came here with your choice already made."

The words land hard and deep. The moon's daughter. A creature who will outlive forests and rivers. Lyla and Colette told me about the witches who make the choice, who bind themselves to the moon's endless cycles. But I'd never connected it to myself. Never thought to ask what it means that I survived the covenant at all, much less that I'm reclaiming my power.

"In The Unbinding," I say quietly, "I heard a voice telling me about a choice I made. About the consequences. I think I'm only beginning to understand what that means."

I pull back slightly, needing to see his face in full. It all feels too large, too absolute. Like claiming this could somehow curse me.

"Immortal," Martin says the word I can't. "Or as close to it as any creature can be. Barring violence, you won't age past your prime. Won't sicken. Won't fade."

I think of my father—his graying hair, the way his hands had started to shake in the final months of his sickness. The way I'd held him while he died, feeling the weight of his mortality like an accusation. I wonder if even then some part of me knew that I would go on while everyone I loved turned to dust?

"I don't know if I can bear it," I say.

I think of Soma and her choice. How she couldn't have known the weight of what she was doing.

"How can you live with it?" The question comes out ragged.

He's quiet for a long moment, his hand finds mind again. "Because the alternative is abandoning them to face those endings alone. Because love doesn't become less real just because it's temporary." He pauses, and I can hear the weight of centuries in his voice. "Because I have you."

The sycamore's leaves whisper above us. Somewhere in the hollow, nightjars call to each other across the ridge. The world goes on, indifferent to the revelation that I will go on with it, long past any natural lifespan.

Martin wraps his arms around me, and we sit in the sacred geometry of moonlight, two immortal creatures who've found each other again. Above us, the sycamore stands witness—a tree that will live as long as we do, marking time in rings we'll never count.

For now, this is enough: his heartbeat against mine, the moon overhead, the understanding that whatever comes next, we face it as we always have.

Together.

21

T he moon has shifted while we sit here, its light slanting through the sycamore's branches at a sharper angle. We've been quiet for a while, each processing what the other has revealed.

But there's one more secret. One more truth I've been carrying alone.

"Martin," I say—the thinness of my voice makes him look at me. "During The Unbinding, I heard Lyla. At least I think it was Lyla. She said that some truths can only be spoken by the dead. Some choices, once made, echo across lifetimes. I don't know if she was talking about me or about herself."

His expression doesn't change, but I feel his body tense slightly against mine. Part of me wants to stop, mentally sew my lips shut like those things in Hallow Lake, but I can't. Because at the same time it feels right to broach this last secret between us.

"When she was young—just before she and my mother left Sibyl Springs—she did something she's been carrying ever since." I take a breath, steadying myself. "She was scared. She thought she was helping. She... tore the page from the registry."

Martin's eyes narrow and he presses his lips to my temple. "I know," he says.

Somehow, his simple admission lands harder than any thoughts of my immortality.

"Lyla called me," he says. "While you were still sleeping. She was ashamed and utterly devastated that she'd felt so powerless to help you the other night. Then she told me. She said that unlike you, she deserves her punishment."

The words settle into me. Deep. Of course Lyla would think that. She always takes everything on herself. She was eighteen, for the love of God, and terrified, having horrible dreams about the registry spelling doom, watching people die around her in awful ways. Her parents from food poisoning. My grandparents in a fire.

"Damn, Lyla. Impulsive as ever," I say. "She thought if she hobbled the book, she could change the course of things."

"Twila," Martin says, wrapping me completely in his arms.

Part of me does just want to be held, told everything's going to be okay. "Do you know what she's done for me?" I say. "All my life. And I haven't always been easy."

"Nothing is easy," he says. "There will be a time when we have to confront what Lyla's done. But not today."

His arms tighten, he rubs his cheek against my head. "I understand wanting to break something to save the people you love. Even when it makes everything worse." I pull back to look at him. There's something in his voice—recognition, maybe. Shared guilt. "When *Moon Child* came out," he says, his voice barely a rasp, "I heard your voice in every line. The way you wrote about the moon like you were writing love letters to something that had never left you." His jaw works. "I thought you'd left me—chose a human life."

"You knew where I was for years?"

"I knew you were out there, yes. Living your life. Teaching." He says it without accusation, but I hear the wound beneath.

"When Soma suggested hiring you, I fought her on it. I didn't want to see you. Didn't want to face the woman who'd walked away from centuries with me for a tenure track position and a series of men who'd never understand what you were." The bitterness in his voice is old, worn smooth by fifty years of polishing. "And then you arrived at Valemont and looked at me like a stranger."

"Oh, God, Martin—"

"I spent years hating you for an abandonment that wasn't even real. So, you see, I understand being faithless, coming to the wrong conclusion in a way that's ultimately devastating."

His hand cups my face, thumb brushing my cheekbone. "And yes, I understand Lyla. I understand doing something that seems right in the moment and then living with the consequences."

I press my palm over his heart, feeling it beat steady and strong beneath my hand.

"I'm choosing you now," I say. "With my memories or without them. I'm choosing you."

"I know." He covers my hand with his, holding it against his chest. "And that's the only thing that makes any of this bearable."

We sit like that for a long moment, his hand over mine over his heart, the sycamore's leaves whispering above us. I catch a glimpse of the pale light behind the tree. Our sycamore, with its deep rings reflecting the years we've been together, will be together. It is today already. Dawn is just starting to break, and I can feel my skin getting cold as the moon's half-face begins its steady fade from the sky.

Martin stands up, then helps me to my feet. We dress in thick wool sweaters and jeans, sturdy-soled boots good for walking uphill. Martin's clothes are contemporary—mine, however, have a distinctly mid-1970s flavor. Left over from when I lived here, Martin pulled them out of a large cedar chest that doubles as a bench in our bedroom. My sweater is forest green Irish wool, heavy cable-knit with clean lines—the kind of thing you'd find in a good outdoor outfitter. And it smells heavily of moth balls. The jeans are Levi's, boot-cut, sitting higher on my waist than modern styles dictate, but well-fitted. Italian leather boots, brown and beautifully worn, make me feel like Ali MacGraw fleeing some doomed love affair through the Alps. I can't help laughing at myself in the mirror, but Martin looks at me with a fondness that speaks of everything he cherished and lost during that decade.

WE CLIMB IN SILENCE, breath clouding in the cold dawn air. The ridge path is narrow, hemmed in by frost-bitten ferns and laurel slick with dew. Every few steps, the light shifts—moon giving way to day in pale gradations of silver and rose. When we crest the ridge, the world opens wide beneath us: Sibyl Springs still sleeping under its gauze of fog, the valley stretched out like a sleeping giant. Nightvale Mountain looms to the west, a dark monolith that's watched us since the moment my bare feet touched the ground here hundreds of years ago.

Martin stops beside me, hands braced on his knees, and looks out over it all. The wind bites through my sweater, making my shoulders hunch, but he never seems cold. Like he wears an invisible cloak of fur.

It's so achingly familiar—Hallow Lake in the far distance, the curl of the river rounding at its side. The faint glint of the old rail line, even the ghostly outline of the hollow beyond the ridge. The moon's half-face is still visible, paling against the rising light, and for a moment it seems to wink at me before slipping away.

I take Martin's hand. Below us, the world is beginning again —softly, without asking for permission. A reminder that we'll have to leave our perfect oasis to take our strange place in it.

Endeavor to protect the vulnerable, the oblivious from what lurks in the blood and bones of this landscape.

Martin's fingers tighten around mine, his thumb brushing over the pulse in my wrist like he's counting something—time, maybe, or heartbeats.

"I used to come here to write," Martin says. "After you were gone."

"I thought you wrote your books from Abingdon."

Martin smiles out over the view. "I came while Soma was at school, to gather my thoughts, feel closer to you somehow."

I look at the sky above Sibyl Springs, now aglow in a blushing orange. A pair of ravens is flying overhead, heading somewhere with purpose. Calling to each other in their varied vocabulary—croaks, clicks, knocking sounds.

"I used to drive to Raven's Roost," I say. "It's high and windswept, like this, but with rocky outcrops and this vast view of the Shenandoah Valley. Locals say ravens circle there tracing invisible currents as if they're keeping watch over something buried."

"Is that why you went there—the ravens?"

I shrug, unsure. "Lyla said that ravens are drawn to magic like lightning is drawn to iron. And I always saw them there, but I don't think I felt any magic, at least not consciously. I did feel like it was the only place that didn't lie to me. Where I was completely part of the environment, like I belonged there. Everywhere else my nose was just pressed up against the glass."

Martin pulls me in front of him, slipping his arms around my waist, so we can take in the view together. I feel his chest swell at my back, his warmth taking the chill away. He puts his lips to my ear.

"In Celtic and Norse mythology," he says. "Ravens travel between the realm of the living and the dead. Odin had two— Huginn, who symbolized thought, and Muninn was memory. They flew the world each day and whispered secrets back into his ears." He nestles his face into my hair and holds me tighter. "I would whisper to the ravens when they came, hoping they'd carry you a message, or bring one to me. But I think the veil was too strong between us at that time."

I shake my head, lean in, and brush my nose with his. "Not strong enough to keep me from reading your books," I tell him. "My dreams about you bled into my mornings, you know. I was so thrilled about the prospect of meeting you when I first learned you were teaching at Valemont—and my department head no less." I can feel his chest drum softly with a chuckle. My fingers find their way into the dark silk of his hair. "Part of me was nervous, because your stories inspired some pretty erotic dreams on my part. Nothing explicit, but I definitely woke up feeling hot and bothered."

His teeth graze the curve of my ear. "Had I known," he says. "I might have chased you around the pool on the night we met again, instead of insulting you."

"I thought you said you should have kissed me instead of insulting me."

"If I caught you—and I would have—you'd have gotten more than a kiss."

The moment hangs there, balanced between humor and ache. Martin rocks me gently as a biting breeze moves along the ridgeline. Layers of sound announce themselves—first the rattle of the changing leaves, then the denser canopy below releasing a deep rustle. Under that I hear a cluck and a grunt. The clap and whistle of a pair of wings.

"Martin," I whisper.

The dove lands on a dead snag and holds open its feathers, stretching wide like a warning flag. The movement is sharp, nothing like the settling flutter of a bird finding its perch.

Its wings beat in a staccato display, catching the dawn light so that each beat sends a flash of white against the dark timber.

The sound is louder than it should be, that wing-clap cutting through the morning air like a hand slapping water.

Then it hisses.

Not the warning hiss of a bird protecting territory, but something sustained and fierce, its small body pulling taut with the effort of it. The white throat trembles, the sound serpentine and wrong coming from something so delicate. Then it turns its head to look directly at us—first at me, then at Martin.

It launches from the snag, wings beating hard in our direction—driving toward us, close enough that I feel the displaced air before it banks and dives toward the hollow below, disappearing into the trees that crown the valley.

The warning was clear: *Something is down there. Something is wrong.*

22

"We should go back," Martin says, uneasy.

The descent is faster than the climb, our boots finding purchase on familiar ground even as our minds race ahead. By the time we reach the courtyard, the sun has fully risen, burning off the last traces of fog. The sycamore stands exactly as we left it hours ago—same ancient bark, same sprawling canopy—but now it looks like what it was: Martin's gift to us. A deliberate theft of time, a few hours carved out of the chaos to remember who we are to each other.

As much as I treasure it, I can't help but to think that all that moonlit revelation and confession, all that talk of immortality and trust, and we left our phones behind like a couple of teenagers sneaking out after curfew. Like we have the luxury of being unreachable.

We don't.

My phone sits on the kitchen counter where I abandoned it, screen lit up like a constellation of missed warnings. Three calls from a number I don't recognize. Two voicemails. A text from Grace sent at 4:47 AM, while I was standing naked under a tree contemplating my goddamned celestial persistence.

Martin emerges from the bedroom with his phone, his expression carefully neutral in that way that means he's already processing something terrible and deciding how to tell me.

"Petal," he says. "She wants me at the cave immediately."

I'm already reading Grace's text, my throat tightening with each word:

Miss Stith, I got your message about Hallow Lake. I know you said come alone, but I'm a little nervous. Is 6 AM okay? It should be light by then. I'll bring my notebook. See you soon.

The world clarifies and every detail sharpens into focus—the apologetic tone, the nervous admission, the obedient agreement to meet alone. All the markers of a good student trying to do what her mentor asked.

Except I never asked.

"The witch," I say.

Martin's hand finds the small of my back but I'm already moving, pacing the kitchen like a caged animal, fingertips raking through my hair. Grace went to Hallow Lake. Grace went to meet something that knew exactly how to sound like me. Someone who fooled Brooks, the concierge at The Montague, and even Nox.

"How long ago?" Martin asks.

"Almost three hours." Three hours of her waiting. Or three hours of whatever found her there.

I want us to split up, go to Hallow Lake myself while Martin meets Petal, but he won't hear it. He knows all of the back ways that only experienced hikers will dare, so we can get there quicker together than if I drive alone. And Martin can move fast, even in daylight, a power I used to have, he tells me. When I traveled beyond the veil, the moon was always accessible to me, even filtered through sunlight. Now, while the sun merely weakens Martin, making him not quite so strong, it blocks me almost completely—like the moon's light is there but I can't reach through to touch it.

As we come up on the lake, Martin slows, but doesn't set me down. I glimpse the lake's black mirror reflecting the sky, and feel a sickly stirring in my belly, like I'm going to heave. The image of the old white witch, her thick, dark blood seeping out from where her mouth has been sewn shut, makes me shiver. I know Martin can feel it, and he holds me tighter, closer. I remember the way her face came toward mine, the way her lips enveloped my lips. The sweet and rancid smell of her breath, the wet curl of her tongue. I would rather kiss a bloated corpse.

It was just a dream, I remind myself. An illusion created by the Bramwell witch to make me doubt myself.

"Was she here?" I ask Martin.

His nose is tipped into the air, taking in the scents around us. "Not anymore."

"Can we follow her? Do you know which way she went?"

Martin finally puts me down, but keeps his arm around my waist. "She was here, but it's as if she vanished," he says. "I can't find the trail of her leaving."

I look down at the log where I used to like to sit. "Could the witch have erased her trail?"

Martin lifts his shoulder, cocking his head. "It's possible, I suppose. But I would detect the scent of that spell as well. It's pretty hard to fool the senses of a wolfen. We were made by our moon witch mothers, after all." He peers down at the water, as if he's looking deep into it. "Something isn't right here."

Near the log, half-hidden in the damp leaf litter, a red thread catches the morning light. I kneel down, my fingers picking it carefully from the ground.

It's not a full bundle. Just thread—like something from a mojo bag Lyla would've made for me when I was a kid. The kind of thing passed down through generations of mountain women. On the log, I see a few crushed fragments of what might have been yarrow. Or vervain. The herbs are too broken to tell, scattered like they'd been torn apart with deliberate violence.

Grace made this. I can feel it. She must have learned how to do it from her grandmother. I can see her gathering the herbs herself, wrapping them properly, and tying the knots with intention. She knew enough to be scared, and she came anyway. For me.

The thread is still damp with dew, or maybe lake water. It comes apart in my fingers, the fibers separating as if they were never meant to hold anything together.

"Martin," I say, and my voice doesn't sound like mine. "She tried to protect herself."

Out of the corner of my eye, I see something moving underneath the water. I grip Martin's arm and he steps back from the lake, pulling me with him. "It's the Others," he says.

"What others?"

"The Others are the damned," he tells me. "They used to wander free, just ghostly miseries looking for animals to torture, but when people began settling the area, my mother had to contain them."

"In the lake?"

Martin shakes his head. "In the bone hollows of the mountains. They must have slipped through a tear in the veil and found their way here."

"Oh, my God," I say. "So it wasn't just a dream."

The white witch's demonic kiss of death visits me again, so vividly obscene it makes my skin crawl.

"She never took your soul and couldn't have if she wanted to," he says.

"How can you be so sure?"

Martin rarely shows exasperation at my memory loss, yet I can feel frustration bubbling at the edges of his speech—not with me, but with the sheer horror and unjustness of it all.

"You're an immortal witch," he says. "She doesn't have that

power over you. And if she did, she would have taken mine with it."

I think of the sycamore and Martin's contention that it will only live as long as we do. "Martin," I say. "She can't have Grace. I won't let her."

It's not just a statement, it's a covenant between myself and God.

PETAL IS WAITING for us at the cave mouth, and I know before we even reach her that she's found something terrible. Not from her body language—Petal's too controlled for pacing or hand-wringing—but from the way she's standing perfectly still, staring into the cave's entrance like she's trying to decide whether to go back inside or never enter again.

When she sees us, something shifts in her face. It's the knowledge that we're the only people who can understand what she's found without needing it explained.

"You have to see this," Petal says, waving her hands in our direction.

We follow her inside. She's left the work lights running from her earlier geological survey—professional LED panels that turn the limestone into something clinical and stark. The cave looks exactly as it had when we found Brooks's fossilized arm over a week ago, still pressed into Ordovician stone like a specimen in God's own museum.

Petal leads us past that first discovery, deeper into the cave system where the walls show different striations and impossible chronologies. She stops at a section where the limestone is paler, almost white in the LED glare.

"There," she says, pointing.

I see it immediately and feel my mouth fall open, ready to let out a scream. It's another anachronism. Another thing that shouldn't exist pressed into rock that predates everything human.

A bracelet. A chain with small charms catching the light—a book, a crescent moon, the Marine Corps anchor, globe and eagle, a compass, an acorn. The kind of thing a seventeen-year-old girl wears every day of her life because people who loved her had chosen each symbol carefully.

Grace's bracelet.

Not lying on the cave floor where she might have dropped it. Not caught in a crevice or tucked into sediment. But *embedded* in the limestone matrix, surrounded by the fossilized impressions of ancient marine life that's been dead for 450 million years.

"The calcite formation around it is identical to what we found with Brooks," Petal says, her voice carefully neutral the way scientists sound when they're reporting data that shouldn't exist. "Structurally integrated. Not surface contamination. Not a hoax. It's *in* the rock, Twila. The same way Brooks's arm was in the rock."

I feel my whole chest contract. It's not my heart breaking— that will come later. This is the sound of hope fossilizing, turning to stone right alongside Grace's bracelet in primordial rock.

"No," I say. The word comes out flat, absolute. "No."

Martin's hand finds my shoulder but I shake it off, moving closer to the wall. The bracelet is right there, close enough to touch if I want to reach through 450 million years of accumulated time and pull it free. Which I can't. Which no one can.

"She's not dead." The words come out sharp, serrated. "She can't be dead."

But even as I say it, I'm staring at the proof. Grace's bracelet in the same primordial graveyard where nothing human should exist.

Martin's studying the wall with that particular stillness that means he's thinking hard and not liking his conclusions. "If the witch threw her back that far—"

"Then I'll go get her," I say. "I've traveled beyond the veil before. I can go back, intercept her when she arrives, bring her with me."

"Twila—"

"I can do it, Martin."

"No." His voice is sharp now, an edge I rarely hear. "You can't."

I turn to face him. "How do you know what I can't do? My other self traveled for centuries—"

"Your time arc never extended that far back. You traveled within your own historical context. This is primordial time. Before consciousness. Before anything that could anchor you."

"Then I'll learn—"

"There's a difference," Martin says, "between being powerful enough to fling someone back through time and being able to travel there yourself, find them, and bring them back with you. That's not even done, Twila. Not by anyone. Not ever."

"How do you know I can't do it?"

The question hangs between us, lit by work lights that make everything look like an autopsy.

"Wait," Petal says, softly. "There's something else I need to show you." She pulls a magnifying loupe from her field bag and leans close to a part of the fossil where some of the charms have overlapped. "Right there," she whispers, placing her pinky next to Grace's acorn charm.

She moves aside so I can see. The acorn, a little larger than a pea, has a hexagon shape inside. It's simple and bisected by a curved line. Grace had shown me that charm in Soma's office and there was nothing of the kind carved into it then.

"It's a distortion symbol," Petal says. "I think it's a magnet pressed to the acorn charm. My granny had one like it."

Martin moves closer. "Yes, it is."

"What does that even mean?" I ask. "Is it for protection, like her mojo bag?"

"Not exactly. It's most often used in conjunction with lunar eclipses." Petal shrugs. "The symbol is supposed to amplify temporal distortion during eclipse windows."

"Will you people please speak English?" I say.

"It's used to introduce chaos into temporal magic," Martin says. "Particularly during eclipses. Think of it like—" He pauses, searching for the right analogy. "If someone's trying to write a specific address, this symbol smudges the ink. The writing still happens, but the destination becomes illegible."

"So it protects against time displacement?" I ask.

"Not exactly. It doesn't prevent displacement. It just makes it... unpredictable. Whoever cast the spell wouldn't get what they wanted, but neither would the victim necessarily end up somewhere safe."

"And like a covenant," Petal says. "It takes a powerful witch to enact, one who better knows what she's doing."

"Grace isn't a witch," I whisper. "And the Bramwell witch wouldn't want her to have something like that. Who else could have given it to her? And what could it have done?"

Martin shakes his head slowly. "The March 9, 1830 lunar eclipse in the Moravian journals," he says. "That's what Brooks was researching. And now a distortion symbol that's used in connection with lunar eclipses."

The implications of that settle over us like cave water—icy, seeping, inescapable. Yet none of us seems to have any idea what it could mean.

"There won't even be another comparable eclipse until next summer," Petal says.

I look back at Grace's bracelet one more time, at that impossible charm laid bare in the LED light. Not an answer yet. Just another question, another layer of mystery wrapped tight around her disappearance.

But it's something. A thread to follow. And right now, that's more than we had five minutes ago.

23

Martin looks like hell.

He eases himself onto Soma's Le Corbusier couch—all chrome tubes and leather—and the unwelcoming furniture finally meets its match. He takes it over despite its objections, and I can almost hear it sigh in surrender.

"You look dog-tired," I say, and catch the ghost of a smile at the corner of his mouth before exhaustion pulls it back under.

We've come back to Soma's office to decipher the Moravian journals—hoping they'll reveal what this means for Grace, for the registry, for us. But the photocopies I made for Brooks feel like distant planets. I know they exist because the math says so, not because I can actually see them. I need the originals. Need to hold them, be alone with them in that room.

"You should lay down for a while." I stand over Martin, stroking his hair away from his forehead. He tips his face up, giving me an immovable look of *no*.

I bend down and kiss him right where Lyla says our third eye rests. "Then why don't I make us some tea?"

That's an idea he doesn't resist.

Like every good moon witch, Soma kept a stash of herbs handy—hers in a severe obsidian box in her console. There's a small kitchenette next to Miss Newberry's office and I take it there, rummaging through its contents, plucking out several sachets that I think will do the trick.

For my tea, I choose mugwort, vervain, passionflower—herbs of vision, clarity, staying present and awake to what must be seen. It will be a white tea. One that's delicate and receptive and reminds me of the moon, for whatever that's worth. As I pour the boiling water into the ceramic mug where I deposited the loose leaves, I say the first thing that comes to mind.

"Moon behind the sun, breach the light that blocks you. Show me what you see."

Nothing seems different, but I feel lighter for saying it.

Then, I turn to the herbs I've chosen for Martin's tea. Those are valerian, chamomile, a bit of skullcap—all herbs of deep rest, surrender, letting go. As I pour the water, I hover over his cup, whispering directly into the steam. It's what I know he needs to hear, even if he won't want to.

"Rest now, beloved. Let me carry the watch."

I steep them each exactly for seven minutes. Seven for the lunar phases, seven for completeness. Not quite a spell, but an intention, and those have worked for me before, although rarely during the day. I place the cups onto a tray with a jar of honey and two spoons—we can't share one as the two opposing teas can never touch (that much I learned from Nox) —and go back into Soma's office.

Martin is no better, but he's trying, and has laid the photo copies of the journal pages on the glass coffee table in front of him. I set his steaming mug down and he reaches for it, taking a sip without looking up.

"It's excellent," he says, taking another sip.

I close my eyes, and put my own cup to my lips. The tea tastes sharp and green, slightly bitter with an herbal complexity. It's hot, so I take several tiny sips, feeling the taste take root, becoming something more than flavor. Within just a couple of minutes, clarity arrives—not like caffeine's jolt, but like a window being cleaned until I can finally see what's been on the other side all along. My thoughts arrange themselves with unusual precision. The fog of exhaustion and fear doesn't disappear, but it no longer obscures my purpose. I can feel the moon's presence, even hidden behind the sun's brightness, like a hand reaching through thick glass to touch mine.

I look over at Martin. His breathing has deepened, shoulders dropping as tension bleeds out of him. The cup rests loose in his hand, nearly empty. His eyes are still on the journal pages but I can see the moment his focus starts to slip, words blurring into meaningless shapes.

Then he looks up at me.

His expression shifts through several registers—confusion first, then understanding, then something that might be hurt or might be fury, I can't tell which. He tries to stand but his body won't cooperate. His legs buckle and he catches himself on the arm of the couch.

"Twila." My name comes out thick, slurred at the edges. "What have you—"

"You need to rest," I say, and I hate how my voice sounds. Calm. Decided. Like I haven't just betrayed his trust.

"Don't—" He tries again to rise, but the valerian and chamomile have already claimed him. His body sinks back into the leather cushions, suspended in that cage of steel. His eyes fight to stay open, fixed on me with an expression I won't easily forget.

"I'm sorry," I whisper, but I don't know if he hears it. His eyes close, his breathing evens out, and he's gone—pulled under by herbs meant for healing, wielded by me like a weapon.

I stand there for a long moment, watching him sleep,

knowing that when he wakes he'll be furious. Knowing I've earned it. Knowing I'm going anyway.

THE DRIVE to the Luna Archive feels endless. I rehearse what I'll say to Martin when he wakes. None of it sounds right. None of it will matter. I did leave him a note–simple, direct. Where I'm going, why I had to do it alone. It won't make him less angry, but at least he'll know I didn't just vanish.

Honey MacDonald doesn't seem too surprised to see me when I show up at the Luna Archive unannounced. Her slit of a mouth turns down at the edges as she steps aside, letting me in. She offers me some tea, which I decline, then disappears behind the wallpapered door. No more than a minute goes by until she reemerges, pushing the cart filled with the journals. Her cohort Wickham is absent, which strikes me as odd. He seemed like the kind of presence that was always here, always watching. As for Honey, she's cordial, but something's off. Her eyes don't quite meet mine, and she keeps glancing back toward that wallpapered door like she's waiting for something to spring from it.

"I'd like to extend my help," she says, but I shut her down more abruptly than I mean to. It doesn't seem to phase her. She's been serving the Blacksburg family for a long time and must be used to taking orders.

When she exits back through the wallpapered door, the room seems to exhale a breath.

The stacks of journals sit before me like a mountain to climb. They're exactly as we left them, with much of the waxy paper that had protected them peeled off, revealing old, but well-tended leather. On my way here, I thought about studying the one detailing the Bramwell family line. The witch's attempts at copying my poetry still burned into the margins, her essence reeking from the pages—the rage and spite. The bitter grasping for power. Only now that I'm here, that's not the journal that calls to me. The one that does is slightly smaller than the others and a deep burgundy color. Like blood mixed with a touch of the night sky.

I sit on the sofa and place the journal on my lap with my right hand on its cover. I feel a whisper from it enter my body through my palm. It feels like a secret between sisters, years in the making and held close to my heart and hers. A bond almost as strong as mine and Martin's. A face appears in my mind's eye. Strong-boned, skin made of pearls, her eyes the color of a thunderstorm in the making.

I open the book without opening my eyes and can see its contents. Symbols and numbers configured into a language— the curve of a shell, a dark circle, lines representing numerals. To be read vertically, up and down the page. They're spells and potions made of herbs and roots. Meant for teas or for burning. My God—they belong to Martin's mother, the moon witch who needed no name because her presence announced her as surely as a trumpet.

I open my eyes and she's standing before me. My body unmoors and a shiver runs through me, as if my own skeleton recognizes her before my mind does. She's as real as Theo Smithfield had been when her spirit visited me a few months ago. As real as Elliot Blacksburg's headless, naked body.

She wears a crown of soft twigs, like from a willow tree, braided into a tight weave with violets and rosebuds growing out from its seams. Her hair is long and loose, spilling out from under the crown and past her shoulders in waves that shift between silver and black depending on how the light catches them. Not the white of age, but the silver of moonlight made tangible. Her cloak is wolf pelt—gray and silver like winter fog, the fur still holding that dense quality wolves develop for mountain winters. It drapes from her shoulders to the floor, fastened at her throat with a brooch shaped like a crescent moon. She wears nothing beneath it. Even her feet are bare, pale against the archive's dark floor.

The dove perches on her shoulder, its white feathers brilliant against the gray wolf fur. It coos softly, and the sound breaks something open inside me. That particular note, that specific cadence—I've heard it a thousand times. In my bedroom at Lyla's, when I was so lonely I thought the only thing that could actually see me was the moon. Outside my window in autumn. On the ridge this morning, warning me. At Soma's garden last summer. Through every moment of grief and every brush with danger—always there, always watching over me.

"Dad," I whisper, and my voice cracks on the word.

24

I want to see him as a person, a being in the spirit realm, not as a damned bird. Feel his arms around me—the soft warmth of his touch followed by that electric current, like when Theo would brush by me.

"You can't," Martin's mother says, although I never spoke aloud.

"Why?"

I look at the dove—the brusque, jittery way it cocks its head is all bird, but the steady black-eyed focus is unmistakably Dad.

"Because he's not in the spirit realm, he's with God and has been since he died. Birds are messengers, that's not merely legend."

When she speaks, her voice has the quality of wind through hollow places, present and vast at once. But it's a real voice, like Theo's. The same voice she had when she was still among the living.

"Why aren't you with God?" I ask her.

"I've always been with God," she says. "I can exist in all the realms. And so could you."

Her use of the past tense in my case isn't lost on me.

"Twila, you don't have much time. You're right that the one of many faces is binding herself to a page in the registry. She's using it to unleash chaos to serve her needs, but in doing so creates opportunities for her destruction."

"Who is she?"

"Who she was she is no longer," Martin's mother says. "She's whatever face she wears, soulless, empty and loveless. Beneath it all frightened and desperate."

That recognition hits like something that falls straight through me. I remember the helplessness of believing myself corrupted. The terrible empathy I felt for the Bramwell witch, awakening to her own ruin.

"You cannot help her," Martin's mother says. "She would not accept your help if you offered it."

The dove, Dad, emits a sorrowing coo, shivering his feathers, marching his feet in place on Martin's mother's shoulder

"Christ forgave the thief crucified beside him." I say. "He promised him heaven."

"Dismas asked. The witch who seeks you has not."

I swallow hard, uselessly.

"What about Grace?" I say. "Can you tell me what happened to her?"

Her eyes shift toward the wallpapered door, and Dad becomes agitated, cooing sharply. "Twila, she's been here, inside these walls, poisoning what was meant to protect you."

Martin's mother steps closer, and the cold pours off her like a veil of winter air slipping through cracks in old wood. "Keep safe my words. She will destroy everything else to keep you from—"

She stops. Tilts her head like she's hearing something I can't.

The dove launches from her shoulder, circling once and crying out—a sharp trill of warning. Martin's mother looks at me one last time, her storm-colored eyes holding mine.

"You were made to understand scattering," she says. "To know what it is to exist in pieces and still be whole."

Then she—and Dad—are gone. Like they were never here at all.

"Don't leave me," I whisper.

The journal in my lap feels heavier. Warmer. Like something living pressed against my hands. I start to open it again, but still when I hear footsteps. Unhurried and certain—coming from behind the wallpapered door.

"Honey?" I call out.

The door creaks open.

Honey MacDonald stands in the doorway, grim as a straight line. Her eyes are dead and flat. Her mouth as expressionless as a wound. In her right hand, she holds a paper knife—the kind used for cutting pages in uncut books. The blade is dull steel, longer than a letter opener, with a weighted bone handle worn smooth from decades of use.

When she speaks, her tone is eerily familiar. Honey's cadence stripped of Honey. No earnestness or affection for her surroundings. No essence.

"She wants you to know," Honey says, taking a step forward, "that you should have stayed with him. But you always were too proud. Too stupid. Too—"

She moves fast and decisively. I'm already turning when the blade catches my throat, a burning line streaking the side of my neck, just below my ear.

My hand goes there instinctively. Comes away slick and red.

For a horrible second I think she's severed something vital. I feel it—blood running warm down my collar, soaking into my sweater and the shirt underneath. But my breathing remains clear and strong.

Honey slices at me again, her teeth bared as she puts her back into it. The steel catches my forearm as I raise it to protect my face—a line of white-hot pain opens like a mouth across my skin.

Blood wells immediately, wicking through my sleeve, dripping onto the burgundy journal still clutched in my other hand.

She slashes again, and I stumble against the cart. The old wheels squeal against the floorboards, wobbling. The journals slide—one thumps open, its pages splaying like a gasp. I shove the cart between us and Honey lunges straight into it, her thigh hitting the handle hard, making the journals rattle.

Only she doesn't cry out. Doesn't even grunt. She just resets herself like some damned zombie.

My pulse jumps. It's mid-afternoon and the sun is still strong and bright. I feel nothing from the obscured moon, not a hint of its blue light.

She comes at me again and I kick the cart at her this time. The wheel catches her ankle and she pitches forward a fraction, just enough. I grab the closest thing—an antique brass candlestick from the side table, heavy and tarnished. As she rushes me again, I swing. The metal comes down on her forearm with a sickening, dull thud made of bone, brass and skin. She drops the knife and it clatters on the floorboards, skittering under the sofa.

Then she's on me.

We slam into the parlor sofa—my back hitting its carved wood frame. Her fingers find my hair, twisting and pulling like she's trying to peel something out of me. My scalp burns like a sonofabitch. Her breath is right on my cheek—warm, wet, and wrong. Like the breath of that thing in Hallow Lake.

And that's when I know there's really nothing of Honey left in her.

I slam my forehead into hers. Pure instinct, crap technique. The impact bursts stars behind my eyes, but her grip loosens. Then I twist, driving my knee into her ribs—a move I learned by accident when I was fighting off a guy who followed me home from a bar once. Slowed him enough to allow me to grind a second knee into his balls.

Only Honey doesn't stop. Her hands scrabble at my face and throat, trying to carve me up with her long, red nails. She snaps her teeth at me, eager to tear into my flesh, while I go at her with both hands—slapping and pounding with the journal still in my grip. A self-defense class I took after the rapist-asshole incident, as I called it, said to go for the eyes, so that's what I do. I shove my thumb into her eye socket and it makes her jerk. But it also tips the couch backward and we hit the floor hard. The jolt shocks my wounds and makes me bite my tongue. I taste copper.

This time, I'm able to get on top and I just start whaling on her with the journal. Hitting her head and face. I break her nose and blood splatters over me like it exploded.

Her hand darts for the paper knife beneath the sofa and I smash the journal on that, too, hearing a sickly crunch that I think is one of her fingers breaking. Then I swing the journal at her mouth, cracking the spine against her teeth and enduring another spray of blood.

Her eyes go wide and she grimaces in what looks like real pain. "Mrs. Blacksburg?" she whispers.

Her lip trembles and I freeze—like an idiot—because that's when she takes her chance. She lunges for the paper knife, but somehow something in me is faster. My hand closes around the bone handle before she reaches it. It's slick with blood, maybe sweat, but I squeeze it so tight it hurts. Then I thrust the blade under her ribs, upward, like I know how to do this.

Her breath catches—no scream—just a soft, surprised *oh*. And we collapse together, slow, as if lying down. Her head rests on my shoulder, and she feels like a stranger who's fallen asleep against me on a train. Her breath stills, her blood flows warm, and I want to throw up.

25

I don't know how long I lie there with Honey's weight against me. Seconds. Minutes. Long enough for her blood to cool where it's soaked through my clothes, for the adrenaline to start draining out of me in sick, shaky waves.

I need to move, but then the smell hits me. Not just blood—I'm already drowning in that—but something else. Ink. Old paper. And underneath it, something acrid. I push Honey off me and turn my head, and that's when I see it.

My blood—the blood from my neck, my arm, soaking into the floorboards—it's moving. Actually *moving*. Crawling across the wood grain like it's searching for something.

Then I see the journals scattered from the overturned cart. The pages nearest my blood are darkening, ink bleeding up from their depths like the paper is exhaling. Words lift off in threads, curling between me and Honey's body. They swarm the air in tightening spirals—angry wasps with a plan.

Every part of me wails in protest. The wounds at my neck and arm are still bleeding freely, and any movement sends fresh blood sheeting down my collar, dripping from my elbow.

But I don't have a choice.

I push myself up, dizzy, and spit the metallic yuk out of my mouth. The burgundy journal is somehow still clutched in my hand, but the other ones—Martin's mother's words about the archive being poisoned weren't metaphorical. The witch has already been here, and my blood just woke what she left behind.

The journal pages are moving—and not by wind or gravity. The pages are turning themselves, and as they do, more ink begins to peel away from the paper like skin from a burn.

The ink rises. Coalesces. Takes shape. The curve of a shoulder. The line of a jaw. The script warps, settles, becoming my handwriting, the outline of a hand.

And every shape wears my face.

MY BLOOD PULLS itself into figures—first three, then a fourth emerges from a thick pool, rising. They're of my blood, but also made of shadow and script, as if prose were poured into a mold and given muscle.

All of them are monsters.

The first is me at twelve, just before Dad died. My shoulder dips to the side, as if his hand is on it, guiding me to the window to watch the full moon. Only my eyes are pin pricks. Like my soul is draining from them at the same time that my dad's life force is leaking from every pore in his body.

Another one of me steps forward, hips swaying—my hothouse summer self. The one who used to take strangers home just to feel anything besides misery. Her eyes are dark Kohl, lips smeared, shirt slipping off one shoulder. She seethes with a hunger that isn't just for pleasure, but obliteration.

The third wears Beckett's old flannel. The girl, on the cusp of womanhood, who screamed into her pillow until her throat bled. Her hands are fists. Her jaw is a hinge barely holding together a world of rage. And I think she's ready to make a move on me, she's dying to, but then I see the last one, who comes out from behind her.

Just a little girl. The girl I must have been before my mom left. Bare feet dirty from playing in the Rivanna River, hair a wild snarl, moon-pale and sharp-eyed. And whole. The Gemini Covenant hadn't split her in two yet, her time arc is still one solid line. She stands on the parlor floor, toes sinking into blood like mud, and cocks her head at me with a disappointment so pure I could drown in it. *You need to die*, everything about her seems to say.

They watch me like wolves scenting weakness. Noting the heat as it floods my wounds, and how my pulse is a drum inside my skull. My fear is poetry to them, sublime. They want to feast on it. They want to devour me while I'm still living. Make me watch them chew each bite.

The flannel-wearing me laughs, and it's Beckett's laugh, only broken at the end. The others are quiet, but I can hear them panting. As for me, air catches half-way, unwilling.

I step back and my bar-girl self moves forward. She advances with a kind of predatory looseness—loose wrist, loose hips, but eyes locked with a surgical aim. And she moves fast, her hands wrapping around my throat.

I can't breathe and feel like I did when that vulture demon put me in a cocoon last summer. Not able to take a breath, not able to die. I try to shove her back and pain lights up my every nerve. My arm is slick, my grip weak, but I'm able to knock her off her center of gravity. I stick out my foot, making her trip, but she rolls with the momentum, landing cat-quiet and smirking.

God, it's obnoxious to see your own worst habits turned into choreography.

The child one starts to cry—a trembling sound like wind across an empty field. And that's somehow worse.

The grief-self lunges, pushing me down hard. I land flat on my back and it knocks the wind out of me. She jumps onto me, pressing into my face, making me taste dust and years and tears I thought I'd already paid for. My head is ringing, and my bar-self gets in on it, thrusting her knee into my rib—right where I'd thrust mine into the rapist-asshole's. Something pops and I feel white, brutal pain.

I try to summon something—anything—from the moon, but it's like trying to strike flint under water. It flickers, guttering near my fingertips, then dies.

The barefoot wild-child watches. Waiting. She snaps her hand in the air, taking power from the sun-hidden moon like it's nothing. Whipping me with the moonlight she's harnessed.

I can only hear my blood rushing, my pulse pounding. The pain goes bright and sharp—a scream caught in a floodlight, nowhere to hide from it.

But I also hear a growl.

"Martin," I say.

Only it's not. Martin's growl is a banked fire. It waits, watches, chooses. This one is declarative, older than bone-memory. It shudders like a sound pulled up through marrow.

And for a moment, it makes the whole room still.

All of us—me and the others—turn toward the door. Wickham stands in the frame like a crooked hinge in the world. The air warps around him, dense and sluggish. As though whatever lives under his skin has chosen this moment to surface.

A tremor shudders through him, forcing the change in an instant. His eyes become golden, not like the amber and whiskey of Martin's, but burning coal. Wolfen eyes.

My wild-child self takes a step back. The grief-self hisses. The bar-girl licks her teeth.

Wickham's lips peel back as the bar-girl springs at him. Because of course she does. Always has to be the one who acts without thinking.

Wickham meets her mid-charge and the room erupts.

His curled fingers find purchase in her ink-wrought flesh. She dissolves partly, then reforms behind him, laughing with my voice. He wheels faster than anything I've ever seen move. Then the grief-self and wild-child move to flank him. They're all starting to work together with an intelligence that's disturbing, able to fight as a unit after having learned to survive on their own. That knowledge is in them.

I recognize the setup—the bar-girl as distraction while the real threat comes from the sides.

"Wickham—on your left!" I shout, and he drops into a crouch just as the wild-child's moonlight whips over his head. She misses him, but lashes me on the shoulder, making me slam into the wall. I have to get up. I can't stay on the floor or they'll swarm me. But I'm dizzy as hell. Still, I manage to make my way up the wall into something resembling a standing position.

The wild-child is walking toward me, slowly, shoulders hunched. "It's your fault Mommy's gone. You know it was you," she says in a voice as high as a bell. "And that bitch Soma killed Daddy with her stupid covenant. Ate his brain. She'll kill Lyla, too. You just wait."

And even though I know it's not real, tears are burning in my eyes.

The bar-girl glances my way. "I bet you haven't told Martin about your slut years. All the barflies 'Stella' took home. Can you even count that high?"

My grief-self starts screaming Beckett's name over and over.

"Shut up!" I scream back at her. I can take the taunts, but I can't take her blinding pain. I'm done with that!

I can't help sucking in big gulps of air through my mouth, then my nose. And that's when I smell it—something sulfurous. The wild-child covers her mouth and giggles. It's burning paper. The scattered journals are smoking, edges curling black. The witch is destroying the archive's knowledge.

"We have to get out of here!" I try for the journals, but they're too hot to touch. So I crawl toward the door, clutching the burgundy one to my breast. Wickham is bleeding like hell from gashes across his shoulder and chest. The manifestations are reforming faster than he can destroy them. He grabs me—rough and urgent—and we bolt. The manifestations start to pursue us, but as we cross the threshold, they hold back. Maybe the witch only poisoned the archive room itself, but we don't stop to find out.

Wickham carries me down the gravel driveway and lays me down in a soft bed of autumn leaves that have collected at its sides. From outside, the Luna Archive looks just as it did when I pulled up. I'd expected it to be burning, folding in on itself, a picture of corruption. But it stands there like the proud southern grandmother it's always been. Almost daring us to think we imagined it all.

I've been bleeding, fading, feeling worse by the second—but now something shifts. I'm no longer drowning, so much as treading water. The sky has changed. That particular quality when the sun starts losing its stranglehold on the day. And there—rising over the ridge—the moon. Still fighting daylight's glare, but present. Real. Reaching for me.

It feels like a hand on my wounds. The blood at my neck slows, then stops. The torn flesh on my arm begins to knit with the moon's patient insistence. My broken rib shifts, pain easing from screaming to aching to dull throb.

Wickham is watching me, his golden eyes reflecting the fresh moonlight. He's healing too.

"The journal," I say. It's no longer in my hands.

He holds it up. The burgundy leather is blood-stained but intact. Martin's mother's words, saved.

Everything else—the rest of the archive, untold quantities of moon witch knowledge—is gone.

26

I need to call Martin. I sit all the way up, my broken rib feeling like little more than a nasty bruise. It's not quite dark yet, but the moon is overhead, just over half full. My blood already feels like it's purring in my veins. I fish my phone from the back pocket of my jeans. It's slick with blood, screen shattered into a spiderweb, but at least it turns on. It's hard to read my messages through the fractured glass, but I'm able to see that Lyla texted, asking me to meet her at Nox's as soon as possible. I dial Martin's number, but he doesn't answer. Still sleeping I imagine. So, I text him, saying I'm alright and telling him where I'm headed.

"Martin never mentioned you were a werewolf," I say.

"Martin and I aren't particularly close. Perhaps it seemed like a strange thing to bring up. Like pointing out that I'm a dwarf."

"It seems strange not to bring up," I say, feeling stung that he never told me. Even if I don't have the right after what I did to him today.

"You're a moon witch," Wickham says. "Maybe he wanted to see if you could intuit it yourself."

"Maybe." I'm angry that I didn't, and realize I'm not just angry at myself, but at Martin. Whatever his motive—whether he was keeping Wickham's nature from me or testing me—I don't like it.

"Are you well enough to drive?"

I nod. "Unless you want to carry me all the way to Widder-shins Hollow."

"Not especially," Wickham says, and holds out his hand to help me up. "We could always fly."

"Moon witches can fly?"

Wickham smiles. "No. You really did lose your memory, didn't you?"

Nice. Someone as sarcastic as I am.

THE DRIVE TO NOX'S, while not entirely free of biting commentary, is turning out to be pleasant. A needed respite after our ordeal at the Luna Archive. Wickham turns through Martin's mother's journal with curled lips and a furrowed brow, while I think about Honey.

"I wonder if she knew what was happening to her," I say.

Wickham looks up.

"She didn't mention it, but I had my suspicions. The Bramwell witch had not only been able to enter the archive, but study the journals. And I knew I didn't let her in."

I can't get the image of Honey receiving the demon's kiss from my mind.

"So, how is it that you and Martin don't know each other better?"

Wickham looks up from the journal. "You think all wolfen are thick as thieves? That we have bowling leagues?"

"Old nine-pin mountain alley bowling...with werewolves. I like it."

Wickham snaps the journal shut and fiddles with the radio

dial until he finds an opera station. *Lacrimosa*, Mozart's requiem whines holy but twisted from the speakers, like a cathedral burning beautifully. Wickham closes his eyes and it's as if he feels forgiven. Almost.

"You know, I despise the term werewolf," he says. "It's all bogeyman, no poetry."

I feel like that was for me, and toss him a smile. He doesn't smile back with his mouth, but I can see it in his eyes.

"Until recently, Martin and I hadn't seen each other in a long time," he explains. "For the most part, he's been here in the Hallowmist, while I was in the Shenandoah."

"Were you made by your mother, like Martin was? Or doesn't it always work that way?"

"It always works that way, so yes. My mother was old school. Even older than Martin's mother."

"And as powerful?"

"Oh, yes. All the old school moon witches were a force to be reckoned with."

"She came to me, you know. At the archive."

"Martin's mother?"

I nod. "He told me I'd known her very well, and it certainly seemed that way," I say. "It's always strange when you don't remember things that other people do. It's like they've seen you walking around naked when you didn't know it."

"Well, just so you know, I haven't seen you naked."

"But you had met me before?"

Wickham looks out over the road and eases his seat back. "Yes."

We're quiet for a while, kind of letting everything sink in. Listening to opera. I want to ask him more about how he knows me, but at the same time, I don't want to talk about me. I've had enough of me today.

"What was your mother like?" I ask.

Wickham busts out laughing. He folds his arms across his

chest and shakes his head, like he's picturing her. "A piece of work," he says.

"In what way...I mean, unless you don't want to talk about her."

"When you've been around as long as I have, there's very little you won't talk about," he says.

"So talk."

Wickham shifts in his seat, still looking out at the darkening road. "My mother lived most of her life alone. By choice. She was—still is, I suppose—what you might call an oracle. People came to her when they needed to see what was coming. Not fortune-tellers looking for coin, but desperate souls seeking real knowledge. Knowledge of themselves, not outside events."

"So, if Martin's mother was like the Nostradamus of moon witches, yours is like the oracle at Delphi," I say. "But with a therapist's couch."

Wickham slaps the dashboard and lets out a throaty *ha*.

"More like an unmasker of truths. And a mighty force for Creation, when she chooses to use her abilities. She's very economical in that way and cautious of the inherent dangers."

I think of Martin's mother seeing what was coming, being killed for her predictions. And of women like her and Wickham's mother spending centuries alone in the wilderness instead of living among people, other moon witches. "That sounds like a particular kind of hell."

"Not for her." Wickham's jaw sets. "You don't get to be as old as my mother without an armor of steel. And a heart to match."

"She doesn't sound heartless."

"I didn't say she was. I said her heart was built differently."

I glance at him, at his compact frame, the way he holds himself. Then I think of something that's been nagging at me.

"If she could make you wolfen, give you immortality and strength—why not change the other thing? Your dwarfism, I mean. If she had that kind of power—"

"Why leave me this way?" Wickham's voice is flat, but has the aftertaste of a very old grudge. "As a credo, my mother has a deep appreciation for imperfection. Almost a fetish for it. She believed my dwarfism was an act of wisdom by Creation—that I was cursed with innate arrogance that needed checking. My pride could have easily swayed me towards darker forces had I not had something significant to humble me, according to her."

The car fills with silence except for Mozart's *Lacrimosa* building toward its crescendo.

"She was right," Wickham says finally. He doesn't sound happy about it.

I think about Martin's mother making him wolfen without asking, about Soma's covenant that fragmented, then nearly destroyed me. About all the ways powerful women have made choices for the people they love. And some they don't.

"Does she know what's happening now? With the Bramwell witch, the registry?"

Wickham's expression shifts. "The question is whether she'll think it's worth intervening, or if she's already determined how this is likely to end."

The way he says it makes my skin prickle. "Has she intervened before in things like this?"

"Once or twice. When the alternative was a complete catastrophe."

WHEN WE FINALLY PULL ONTO the rough road to Nox's place, I start to feel nervous and queasy. Martin's talked to Lyla, but I haven't. And I've neither heard nor seen Colette or Nox since they tried to burn me alive. I don't know if they'll still be weary of me, or feel guilty, or scared that they'll have to face Martin eventually. But if Lyla asked me to come here, then I have to believe that everything will be alright. Still, I don't pull all the way up to the cabin. I park where Martin usually parks his Jag, so that Wickham and I can walk a few minutes and I can get my head on straight.

"Don't worry," Wickham says. "You're not the first innocent witch who's had to face her would-be executioners."

"These are my best friends, Wickham."

"Our executioners usually are."

We walk up the path, quiet as church mice, Wickham breathing in the outdoors like Martin does. He looks at odds here in his dark clothes and I sense he's dying to peel them off and go running into the wilderness, chasing after night dwellers.

When we round the rhododendron bushes, Nox's cabin comes into view, porch light on and torches lit. The place looks better, well tended again, but maybe that's just because it's evening. Colette's Volvo is parked outside next to Lyla's Subaru. The screen door opens and I see Lyla peek her head outside. She steps out onto the porch in full view and the two of us just freeze for a moment. Then we start running at each other, colliding mid-way, hugging tight and awkward until we end up sinking to the ground. Both of us burst into tears, going right into one of those gasping ugly cries that makes the snot pour out of our noses.

"Baby kitten," she says, petting my head and kissing me all over my face. "I'm so sorry."

"No, I'm sorry," I say. "I should've known better. I shouldn't have been so damned weak. Not when we know she's out there and what's at stake."

"I would've flung myself on that fire with you," she says. And I know it's true.

I notice Nox and Colette are standing out on the porch now. Nox nods to Wickham, who steps aside me and Lyla like our emotions are a sickness he doesn't want to catch. Colette gives me a small wave, uneasy, and Nox puts his hands on his hips and looks right at me. He's not exactly apologetic about things, but neither is he looking at me like he did when he thought I was corrupted. What's unsaid, but as present in our minds as the smell of burning black salt and herbs is how foolish we've all been. How easily manipulated, even when we knew what the Bramwell witch was capable of, have experienced it, fought it more than once. Yet she nearly turned me against myself and turned us all against each other.

"She can't corrupt me," I say. "I know that. I hope you know it, too."

"It was good to find out," Nox says. "The Lord works in mysterious ways."

"It wasn't the Lord's work. It was hers."

Nox lights a cigarette and lets it dangle from his lip. Then he crosses his arms over his chest. "You think the Lord didn't work his way in there? You wouldn't be standing here if He didn't."

I untangle myself from Lyla and help her up from the ground. Then I walk over to Nox. "You think you can give me one of those cigarettes?"

He shakes one out of his pack and hands it to me, reaching for his lighter.

"I'll light it myself if you don't mind," I say, and Colette covers her mouth. She's hiding her laugh, but it's contagious and as much as I want to stay serious I start to laugh, too. Lyla chimes in and finally Nox, who just grins like the Cheshire Cat. Wickham sits down on the porch steps waiting for it all to pass.

"You hungry?" Colette looks me up and down, noticing under the porch lights that my clothes are caked in dried blood. She doesn't seem particularly surprised.

"Yup," I say. "I could eat a wild boar, hooves and all."

Colette reaches her hand out and brushes my cheek with her fingers. Then she comes in for a hug that feels weeks overdue.

"We really thought we were saving you," she says.

We stand there rocking for a few moments until she slows, then stops. She pulls back, not looking at me, but over my shoulder. I don't quite know how to read the look on her face and turn around. Up ahead, by the rhododendron bush stands Martin. His eyes are glinting in the darkness. A storm ripples under his skin and I see the subtle change in his shape.

"Maybe you should all go inside," I say.

___

artin stands as still as a statue, not a breath stirring. And yet everything about him vibrates with intent. What he sees, what he's feeling, what he wants to do.

Lyla puts her hand on my shoulder and shakes her head, but I tell her to go on. I peel off my bloodied sweater and hand it to her. It's cold out, but I'm burning up. Wickham is already ushering Nox and Colette inside, waiting for Lyla to follow. Reluctantly, she does. The door closes, and now it's just the two of us...and the moon.

The silence is the kind that thrums with everything unsaid between us. Not even the night birds give their calls. The trees don't rustle. Like they don't dare. Or maybe it's just my imagination.

The moon overhead sings in my blood, and my wounds from the Luna Archive are fully gone. But fear simmers through the whole of my nervous system—of Martin, but also of me. Because I'm not sure what I want out of this and I'm not sure of my own strength. Then Martin starts to close our distance fast. I don't move back, as much as I want to, and he comes up, invading my space. Daring me to back down.

I won't.

He reaches out—maybe to grab my shoulder, maybe just to touch me—and I strike. Palm to his chest, hard enough that he actually steps back. It came out of nowhere. I thought I wanted to talk him down. But the blunt force of it just felt good.

His eyes flare. A growl builds in his chest. My heart is pounding so hard it's giving me a headache.

"Say it," I tell him. My voice doesn't shake even though everything inside me does.

He doesn't speak. Just that deep breath, that tremor running through him that could go either way—toward control or chaos.

"Say I betrayed you. Say you wish I'd died. Say you hate me for all those years I was gone. *Say something.*"

I watch him inhale another deep breath. The kind you take when you're on the verge of doing something you're going to regret.

"Not good enough!" I slap him across his face, so hard it makes his head snap sideways. His eyes when they come back to mine are pure gold.

"Say it!" I say, because apparently I've lost my mind.

My second slap lands and this time he grips my upper arm and lifts me up like I'm made of corn husk. He spins me, rushes forward, and pins me against the cabin wall. The wood creaks under the impact, and I feel splinters press through my shirt.

Light flares between us. Hot enough to make him release me. His hand smokes where the moonlight touched, and we're both breathing hard. Both shocked that I did that.

And then he comes at me again and this time there's no restraint. He picks me up and throws me over Nox's front yard. I land and roll, hitting the shed. He's not done.

Neither am I.

We move through the clearing between cabin and forest, outside of the blessing. Not quite fighting, not quite dancing like Muhammad-Damned-Ali either. He catches my wrist and I twist it free, as if the moon made me as slippery as an eel. When he bares his teeth, I strike at him again and he deflects with such force I nearly fall down.

Noting my momentary weakness, he sweeps my legs and I roll and come up. I see my eyes in his, blazing silver-white.

There's movement in the cabin. Probably Wickham physically restraining Lyla from coming out. Good. This isn't for her or any of them.

"Come on," I say. "Don't be so gentle."

And holy hell he delivers, slamming me high into a tree trunk. I slide down, the bark cutting me, blood slicking my back. Stings like a motherf— and I reach up above our heads, bringing down a lash of moonlight that burns across his shoulder. Martin catches my throat—not choking, but holding, making me feel how easily he could—and I give him the rapist asshole treatment, driving my knee into his ribs with enough force that even he grunts.

We're both bleeding now. Nothing serious. But damn how it hurts and thrills and feels so cathartic I could scream.

Martin moves at me again, fast enough that I hardly see him coming. Then he takes me down. We hit the ground so hard I swear I can feel it shudder, leaving me gasping for breath. He has me pinned in the dirt, his full weight on my chest and hips, his eyes boring into mine. Panting hard, both of us. I can feel his curled, steely fingers pressing into my shoulders.

"Do it," I say. And hell, yes, I mean it. "If you're going to punish me for surviving alone, for keeping secrets, for being with other men—and there were a lot of them—then do it."

His hands tighten. His fingers pierce the fabric of my shirt, just beginning to break skin. I feel the hot blood start to seep. The pain is bright and clarifying.

But his eyes are flickering. Something shifts in his face, breaking underneath.

"You can't, can you?" I whisper. "Neither can I."

His hands loosen. He doesn't release me, but I can get out from under him if I want to. There's forty-nine years of loneliness in his eyes. Months of grief and frustration. I didn't do all of it, but I'm responsible for some, and I know he's let me off easy.

I rest my hands on his forearms, but not to push him away. Just to touch him. "I don't know why she–I—kept things from you," I say, and my voice is raw. "I don't remember making those choices. But I did the same thing today, and I can tell you why —I thought if something killed me, at least you wouldn't be there watching. At least you'd still be alive. I can't bear the thought of you becoming some spirit that only comes to me here and there."

"That decision," he says. "That's abandonment,"

The words hit like another blow. Because that's all I've ever known how to do.

"I lost you once to magic I couldn't control, and forces I couldn't fight," he says quietly. "But when you put that tea in my hands, and watched me drink it—that was your choice."

I have no defense. "I know."

"Do you?" His eyes are burning. "Because I woke up and you were gone and I had no idea if you were already dead. If the last thing you'd done was lie to my face."

The words hollow me out. Betrayal compounded by helplessness. My eyes well up and I squeeze his arm. "You should have hit me harder."

That, at least, elicits a faint smile.

His weight on me is different now than it was during our fight. Still heavy, still undeniable, but I'm aware of it in a way I wasn't before. Of how close we are. Of his breath on my neck. Of my heartbeat against his chest. Of how thin the line is between violence and something else entirely.

He feels it too. I know because his hand moves from holding me down to holding me. The difference is everything.

"I can't fix what Soma did," I say quietly. "Or what I did." We're laying under the moonlight, our blood dried, our skin nearly healed. "I can't give you back those years. Can't make us whole. Can't bring her back. Can't change what I don't remember. But I can tell you what I learned today."

I place my head on his shoulder and feel him rest his hand on my back.

"I hate what I did this afternoon. But I think something, someone—maybe my fractured self—was telling me to go to the Luna Archive alone."

His lips twitch. He doesn't want to hear it.

"You trust me, right?" I say. "Because I trust you, and I promise this wasn't about trust."

My hand moves over his chest, my fingers tracing the delicate pattern of the lash I'd struck across his shoulder. It's barely there anymore.

"You told me I always find a way. And that's what I was doing—finding a way."

"Did you?" he asks. "Find a way."

There isn't exactly a tone of accusation in his voice, more an acknowledgement of what appears obvious. I came back covered in blood, could have been killed, the Luna Selenography at the Archive has been largely destroyed, and we might have fared better if I'd taken him with me.

"Your mother appeared to me while I was there. Her grimoire. It was part of the archive...it just called to me."

Martin rolls me off him, looming over me with an intensity that burns away nearly all of his tenderness.

"What did she say?"

"She said I was made to understand scattering. To know what it is to exist in pieces and still be whole."

Martin's eyes search my face and he takes my hand, weaving his fingers through mine.

"You said something similar to me once," I tell him. "When I said I felt like I was coming together like a late-stage Picasso. You told me that maybe that's what I'm meant to be."

"I was merely trying to be encouraging," he says.

I can't help giggling, but Martin's not ready yet.

"Come on, it's a little funny," I say. "My point is, I don't think your mother was merely trying to be encouraging. I think she meant what she said literally."

Martin purses his lips and nods, if barely.

"I'm still so angry with you," he says.

"I know," I say. "I'm angry, too. For you testing me with Wickham. For not telling me things under the ruse of oversight. Don't deny it. And I'm angry at myself most of all."

"I don't—" He stops, tries again. "Don't make me do that winter again."

The words land like a knuckle pressed into a bruise. The silence that follows is different. Something like the floor returning under our feet.

He shifts his weight and helps me sit up, careful of my neck, my arm. Our eyes flicker over each other, taking stock and shelter.

"Sweet St. Romedio," I say. "We're a mess."

I reach for him, to touch his face, and he catches my hand mid-air, holding it softly on his cheek. He holds it there like warmth is rare and borrowed.

"Have we fought like this before?" I ask him.

He huffs in a way that could be a laugh if he had the energy for it.

"This?" His mouth lifts on one side. "This was nothing."

The cabin door opens, and Wickham emerges, assessing the situation with those leery eyes of his. Then Lyla, tears still wet on her face. Colette, hand covering her mouth. Nox remains inside, probably praying for our damned souls.

"Busybodies," I say.

"That went better than expected," Wickham says, dryly.

The burgundy journal sits on the porch steps where Wickham left it. Martin's mother's words, saved. The only thing we managed to keep from turning to ash.

Martin helps me to my feet. We're both filthy, blood-crusted, healing but not healed. He picks up the journal, turns it over in his hands. The leather is stained darker where my blood soaked in during the fight at the archive.

"Can you read it?" I ask. "The symbols, the language—"

"Yes." He opens it carefully, pages crackling. His eyes move over the strange vertical script, and something shifts in his expression. Recognition, maybe. Or sorrow. "I'd know my mother's hand anywhere."

Colette's already moving back inside, her footsteps purposeful. Within minutes I can smell it—onions hitting hot oil, the sharp green of herbs being stripped from stems. She's cooking. Of course she is. That's what Colette does when the world tilts sideways: she feeds people.

"You should clean up," Lyla says to me, but she's looking at Martin when she says it. Making sure. Making sure he's safe to be around. Making sure I'm safe with him.

"We're fine," I tell her. And maybe we are. Maybe we're not. But we're here.

Martin's still reading, standing in the clearing with the journal open, moonlight falling across the pages. His shoulders are tense, and I know that focus—he's hunting for something in those symbols, in his mother's words.

I should go inside and wash the blood off. Should help Colette cook or let Lyla fuss over me or do any of the normal things that follow abnormal violence.

But I stay for now, watching him read. Waiting for whatever he's going to find in those pages—because I can see it on his face, the way his breathing has changed. He's found something.

Or something's found him.

28

I keep stealing long glances at Martin as I play sous chef for Colette. She's cooking like she means it, throwing together one of her comfort food extravaganzas.

"Chop the salad," she says, ordering me around like a drill sergeant. But I can't stop trying to read deeper into the look on Martin's face, and nearly slice off my fingertip. I have to hold my hand out the window, letting the moon clot the blood.

Lyla sets the table and I bring out the heavy-bottomed pot of chicken and dumplings. I taste the broth one last time, and it's so thick with celery and sweet onion that I feel like it's trying to tuck me in and tell me I've had a long day. Which, come to think of it—I have.

Colette follows me with steaming skillet cornbread, fresh out of the oven, and sets it between the green beans and pickled peaches.

She calls for Nox and Wickham to come back inside. While giving the place an extra blessing, they made a pitstop at the cellar for some homemade black walnut and honey moonshine.

We gather around Nox's table and he says grace before we

dig in—giving thanks not just for the food, but for me still being around his table. Martin holds my eyes a little too long. *What?* I mouth. He shakes his head. Not yet.

"You find anything in that book?" Lyla asks him, casting a side eye as she spoons the stew into her bowl.

"There's a lot," he says. "Spells, tinctures, ruminations. Some drawings she made."

"Like those little symbols," Lyla says.

"Those, and more detailed sketches. She was very good."

"Speaking of very good—Colette's done something holy here," Nox says. "If heaven don't taste like this, I ain't goin'."

Wickham raises his sweet tea high into the air and we all follow, clinking glasses. But as delicious as it all is, I'm focused on the journal. I want to get Martin alone as soon as I can and ask him about the strange, arcane language his mother wrote in. A language I could almost understand when I was at the Luna Archive. Part of me feels like it was written just for me, but maybe that's just wishful thinking, since that's the only journal that survived.

AFTER WE FINISH CLEANING up from dinner, Martin catches my wrist as I'm carrying the last of the dishes to the sink.

"Come outside with me," he says.

He needs to move, needs air, needs to do something with his hands before whatever's been building in him all evening breaks through his skin.

I follow him out to the yard where an old stump sits about twenty paces from the porch—scarred and pocked from years of use. He pulls a couple of throwing knives from his belt. The handles are worn smooth, the blades catching moonlight.

"These belong to Nox?" I ask.

Martin shakes his head. "They were ours. But I keep them here. You remember how?" He offers me one.

I take it, feeling the balance. "I used to do this with my dad when I was a kid, so yes, but I assume you're talking about something else. Spoiler alert: I was never very good."

He demonstrates—the stance, the grip, the release. His knife buries itself in the stump with a solid thunk. I throw. Mine lands handle-first and clatters to the ground.

"You're thinking too much," he says, retrieving both knives.

We throw in silence for a while. His always true. Mine getting closer. It's meditative—the repetition, the focus required, the small violence of blade meeting wood.

My knife finally hits the mark—not center, but close enough. Martin's turns me slightly. Adjusting my stance. His chest solid against my back. His hand over mine on the knife handle, showing me the angle.

"Like this," he says quietly, and I can feel his breath against my ear.

The knife leaves my hand. Dead center.

We stand like that for a moment—his body a warm line against mine, our hands still raised together in the shape of the throw. Then he steps back, and the night air rushes cold where he was.

"There's something else," he says finally. "In the journal."

I wait. Watch him struggle with whatever he's been carrying since he opened that burgundy book.

"One of the drawings," he says.

He reaches into his pocket, and pulls out a folded page. He doesn't hand it to me right away. Just holds it, looking at it like it might bite him.

"Martin."

He unfolds it slowly. Even in the moonlight, or maybe because of it, I can see it clearly—the careful pencil work, the attention to detail. A young woman in homespun dress, hair pulled back simply with dark curls that have escaped. Her face is unmistakable.

"That's Grace," I whisper.

"I know." His voice is tight. "Which means she survived the displacement and was flung to 1830."

The relief that floods through me is so powerful my knees nearly buckle. "She's alive."

"Was alive," Martin corrects gently. "In 1830. Twila, this drawing is two hundred years old."

"But if she made it there, if she survived long enough for your mother to draw her—"

"Stop." He looks at me directly, his eyes hard, full of alarm. "You can't travel to 1830."

"I know there are risks," I say.

"You could encounter the version of yourself that I knew, and we don't know what that would mean."

"Martin, I've already traveled that far back. Last summer when Colette anchored me beyond the veil. I traveled even farther, if you remember. And I never encountered her. I was her."

"You don't know that. You don't know if you could fracture further and get trapped there. You don't know if you're walking into a trap the Bramwell witch set." He pulls one of the knives out of the stump, then takes the drawing back, folding it carefully. He takes a few steps and flings the knife again. It lands deep. "There's a possibility that you won't come back. Or we'd be trapped in a cycle from which we can't extract ourselves."

The idea of living together until July 14, 1976, then being torn apart by the Gemini Covenant—in perpetuity—seems like a fresh hell. Especially since our restrictions for traveling beyond the veil, namely doing our best not to affect historical outcomes, is a strict code for our kind. It's not like I could find Martin in the past and warn him about what's going to happen. I retrieve the knives from the stump, needing something to do with my hands. When I return, I press one into his palm.

"Tell me the rest," I say. "Whatever else you found."

He throws. The knife vibrates in the stump's center. "There's a tincture she recorded. I think—" He stops, starts again. "I can't be sure, but she may have made it for you. The ingredients, the moon phase required, the sparse preparation method. It reads like instructions meant for someone who would know how to interpret them."

"What does it do?"

"I don't know. But knowing my mother as I did, as you did, it's to make visible what is hidden." He turns to me. "I think there may be a message in that journal. Something only you can see, and only after you've made this tincture."

The skin on my arms prickles. "Why didn't she just tell me? Back at the archive?"

"Twila, my mother's magic isn't just for words. It's meant to be experienced."

I think about how her writing almost seemed to penetrate my very being when I tried to read it at the Luna Archive. "When can we make it? You said it was for a specific moon phase."

"Twila—"

"If there's a message your mother left for me, I need to see it. Maybe it involves Grace—" I can't finish that sentence. "I made a promise, Martin. I told God I wouldn't let that witch have her."

Martin throws again, harder this time. The blade sinks in almost to its handle. "The moon phase. We would have to make the tincture tonight. Tomorrow night at the latest. But Twila— whatever message is in there, whatever my mother wants you to know—it won't change how I feel about doing something reckless. Even if it involves Grace."

"But if we can help her—"

"Maybe she's already been helped. The drawing—that could be my mother's way of letting us know she's alright."

"Or that we have to bring her back," I say. "Martin, she

doesn't belong there. She has a family, people who love her and are waiting for her to come home. She could die of an infection, of typhus, of the damned flu for the love of God!"

Martin takes my hands and leads me away from the stump, from the moon shadows cast through the dense freckling of tree leaves overhead. We stand in Nox's yard under the direct light of the moon.

"I know she appeared to you today, but you don't remember my mother," he says. "I do. Whatever you think she might have meant by helping you save the journal, making sure we saw the drawing, I can tell you what I know."

He pulls me closer, and I feel the last of his anger ease away, disappearing into the night like the ghost of a blown-out flame.

"She'd told me, told us, to always turn toward one another, not away. To hold each other above even those closest to us, including her. I'm asking you right now to put me above Grace. Above my mother. I promise the same. It's the only way we can help the people we love."

I look up at the moon—for guidance, I guess. I wish my dad would flutter down from wherever he is and help me make sense of all of this. I wish I hadn't made such a trophy of being an outlier all my life.

"A trophy's just a mold of plastic and metal," my dad would say if he was here. "Not something to hang your heart on."

I meet Martin's eyes and look deeply into them. I don't let myself even glance away. I think about when Martin wanted to deal with Soma on his own and I wouldn't let him. The way every time we've stood together we've come out on the other side. "I'll do that," I say. "Whatever we decide. We'll do it together."

I push up onto my toes and kiss his lips softly, sealing our promise. "I swear it on my living soul."

29

"Moonwort, eyebright, silver shavings, and spring water," I say. "That's it?"

"Brewed just before a full moon crests," Martin says.

I glance at Nox's cabin, seeing Colette in the window. Neither of us wants to do this with an audience. Seems private somehow.

"Meet me in the root cellar," Martin says, and disappears around the back of the house.

I slip in through the front.

"Everything alright?" Lyla asks.

"Fine," I say. "We just need a little time alone."

Lyla purses her lips and throws a glance at Colette. Wickham's got his face in an old hunting guide and doesn't look up. A quiet little smile ghosts his mouth.

"I'm sure Nox wouldn't mind if you went into his room," Lyla says. "Had your talk or whatever it is you want to do in there."

Nox, fully reclined in his recliner, pops an old mix tape into an older boom box. Sepultra's *Inner Self* starts to play. "Bedroom's a heapin' mess," he says before the music shifts from clean, echoing guitar notes to crushing mirrors. "Ain't fit for company."

I go into the kitchen and clatter around, pouring a couple of elderberry cordials and slipping the necessary herbs into my pocket.

"You need help?" Lyla asks, watching me exit the kitchen carrying a tray with salted nuts, a candle, and the glasses of liquor.

"For God's sake, Lyla," Nox says. "I think they can manage a little romance without your help."

"It's not the romance I'm worried about," she snaps. "And will you turn that racket down?"

Nox snickers, ignoring her request. Just talks louder. "You let Twila handle Twila. She don't break, she cuts."

I push the screen door open with my hip and hurry to the root cellar. Martin's nowhere to be seen, so I prop the door open and light the candle. The small flame swells—and there he is at the bottom of the stairs. Sitting on one of the barrels like the night itself had made him, a camp stove and a copper kettle set on a crate at the ready.

"Jesus," I say. "You scared me."

"At least you didn't scream."

"That would have brought the whole chorus out here. They think we're sneaking off to get naughty."

His smile is a low, private thing.

"Maybe later," Martin murmurs. "I wouldn't want to make a liar out of you."

I pull the moonwort and eyebright sachets out of my jeans pocket and place them on the crate. Martin brings the spring water in a pitcher and lays some silver shavings on a square of worn suede. The moonwort leaflets are crescent shaped, paired neatly along the stem. Dried, they're fragile, almost translucent in places, with a ghostly quality. Brittle and papery, they crumble easily when I rub them between my fingers, depositing them in the copper pot. They don't smell like much, just a faint leafy note, the echo of something that once lived.

The eyebright is delicate and wispy. I sprinkle it on top of the moonwort and add the spring water into the pot, as Martin ignites the camp stove. We wait, our shoulders pressed against each other, our hands entwined. I can feel his pulse through his wrist, or maybe it's mine—our hearts pushing into each other's skin.

The root cellar breathes around us—earth and time made into walls. Mason jars catch the moonlight coming through the propped door, throwing rainbows across the dirt floor. Nox's preserved peaches glow like a captured sunset in their glass prisons and strings of dried peppers hang from the ceiling beams like rosaries. They cast delicate shadows that sway with our movements, as if the cellar itself is alive and listening.

The camp stove flickers blue beneath the copper pot, and steam begins to rise, writhing between us like a living thing. Martin's face is half in that soft mix of fire and moonlight, and I can see the tension in his jaw softening. The smell of earth mingles with the heating tincture—mineral and verdant, ancient and new at once.

It feels like we're in the belly of the mountain itself, in a space that exists outside of time, where the only things that matter are the steam rising between us and the secret we're about to uncover together.

Once the water erupts into a raging boil, we add the silver.

A thin, greenish steam with a subtle bitterness dances up from the pot and into the air. Martin's mother gave no further instructions, but I lean in toward the steaming pot anyway. The words come—neither planned nor memorized, but rising like the vapor itself:

"What's hidden wants the light—
my father used to say that when I'd lose
my house keys, my good sense, my way.

MOON'S DAUGHTER, *show me what your son*
kept close. I'm asking nicely.
I'm asking the way you ask
a mountain to move: with breath,
with belief I don't quite own yet.

LET *the steam be a veil I can pull back.*
Let the words rise like moths
drawn to what they shouldn't touch
but can't resist. Your hand
wrote this, Mother. My hands hold it now.
Between us—this vapor, this moment,
this marriage of shadow and light."

Martin's eyes haven't left my face. I can feel the weight of his attention like a hand at the small of my back. He opens his mother's journal and I gently blow the steam into its pages. Those begin to turn, as if there's a real breeze blowing through. They land on a section so dense in script it looks like a page from a Tolstoy novel. Only one written in peculiar hieroglyphs.

I loom over the journal, my shadow reaching across the open pages. I can feel the message trying to come through, but it doesn't.

"Can you make anything out?" Martin asks, and I shake my head. He leans in for a better look, and his chest nearly touches my shoulder blade. I can feel the heat of him, smell cedar and night air, his particular scent of clove and bergamot. For a second I forget to breathe. As soon as his shadow overlaps with mine, the script begins to change.

Faint shapes appear in the hieroglyphs—not words yet, just a subtle luminescence, like foxfire on rotting wood. Certain symbols pulse with warmth—I can feel it radiating through the paper against my fingertips.

"Do you see that?" I whisper.

I press my finger to the first warm symbol. Heat blooms under my touch, and for a moment I feel Martin's mother's hand beneath mine—steadying, guiding. The hieroglyph transforms: *In.* Elegant script that holds for three heartbeats before fading back.

"Again," Martin says, his breath warm against my ear.

I chase the next glow, then the next. *The hollow of deep time.* The words appear and vanish like fireflies, and I have to hold each one in my memory while hunting for the next. Martin's hand moves across the page with mine now—sometimes steadying the journal, sometimes finding symbols I've missed. Other times both our fingers land on the same warm glyph and press down together.

The root cellar shivers around us, and smudged ghosts from the hanging herbs sway across the earthen walls. I can smell winter apples and old wood and the fading herbal bitterness of the tincture.

I buried silence.

The words come slowly, demanding patience. Each touch reveals a fragment, a piece. The message builds itself in my mind even as the pages remain stubbornly hieroglyphic. Martin presses against me. Our shadows have become one.

Where the daughter walked with grief and wonder, there lies what was entrusted to my keeping.

My hand stills. Martin's mother is talking about me. About places I've been. Perhaps moments I don't remember. Martin's breath catches—I hear it, feel it against my neck.

"Keep going," he murmurs. His voice has gone rough.

The shield is woven of moonlight and shadow—it will not yield to force, only to blood claim.

My fingers find the next cluster of symbols. They're warmer than the others, almost hot. I touch one and nothing happens. Martin places his hand over mine—his fingers are cold from the night air but his palm burns. The words kindle under our joined touch. *When she who reads the earth's old bones speaks of protections that should not hold, you will know the place has been found.*

"Petal," I breathe.

The final page has only two symbols, but they burn brighter than all the rest. I reach for them and feel resistance—like trying to push through water. Martin's hand covers mine again, fingers threading through, and together we press down.

The eclipse opens all doors, but some lead forward by going back.

The words hang there longer this time, glowing against the dark page. Then they fade, and the hieroglyphs settle again into their ancient pattern as if they'd never been disturbed.

We stay bent over the journal, breathing in unison. The message is beautiful and incomplete. A riddle wrapped in poetry. We're supposed to wait for Petal, that much is clear. Listen to what she's found. And the eclipse—the eclipse is the key to something, though I don't know what yet.

Martin's thumb traces a small circle on the back of my hand, still resting against the page.

"My mother," he says, "always did like making people work for answers."

I almost laugh, but the sound catches in my throat. Because somewhere in that cryptic message is Grace, is the registry, is whatever comes next. And all of it is wrapped up in an eclipse that happened nearly two hundred years ago.

Outside, the last song on Nox's tape—'Hells Bells'—fades out, drifting toward us from a cracked window. That final guitar chord and bell toll slowly decaying into nothing, the sound dying away until I can't tell when it actually stopped or if I'm just remembering it. In the sudden quiet, I become aware of how close Martin and I are sitting, the way our breathing has synchronized. Neither of us has moved to break contact. The candle flame gutters and throws our single form huge against the earthen wall —dark and whole and impossible to separate into two.

30

I wake wrapped in the old blanket Nox keeps in his Bronco, the red and black wool heavy and warm against the chill of dawn. Martin's still asleep beside me, one arm across my waist, our bodies fitted together under the old oak where we'd been throwing knives just hours ago. The blanket smells like wood smoke and a few decades of mountain living. Above us, the oak's branches are black lace against a sky going pearl-gray at the edges.

Beside me sits a clean folded sweatshirt and matching pants —Lyla's—topped with a note in her loopy hand:

Lord above, the two of you sounded like rutting foxes. Nox says use the rainwater shower outside; the one in his room is spitting out sulfur again. The water's freezing. Consider it penance.

In the distance, behind the rhododendrons, I hear the unmistakable rumble of an old Jeep Cherokee pulling up. The door groans open and thunks closed. Petal's boots hit the ground in that clipped way of hers, each step landing exactly where she means it to. I hear the rustle of her shifting her field bag on her shoulder, then a small sigh—here at last.

"Morning," she says, standing over us. Her voice has the

same quality as her footsteps—steady, grounded, matter-of-fact.

Martin exhales next to me and rolls onto his back. "Petal, it can hardly be called morning yet."

"You said to come first thing. And it was urgent."

We texted Petal last night, just after deciphering the journal.

"It is," I say, pulling on Lyla's sweatshirt and pants under the blanket. "It's more than urgent. I wish to God it wasn't."

MARTIN MAKES some coffee on the camp stove in the cellar, away from windows and tuned-in ears, in case someone's already up. Lyla, in particular, is an early riser and I want to understand what we're dealing with before we start sharing what's going on.

While the coffee percolates, I actually do take that rain-water shower. Its icy needles are almost torture, but I need it. I return dressed in Lyla's sweats, teeth chattering, and Martin swaddles me in Nox's blanket. He's pulled his dark indigo jeans on, plus his olive Carhartt work jacket, but no shirt underneath. That was a casualty of our fight yesterday. Petal sits on a bench next to a barrel of winter apples, and the dented metal perco-lator starts to burble. Martin pours the coffee into mason jars, the liquid dark and thick as balsamic vinegar. The glass is hot, and I have to hold it in the blanket. Smells wonderful though.

Petal cups her jar in both hands, waiting. She's good at waiting—geologists spend half their lives letting rocks tell their stories in their own time.

"We decoded my mother's journal last night,' Martin says. "There was a message hidden in it. Cryptic, but one part was rather obvious. 'When she who reads the earth's old bones speaks of protections that should not hold, you will know the place has been found.'"

Petal goes the kind of still that means something's clicked into place.

She sets down her jar and pulls a field notebook from her bag, flipping it open. The pages are covered in sketches, measurements, and coordinates, all in her small, precise hand.

"The protections in that cave aren't usual," she says. "Not even from what I know about how your mother used to operate."

"How is that?" Martin leans forward.

"It's *active*. Most old spells, even powerful ones, they fade. Become residual. Like a heat signature after a fire's gone out." She taps her notebook. "But this? This is still burning. The rock itself is warmer in specific patterns—circles within circles, radiating from a central chamber."

"A living ritual," I breathe. I can feel Martin's whole being shift next to me. As if his body has become heavier with every revelation.

"Not just one ritual. Layers." Petal's eyes are bright with excitement. "I found symbols in the stone that shouldn't be there—not carved, actually. *Grown*. Like the rock formed around them. And the arrangement..." She flips to a page covered in concentric circles, each marked with notations. "This took years to build. Maybe centuries. It's not your run-of-the-mill protection spell mechanism—it's a vault."

The word hangs in the cool cellar air.

"Something's locked in there," Petal continues. "And whatever spell was used is still holding. The protections recognize me—I could feel it. They let me move through the outer chambers, let me take readings. But there's an inner sanctum I can't access. Every time I get close, the temperature drops so fast my instruments fog over. The air gets heavy, like bad breath and river mud all mixed up together. And I feel..." She pauses, choosing words carefully. "Watched. Not threatened, exactly.

More like being assessed. Permitted to be there, but warned not to touch."

Martin and I exchange a look. The registry. It has to be.

I think about the message: *The shield is woven of moonlight and shadow—it will not yield to force, only to blood claim.*

"Can you get to the inner chamber?" I ask.

"Maybe. Not so far," Petal says. "But that's not really what you're asking, is it? You want to know if someone else could get in. Someone with... different intentions."

"Could they?" Martin's voice comes in like a cut.

Petal closes her notebook slowly. "Not alone. The protections are specifically designed to stop intrusion. But if someone forced another person—someone the protections would accept —to breach the inner sanctum for them?" She meets our eyes. "Then theoretically, the vault could be opened."

The coffee has gone tepid in my hands. In the silence, we can hear Metallica starting up again from inside the cabin— Nox must be awake.

"We need to go," I say. "Right away."

"Hold on there," Petal says. "There's something else you need to understand. The vault part of the cave isn't accessible during the day. At all."

"What do you mean?" I ask.

"I mean the protections are keyed to lunar cycles. During daylight hours, the inner chambers are completely sealed—the temperature drops below freezing, the air becomes toxic. I measured carbon dioxide levels that would kill you in minutes." She flips to another page of readings. "But at night, under moonlight, everything changes. The temperature normalizes, the air clears, the passages that were solid rock during the day become navigable."

Martin's eyes narrow. "My mother built a vault that only opens under the moon."

"Not just opens—becomes survivable." Petal traces her

finger over a graph showing temperature fluctuations. "I charted this over three days. Sunrise to sunset, the inner sanctum is a death trap. Moonrise to moonset, it's merely dangerous. But during the full moon?" She looks up. "The protections are at their most permeable. The stone itself seems to... breathe. That's when someone with blood claim could potentially reach the center."

"We have a full moon tonight," I say.

Petal sets down her notebook and wraps both hands around her coffee. "And there's something else. The outer perimeter—the forest surrounding the cave entrance—it's being watched. I didn't see anyone. But the trees are marked."

"Marked how?" Martin asks.

"Symbols scratched into bark. Fresh, maybe a week old. Not spell or ritual work—more like... someone or something has been circling the site, testing how close they can get before the protections push back." She meets our eyes. "The blessed protections don't just guard the cave. They radiate outward in layers. And the marks? They're right at the edge of that repulsion field. Whoever made them got as close as physically possible without triggering a full defensive response."

"Assuming it's the Bramwell witch," I say, and my voice sounds distant even to myself. "What would a full defensive response look like?"

Petal shrugs and looks deep into her coffee. She has no idea.

"Knowing my mother," Martin says. "The protection would be simple and devastating. She'd lose her power entirely while in range. The protections would sever her connection to the spirit realm, to the Others, to everything she's bound herself to. She'd become purely human, vulnerable, mortal—until she retreated beyond the boundary."

The coffee has gone gelid in my hands. Through the propped cellar door, I can see the sky brightening into full morning. One day. That's all we have before moonrise brings the full moon this evening, before the vault breathes open, before whoever's been stalking in the forest makes their move.

Martin's hand finds mine in the folds of the blanket. His thumb traces that same small circle on my wrist—the gesture from last night, when our shadows had to merge for his mother's words to appear.

"Then we go tonight," he says quietly. "Before she does."

I nod, though we both know it's not that simple. We're racing toward the full moon with a plan that's mostly hope and desperation. But it's all we've got.

31

F ull Moon

"WHAT'S HE DOING HERE?" Petal whispers.

We've entered the cabin just as Wickham glides into the living room from Nox's bedroom. His head a black mess of hair that makes him look like Edgar Allan Poe risen from some dark dream. Judas Priest is playing low from the boom box, a dull, distant wail—metal echoing through a mine shaft.

"Wickham pretty much saved my life," I say.

Petal rolls her eyes. "He does that from time to time. He does other things, too."

"Petal," Wickham says, and there's something almost startled in his voice—strange coming from a man who never seems to startle. He looks her up and down like she gives him a migraine, then shakes it off, easing himself onto the windowsill bench. "Still carbon-dating sacred stones and drilling cores through holy ground?"

"Sure," Petal says. "And you're still allergic to joy. Look at us. Consistency."

Colette's in the kitchen already cooking, of course. I can smell a mean biscuits and gravy taking shape in her hands. I should go offer my assistance, but the dynamic shaping up in the living room has piqued my curiosity. Lyla's in there with her anyway—snipping at her for putting too much salt in the gravy. I know it's not about the gravy, it's about me. The specter of my near burning is fading, but hasn't faded entirely.

I watch Nox as he actually gets up off his recliner. He tucks his faded-gray waffle-knit thermal into his canvas work pants and fixes the collar on his open flannel shirt before walking over to us. Then he holds his hand out to Petal like he's some kind of southern gentleman.

"Silas Jasper Treadway," he says.

Petal tips her head. A nod of recognition. "Petal Faye Whitaker."

"Might I say, *The Living Bedrock: Thermal Anomalies in Sacred Site Geology* is an extraordinary piece of work."

I swear if Nox had a hat on, he'd take it off and hold it against his heart like he's reciting the Pledge of Allegiance.

"But as good as it is," he continues. "It barely scratches the surface of *Where the Earth Keeps Secrets: An Unconventional Survey of Appalachian Sacred Geology.*"

Petal inhales sharply. She licks at her lips, almost shy. "Thank you, Mr. Treadway. *Dark Dominion: The Spirits of Appalachia* is the most overlooked piece of folkloric scholarship that's ever been written about our region."

"It's the only damn book I ever wrote," he says. "You've written five, and numerous papers. A few of which shook the wrong pillars in the wrong offices. *The Persistence of Place: Why Certain Sites Resist Standard Geological Classification* in the Journal of Geological Anomalies was a classic. Unflinching, rigorous. That one took muscle and teeth to push through."

"It was a hell of an uphill climb, I can tell you that," Petal says. "You've read my books and papers?"

Nox nods. "Every one."

Lyla passes through, dropping a muttered, "Get a room," as she sets a pitcher of orange juice on the table.

Martin finally joins us after his turn in the rainwater shower. He comes in through the back door, his hair wet and finger combed. Nox has given him one of his heavy metal concert t-shirts to wear. An old black Dio from their "Holy Diver" tour, the central demon image cracked and faded to almost nothing. It shouldn't suit him, but it does.

Colette emerges from the kitchen carrying a cast iron skillet of biscuits, golden and splitting at their sides, trailing the smell of butter and salt. Behind her, Lyla brings the gravy in a blue enamel pot, thick and peppered and studded with crumbled sausage. They seem to have made up.

"Y'all need to eat before we do whatever foolish thing is in the planning," Colette says, setting the skillet on the cafe table with a decisive thunk.

The room holds—it's the moment people stop dancing around something and finally face it head-on.

Martin catches my eye across the room. I nod.

"We found something," I say. "In Martin's mother's journal. And Petal found something in the cave."

Nox kills the music—Judas Priest dies mid-wail. Wickham straightens from his slouch against the windowsill. Petal pulls out her field notebook, suddenly all business.

We gather as best we can—the cafe table only seats a tight four, so Wickham stays on the windowsill bench, Nox leans against the wall near him, and Martin stands behind where I sit. His hand rests on the back of my chair, his fingers grazing my neck.

Colette serves biscuits and gravy while we talk, spooning the thick sausage gravy over split biscuits, handing around plates. The food should ground us, make this feel manageable. Instead it just reminds me we're still vulnerable, still made of flesh that can break. Sometimes in ways even the moon can't mend.

"The registry," I begin, slicing my fork through a biscuit. "It's in the cave. The one where we found Brooks."

No one speaks. They're all thinking the same thing I am— Brooks's arm pressed into stone older than memory, his pocket watch still ticking in the Ordovician. The cave isn't just a place. It's a mouth that swallows time. And the registry...that's time in and of itself.

"The witch—what she's done with that single page," Nox says. "That kind of power comes from decades of binding rituals. Blood, intention, pieces of her soul fed into that page, binding with her."

"It's a helluva power source," I say slowly. "More than that. It's a conduit to the registry's accumulated magic— millions of years of moon witch history compressed into divine script. Even separated from the whole, that one page carries a lot."

Martin grits his teeth. "That page contains elements of the registry's architecture—the mechanisms that make it a living document capable of rewriting what it records. That's what she's been binding herself to. Which tells us what she'd be capable of with the complete registry restored."

The unspoken hangs between us: godhood.

"There's a vault," Petal says quietly, her notebook open but her hands still. "A couple hundred years old at least and still active. Still burning. Martin's mother built something that shouldn't be possible—protections that layer over protections, circles within circles. I've been in the outer chambers. They let me through. But the inner sanctum..." She meets my eyes. "That's keyed to blood. Twila's, we think."

I watch understanding move across faces. Lyla's hand

makes a full stop halfway to her mouth. Colette sets down the gravy pot with care, like sudden movement might shatter something.

"Beulah, my grandmother," Lyla says, her voice small. "She was our archivist. The knowledge of the vault could have been passed down to her in case it ever needed hiding. And Beulah could have only hidden the registry right before I left Sibyl Springs. Right after I tore out that page. I was one of the last people to see it."

"Ly, it makes sense that Martin's mother would have given our archivists access to the vault. A place to hide the registry if it was in danger. Beulah was hiding the registry from something, someone."

"A lot of strange things were going on then," Wickham says.

"Plenty of strange things going on now. And they're about to get stranger," Martin says, his voice low and even. "There's a full moon tonight, and the vault is only accessible then. Only survivable. We have one window to get inside before—"

"Before the Bramwell witch does," Wickham finishes.

"She's already circling it," Petal says, tapping her notebook. "Marked trees at the perimeter. Right at the edge of the repulsion field. As close as she can get without the protections turning her own corruption back on her."

"She's always been good at finding a way," Lyla says quietly.

The weight of it settles over the room like snow, hushed and cold and accumulating fast. The warm food, the morning light, feel like props. Something is building—not in this room, but somewhere else. In the forest around that cave. In the hollow of deep time where the registry sleeps. A memory or prophecy. I can't tell the difference anymore.

"So we go," Nox says. A statement that lands like a boulder.

"We go," Martin agrees. I can feel how tight he's gripping my chair.

"The moon rises just after six," Lyla says. "Right at sunset."

Less than nine hours. Nine hours before I walk into a vault Martin's mother built centuries ago. A vault only Beulah had ever entered, and that only I can access now.

"I can get us close," Petal says. "Through the outer chambers. But past that..." She doesn't finish. Doesn't need to.

Past that, I'm alone. Walking into a place made for me by someone I can't remember, holding something Beulah, a woman I never even met, trusted to spirit and moonlight and the hope that I'd find my way back.

Colette pushes her plate away, the food barely touched. I've never seen her not finish her own cooking.

"There's blessing work I can do," she says. "Protection spells. They might buy us time."

"Time for what?" Wickham asks. "We know she can't enter the cave herself. We know only Twila can access the vault. So what's the plan when we get there and find out she's already waiting?"

No one answers. Because there is no plan. There's just the terrible math of it: the witch wants the registry, only I can retrieve it, and she'll do whatever it takes to make me give it to her.

The biscuits and gravy have gone to goop on our plates. Outside, I can hear crows calling to each other—three sharp cries, then silence.

Martin places his hands on my shoulders, heavy and hot-palmed. "We go at moonrise. All of us. We stay together as long as we can."

As long as we can. The words hang there like a warning, a promise we already know we can't keep.

I think about the vault breathing open under the full moon. About walking into darkness and magic. About my hands reaching for something that might save us or destroy us or both at once.

And about Martin's mother knowing this moment would come, planning for it, leaving messages in journals and protections in stone for a daughter-in-law she knew intimately, and loved deeply. She even built safeguards for knowing I would someday forget everything we'd shared.

Or maybe someone else has built a different trap entirely.

———————

32

We've pulled the cafe table up close to the galley kitchen so that Lyla, Colette, Petal and I can work without being on top of each other. Our sleeves are rolled up to our elbows and our hands are dark with herb oils—green and brown and rust-red from the iron.

"I wouldn't go too heavy on the vervain," Petal says, brushing Colette's hand as she reaches for the herb. "We need some lingering energy to ground the salt."

Colette purses her lips and goes for the vervain anyway.

"I'm not trying to get in your business, Fillmore," Petal says. "My granny didn't teach me the spells—said it wasn't her gift to pass down. She showed me to listen to what the mountains were saying."

"So, what are the mountains saying?" Colette asks her.

Petal pinches exactly the amount of vervain Colette has prescribed and mixes it with the salt.

"That I should shut my trap and let you do the spell-making."

"Well, isn't this just like a coven," Lyla says, and we all bust out laughing. Covens, I've been told, are not only viper pits, but for amateurs and weaklings, pretenders who couldn't light a match on the moon itself. Moon witches and wolfen—we're a race of beings touched by the divine.

"God, I hope so," I whisper, though mostly to myself.

Despite the sister moon witch bickering between ladies who've not only known each other forever, but whose families have dug in the dirt together for generations, there's a goodness I feel in this place, these women. Our singularity of purpose, our hope for the best, even our fear for the worst. There's an unspoken holiness made real by the work of our hands, the promises we've made to ourselves and each other. Even the kitchen smells like church. Along with forest and something burning that isn't fire. Steam from the oil pot hazes the afternoon light and Colette stands at the stove, stirring. I watch her add angelica root, hyssop, frankincense resin—each one dropped in with deliberate care.

The counter tops and the table have been scrubbed with salt water and laid with a white cloth. Light slants through the window, catching sparkles of dust that drift like lazy stars.

I notice Petal peeking out the back window, like she's doing it all casual. The men and women have split up, with Martin, Nox and Wickham by the root cellar, pulling together weapons and other tactical defensives that can work against whatever creatures the Bramwell witch might sic on us. We have to assume she'll pull whatever she can through the tear in the veil —whatever hungry, violent atrocity might serve her purpose.

But that's not why she's looking. Nox has brought out his rifle and is sitting on a stump, loading it with blessed salt and iron filings. He figures it worked on Vyrithra and might work on whatever else might come through.

"There's something about a mountain man, isn't there?" I say, and everyone but Petal snickers. She does offer up a sly smile, though.

"My Uncle Silas, and uh...Wickham?" Colette says.

Petal looks up from the table, holding up a piece of angelica root sliced into a coin. "This thin enough?"

Colette inspects it and approves, dropping it into the pot.

"As for Wickham," Petal says. "Did you know that little bastard once called me profane?"

Petal nods, pursing her lips. "To me, magic and geology are the same thing—just forces that shaped the world. But nooo, that's blasphemy, studying what he reveres."

"So, religious and philosophical differences ended things between you two?" I say.

Petal raises an eyebrow at me. "Sweetheart, that was thirty years ago," she says. "And there wasn't much to end." She drives the point of her knife into the chopping block, leaving it vibrating upright. "The man's insufferable. But he is well hung. God is unjust—that's all I'm saying."

The teasing fades, and the silence that follows is thick as molasses when it's been left too long on the stove. The wilds have always listened when women like us gather. They've always known when the work was turning from talk to spell-making.

Colette starts it—soft, almost under her breath, like it's not even meant for us.

Come Thou fount of every blessing Tune my heart to sing Thy grace

The melody is old, modal, the sound of faith made audible. Her voice carries the tune like a promise—one that's mournful but with all the trimmings of hope.

Streams of mercy, never ceasing Call for songs of loudest praise

Lyla sits across from me, red cotton thread in her lap. She's braiding it with nettle fiber and black wool, her fingers working the pattern without looking. As she braids, she speaks names under her breath. Her grandmother Beulah. Her great-grandmother Lydia, then Rutha and Nonie, Hester, Glenna, Effie and Elspeth. Names going back and back, women in her family who held our history and survived impossible things. Each name woven into the thread like a map—proof that survival is possible because it's already happened.

She cuts the cord into seven lengths, ties nine knots in each one. Each knot a seal, a binding. Her hands shake like a gremlin, as she'd say, but they don't falter.

Here I raise my Ebenezer Hither by Thy help I'm come

I'm at the bowl, measuring nothing, working by feel. Rowan berries that Nox brought from the ridge, vervain from Colette's garden, iron filings that smell like the rust of old nails. Salt. My hands move automatically, mixing the fine and rough textures together.

Petal pulls something from her field bag—small fragments wrapped in tissue paper. "From the cave," she says quietly, unwrapping them. Limestone chips, tiny pieces of the cave itself. "The protections let me take these. Maybe they'll recognize their own."

She adds them to the bowl, her geologist's hands treating folk magic like field work—careful, methodical, respectful.

And I hope, by Thy good pleasure Safely to arrive at home

Colette's song fills the kitchen, the melody coming back on itself, hypnotic. The oil heats and the smell intensifies, becoming resinous, clean. Steam rises like the kitchen is making prayers of its own.

We fill the muslin sachets together. My hands brush Lyla's, Lyla's brush Colette's, Colette's brush Petal's. The motion becomes rhythmic, meditative. Pass the bowl. Fill. Pass again. The sachets grow heavy with protection, with intention, with the weight of our combined need.

"What walks in dark, stays dark," I say. "What loves us, stay near. Light for the living, silence for the dead. Let the old wounds sleep and the new day come clean."

Lyla sews each sachet closed with the binding cord, her needle flashing in the light. Nine stitches each—three times three. A trinity of trinities. Her hands quake hard when she finishes and I cover them with my own.

Colette anoints each sachet with the oil, making a simple cross on the muslin. Her lips move in prayer, then she ties the remaining cord around each sachet's neck. Three knots, firm and final.

Prone to wander, Lord, I feel it Prone to leave the God I love

Seven sachets laid in a circle on the white cloth. One for each of us. One for each person walking into whatever's waiting.

We join hands around them. The words come from all of us, layered, overlapping, our voices finding harmony without trying:

"Protect these bearers as they cross from the light. Let them pass through danger and return. Let them walk in darkness and not be consumed. Let the threshold know them: These are claimed. These are guarded. These are loved. Let the earth remember. Let stone recognize stone. What is rooted cannot be easily torn away."

The words aren't from any book. They come from the place where devotion and desperate hope and geological certainty all meet and become the same thing.

Colette's song is done. She's tired and leans against the counter. Blue crescents lay under her eyes and I realize we all must look that way. The kitchen is quiet except for the small clinks of the copper pot cooling, the last of the steam dissipating. Our hands are stained. Colette's eyes are wet. Lyla's breathing is uneven. Petal stares at the sachets like she's trying to understand them as data and failing, which means they're working.

The sachets sit on the white cloth like vows made physical —the only answer we know how to give when someone we care about is about to walk into darkness. We all know the truth without saying it.

It won't be enough.

But we make it anyway.

Because making it matters—our hands working together. Because speaking protection into being is what women have always done when the men go to sharpen the knives and prepare for violence we pray won't come but know probably will.

I pick up the sachet meant for Martin. It's warm from the oil, rough from the herbs, heavy with all the things we've bound inside it. I close my hand around it and feel the weight of what we're asking it to do.

Keep him safe. Keep us all safe. Let us cross through and come back.

Simple asks. Impossible asks.

The only asks that matter.

Outside, I hear the sound of metal on metal—the men at their own preparations. And beyond that, just at the edge of hearing, is the coo of a dove. I run to the door, letting the screen slam behind me, searching tree to tree. I finally spot him roosting on top of Nox's shed.

"Lyla," I call out. And she comes to my side. "You see that?" I say, pointing. And she says she does.

"That's Dad."

He rustles his feathers and flies over our heads, diving deep behind the house and over the stream.

33

I spot the white dove perched just beyond Nox's blessing, watching us with eyes that are almost human. Each coo rises and falls like a remnant of Dad's voice: the same slow, careful cadence he used when lecturing me about not wandering too far away, or when laughing quietly at my insistence on having the last word.

Lyla gasps, her hands covering her mouth. "He's back," she whispers.

"He was with Martin's mother when she came to me at the archive," I say.

Lyla's chest starts to heave and she folds her hands together, doing everything she can to hold back tears.

"You remember that pawpaw in the yard with the crooked trunk?" she says.

It was hard to forget—oblong leaves draped over its branches like the tongues of some quiet, watchful creature, and heavy-hanging fruit. Dad's favorite tree. One he liked to sit under when he was dying. Said the fruit reminded him of big, beautiful breasts and he wanted to go out like a man—staring at them without apology.

"Some mornings that first year after he passed," Lyla says. "I'd see a white dove perched among the low branches. That was a year of non-stop rain, if you recall, and the collar rot took it. Brunie's boyfriend had to come by with his pick up truck and pull it out at the roots. Dove never came back after that and I couldn't figure out why that made me so sad."

I hated Lyla for months after she took down that tree.

"Ansel," Lyla calls out to him.

He flies to the next tree, further away, like he wants us to follow. He's past the blessing and Lyla and I look at one another. We don't need to say a thing. The man never steered us wrong and we're going.

The path beyond Nox's property slopes down through rhododendrons laden with late blooms, their leaves catching the midday sun. The dove moves ahead of us in easy stages, never rushing, just leading the way he always did when I was small and he wanted to show me something—a patch of wild strawberries, a bird's nest, the first frost on fallen leaves.

The air smells like earth and water and the last warmth of October. Everything is gold and amber, the trees dressed in their dying colors but still beautiful, still full of light. It's the kind of afternoon that makes you forget about endings, about what's waiting in the dark.

"I know where we're going," Lyla says after a while. "The hot spring. Haven't been there since..."

She doesn't need to finish. Since she and my mom went there together just weeks before they blew town. For years, there was a picture of them from that day stuck on our refrigerator. Two beautiful young women in white string bikinis. It was the only picture that had remained of my mom—I don't know what Lyla and Dad did with the rest. And now it was burned to ash.

The dove calls out a single bright note, like he's saying *yes, that's right, keep coming.* So we do.

"Not so fast, Ansel," Lyla says, minding her step as we navigate the tree roots.

We follow the creek where it narrows and turns, the water clear enough to see smooth stones on the bottom, the way light bends through the current. There's a peace here, a rightness. Whatever's been building at the hollow, it hasn't reached this place yet. Or maybe Dad's presence is keeping it at bay.

"We loved coming here," Lyla says. "Used to all the time, especially in winter if you can believe it. The hot water and cold air together make you feel alive."

The spring appears through a break in the laurel—steam rising from dark water, the smell of sulfur and minerals, the stone edges worn smooth by decades of use. The dove lands on a rock at the spring's edge and settles there, his white feathers radiant in the dappled light.

"This is where you took that picture," I say.

Lyla nods. "Your mom and me. Right here, that June."

The two of them smiling at someone holding a camera, the steam rising behind them like they were emerging from some primordial dream. Before either of them knew what was coming.

"Tell me about her." I realize it's the first time I've ever asked.

Lyla lets out a sweet, small groan, like she's got a stomach ache. She half-sits, half-leans onto a boulder and crosses her arms.

"Everything we ever had that ever meant anything—I mean besides each other—burned up in my house," she says to me. "Your dad's couch, all your art projects. There was one you painted of you and me and your mom and dad catching fireflies out in the yard. There was all this motion in it and the fireflies were everywhere, and you even painted a full moon. But you didn't give us any faces and I asked you why and you know what you said?"

I shake my head.

"That you were an artist and that was your vision." Lyla closes her eyes and giggles.

"I don't remember that."

"You don't remember much about anything before she left."

We're quiet for a few moments, listening to the spring hiss and bubble.

"Your mom thought that was so funny—the no faces, all that. But even as she was laughing, I could see there was something wrong in her eyes."

"She didn't leave long after that. Maybe it was my painting that finally did it."

"Stop it," Lyla says. "Your mother loved you so much it scared her. She didn't trust people. Not your dad, not even me. Always expected to be turned on, let down, left."

I can relate to that.

"Her family was a mess," Lyla continues. "Sometimes I even thought them having died was the best thing that could've happened, and I know that's a terrible thing to say. Almost seemed like they'd been asking for it. But you wouldn't know it on the outside. They were charming and powerful and selfish as this spring is hot."

"They were certainly able to give away a child without blinking an eye." I picture Soma, all white hair and a face like a blue moon. "Made sure the whole ugly business was handled quietly."

"Well," Lyla says. "They threw great parties. And they sure knew how to punish you hard if you went against them."

"Is that what my mother did? Went against them?"

Lyla takes a deep breath. "No. Not once. I think they died before she could. She was little, after all."

I look right at the place where Lyla and my mother stood to have their picture taken. I try to imagine her here—Lavinia Bramwell with the dark honey hair and ghost-lit eyes. Just like me. But I can't. Not even her image from the photograph comes to mind, and it's like I'm looking at the painting Lyla described.

"Why did she leave?" I ask.

Lyla reaches out and takes my hand. "I don't know. When I look back, sometimes it seems so sudden and then other times I think I saw signs. For a long time I worried it was my fault."

"Lyla," I say.

"Look, she and your dad, as the years went on, they just didn't have much to say to each other," Lyla explains. "Your dad was fun and good lookin' and he loved her." Lyla shrugs and looks away.

"I guess she didn't love him."

"I guess not," Lyla whispers.

The dove looks down on us from the bare branch of a young dogwood. He makes no sounds, just stares at us, listening. The one thing that has always been branded onto my memory is how devastated my dad was after my mom left. Not wanting to fish for crawdads with me in the Rivanna, not wanting to go to the movies. His favorite whiskey sat untouched in the cupboard. He couldn't even be bothered to drown his sorrows in it. Went through his days like a walking corpse. Like I did after Beckett died. It took Lyla's persistent pursuit of joy to pull him out of it, make us anything like a family.

"She could've just left him and moved down the street," I say.

Lyla nods. "If there's one thing about Lavinia, she never did things half way. I have to think in her mind she thought you were better off without her."

A child is never better off without a mother who loves her, but I don't say that. Especially since Lyla took over as my mother and loved me so well it hurts. I haven't always made her feel that way.

"Hey, you want to get in?"

"No," I say. "It's chilly out. I'm not stripping down to nothing and walking back wet."

"Just our feet." Lyla slips off her clogs and orange woolen socks, then rolls her jeans up to her knees.

I follow, pulling off my boots and pushing Lyla's sweatpants up over my knee caps. We sit on the edge of the spring and go toes-first into the hot water. It burns, but it also feels so good I almost sing Hallelujah.

"Beulah used to bring me here on Sundays when I was a kid," Lyla says. "It was her thinking place. She'd sit right here and I'd wade in the shallows. Sometimes your mom came along. She'd wade deeper than I would, stay under until her skin turned pink."

"Sounds like something I would do," I say.

Lyla hooks her foot with mine and swings it in the hot water. "You look like her alright. But no, you and Lavinia are different. Where she goes silent, you go loud and hot."

I think of the way Martin and I went after each other and I'm not sure that's a compliment.

"You always fought for yourself, for the people you love," Lyla says, as if she heard what I was thinking. Then, it's like a curtain comes down over her face. "You don't just disappear."

I knew how badly my mother hurt Dad when she left, but I never saw until now how much she hurt Lyla. With a heart three times the size of most people's, Lyla set aside her own pain to make sure Dad and I came out alright. And here she was, someone who'd lost just as much as we did but never complained.

"I know how much you think about Beulah," I say.

A big smile slices across Lyla's face.

"Well, Beulah wasn't like other grandmothers. Not like your dad's, who made him marshmallow treats and took him to the train museum in Roanoke."

"You don't say," I tell her.

Lyla pokes me. "Beulah brewed teas and tinctures and told me stories, like a good moon witch. Thinking I'd take over as archivist. She spent a lot of her time writing things down, and encouraging me to do the same." Lyla shoots me a look that suggests Beulah and I would've gotten along great. "Your mother used to tease her about it. Called her 'the keeper of everyone's business.'"

"Were they close? My mom and Beulah."

Lyla nods. She picks up a round, flat stone and turns it over in her palm. For a while we just sit there, feet moving together in the mineral heat, steam rising between us.

"I said terrible things to you," I say finally. "After Beckett died."

Lyla's quiet.

"The way you'd come looking for me in the middle of the night. Shoo away the nightcrawlers I was using to show myself the worst possible time. I hated you for that. Said you weren't my mother and to stop trying to be." My throat tightens up. "That you weren't anything to me."

"You were hurting," Lyla says softly.

"That's no excuse." I watch the steam curl off the water. "You just kept coming back. I didn't even recognize the girl I saw in the mirror anymore, but you still did."

Lyla squeezes my foot with hers underwater. She leans over and kisses my shoulder. "You were never that person you thought you were. Not to me."

The dove makes a low sound in his throat.

"Your mother was different after Beulah died," Lyla sighs. "She'd disappear for hours. Come back with dirt under her nails, scratches on her arms. I'd find her standing in the yard at three in the morning just staring at nothing."

"Did she say where she went?"

Lyla shakes her head. "Once I followed her. She walked all the way to where her family's house had burned. Just stood there in the middle of nothing—only some old ash and char left. I watched her from the tree line for maybe an hour, waiting for her to do something, anything. She never moved. Didn't cry, didn't swat away the mosquitos. Just stood there like she was waiting for something to crawl up out of the ground."

My skin on my neck pinches. "Is that why you convinced her to leave?"

Lyla's quiet for a long moment. "I told myself I was protecting both of us. That if we stayed, whatever took Beulah and my parents and her family would take us, too." She takes her feet out of the water and rolls her jeans back down. "But maybe I just couldn't stand watching her disappear piece by piece."

"You think leaving helped?"

"For a while." Lyla reaches for her clogs. "And then she left anyway. Left you and your dad. And I've spent twenty years wondering if I made it worse. If by running, I just gave whatever was chasing her a longer road to catch up."

The dove shifts on his branch. Rustles his wings to get our attention.

"Seems like Ansel wants us to get going," Lyla says.

We follow the dove along the path back to Nox's. Spider silk catches the light like thread from another world. The rhododendrons sway as we pass, their leaves glinting darkly. The path that felt so peaceful on the way down now seems different. Like the trees are paying attention in a way they weren't before.

"You smell that?" Lyla asks.

I do. Something faint and bitter underneath the earth and water smell.

"Probably just someone's chimney," I say, but neither of us believes it.

The dove lands on a low branch ahead, waiting. When we catch up, he flies to the next tree, then the next, leading us back toward Nox's property the way he led us away from it.

Lyla stops suddenly. "Twi. Look."

At the base of a sweetgum tree, there's a scattering of dead insects—dozens of them. Beetles, mostly, and some kind of wasp with papery wings. They're arranged in a rough circle, like something passed through and they all dropped at once.

"That's not right," Lyla whispers.

We keep walking, and there are more. A cluster of dead moths clinging to bark. A pile of cicada husks that look fresh, not like the ones that litter the ground all summer. Even a few dead honeybees, their bodies still golden.

Lyla crouches near a fallen log where more insects lie scattered. She doesn't touch them. "Something passed through," she says quietly. "Something that takes life and leaves nothing behind."

The dove calls out—sharp and insistent.

"Come on," I say, taking Lyla's hand. "Let's get inside the blessing."

We walk faster, not quite running but close. The insects keep appearing—in the leaf litter, on stones, clinging to bark. Some of them are still twitching.

When we finally see the chainlink fence that marks Nox's property line, the blessed salt still glittering along its base, I feel my chest loosen. The dove is already perched on the roof of the cabin, white against the afternoon sky.

We step across the threshold together, and Lyla looks back at the path we took.

"You think it was following us?" I say.

"Or maybe it was looking for something." She meets my eyes. "And didn't find it yet."

Lyla starts humming something low and lilting—one of her blessing chants. Trying to reinforce whatever protection Nox has already laid down.

The dove watches from the roof, unblinking.

The cellar doors are open, angled back against the grass like broken wings. I can hear the ring of metal on metal coming from below, and smell wood smoke and hot steel. I walk over and look down into the dim space.

Nox and Wickham have their heads together, their backs to me. Several rifles are strewn around them.

And Martin is there, Nox's t-shirt clinging to his skin. He's kneeling over a worn whetstone set on a workbench. He drags a knife along the surface in a steady, deliberate rhythm, the edge singing against the stone. The scent of forge-fire, wet iron and sweat hangs sharp enough to taste. His hands are sure and unhurried, the muscles in his forearms coiling with each stroke.

After the mineral softness of the spring, this is all edges.

He looks up as he finishes, because he smelled me, of course. He comes to me, wiping his hands on a rag.

"The blade only becomes sharp when it meets resistance," he says. "Everything else is just waiting."

"I'm through with waiting," I say.

34

I don't wait for words. I cross to Martin and wrap my arms around him before either of us can speak. He's soaked with sweat, his shirt clinging to his back, but I press my face against his chest anyway, breathing him in, listening to his heartbeat. His hands hover—uncertain, still dirty from the whetstone.

"Go ahead," I say into the brine of his skin. "We got a lot dirtier than this running around in the wilderness together."

His hands don't just settle on my back—they take me in. Pull me into that quiet space beneath his chin, where the world always feels a little less cursed. His palms are rough from the whetstone, gritty with metal dust, and they leave a trail of texture as they move over my spine.

I press my face harder into his chest, and his arms tighten in response. Not the gentle embrace of this morning, but the desperate grip of someone who's stropping weapons because he knows what's coming. We stand like this while the afternoon light slants down on us. I can hear Lyla humming her blessing chant somewhere from the house. The dove cooing from the roof. "You said what we did was nothing," I say. "The fight. You said 'this is nothing.'"

His hands settle harder against me.

"What did we fight about before July 14th, 1976?"

Martin doesn't say anything right away, and I just ride the swell of his chest as he breathes. Then his hands move up to cradle my head, tipping my face back so he can look at me. There's ash smudged on his cheekbone and his eyes have that predator's shine they get when the wolf is close to the surface.

"Come with me," he says, pulling back but keeping hold of my hand.

I glance toward where Nox and Wickham are still working near the root cellar—the ring of metal on metal, Wickham's gravelly voice saying something about balance. Too close for the conversation we need to have.

Martin leads me across the yard to Nox's shed. The door isn't locked—nothing here is, really. He opens it and we step inside, into Nox's private sanctuary. It's a liberty, but I think Nox would understand.

The shed smells like old paper and tobacco smoke that's seeped into everything over years. A single lamp casts warm light over books stacked on the floor, crammed into shelves carved directly into the walls. Above us, a topographical map of the region is pasted to the ceiling, its contour lines like a fingerprint of the mountains. This is where Nox comes to think, to read, to be alone with the knowledge he's spent decades gathering.

Martin closes the door. The space shrinks around us, intimate and close. There's barely room for both of us without touching.

I scan the shelves and spot them—Martin's books. The whole collection. His historical fiction novels with their weathered spines, their companion non-fiction works on the real Appalachian history that inspired them. I'd read them all before I ever came to Sibyl Springs. Before I knew the author was not only the man who ran my department, but had been my whole world.

"Nox has first editions," I say, touching one of the spines.

"Nox is thorough about the things that matter to him." Martin leans against the small wooden bench, watching me.

I pull out the novel about the French trapper in the Virginia wilderness. Then its companion. It had changed how I thought about historical fiction, about myself and my poetry. How I thought about everything. "You said you wrote this for me."

"I wrote all of them for you." His voice is quiet. "Every story. Every word. They were all ways of talking to you when you weren't there."

I turn to face him. The shed is so small our knees almost touch. "We can talk now. Really talk. No enforced secrets."

"I know."

He takes the books out of my hands and sets them down. Then he takes me into his arms again. We're quiet for a moment. "We fought because there was nothing to fight about," he finally says.

I pull back to look at his face. "That doesn't make sense."

"It makes perfect sense," he says. "We were following our laws, and my mother made sure to remind us of that obligation. We both understood why you couldn't tell me things. Why I had to live with not even knowing your family name, when you were born, where you were coming from. Or what dangers you knew awaited us."

"So what was there to fight about?" I ask.

"Nothing. Everything." He exhales slowly. "We'd be fine for years sometimes. And then the frustration would surface."

"And there was no one to blame."

"No one to blame," he agrees. "You were following the law. I was upholding it. But we'd still get angry. Not at each other. At the situation. At the impossibility of it."

Makes sense, and gives me a pretty good visual of just how ugly those fights might have been.

"We'd tear into each other because there was nowhere else for it to go." His forehead drops to mine. "No villain to punish. No rule to break. Just this constant low-grade tension that had no resolution."

"We could have just had more sex."

His whole being quakes with laughter and I love the feel of it. "We did that, too. Most of the time it worked."

"The fighting. The violence" I say. "It must have felt like the only time we could be completely honest with each other."

Martin takes the curve of my ear between his fingers, rubbing it softly.

"After, we'd hold each other. And for a little while, the tension would be gone. We could just be." His other hand traces my spine. "I hated it. And needed it."

"I hated that I liked it," I say. "It was like a muscle memory."

"Always came back. Just as it did today. Because the situation never changed. You were still traveling. We were still bound by law." His voice drops. "Until that one July, when you disappeared."

I let that sit between us. Forty-nine years of him waiting. Not knowing if I'd chosen to leave or been taken from him. I place my head on his chest again, feeling his heart thrum against my cheek, hearing his blood rush through his veins. Books pressing in around us, words surround us on every side. Words are who we are.

I tip my head up to look at him and put my hands to his face, kissing him softly. "I never want to do that again."

"I'm not sure it's that simple. We're not people."

The words just sit between us. I think about my mother standing in the ashes of her family's house. Silent. How she left without a word, just disappeared. About Grace, displaced through time. About Soma, five years old and making covenants she didn't understand.

"I'm not asking for simple. I'm asking you to promise me we will never do that again."

His arms lock tighter around me. He doesn't promise. Can't promise, maybe. He knows us better than I do. But he holds me like he means to try.

I burrow my face into the hollow of his neck like a little animal. Feels good though. We stand like that in Nox's shed surrounded by books and maps. Fragments of our history, a story he tried to tell me even though he had no idea where I was.

My eyes flit to the little window and stay there. Outside, the sky has turned dark, though it's too early for twilight. It's the dark of a thundercloud, not a setting sun.

"Martin," I say.

He looks out the window, his eyes narrowing at the sight. Then takes my hand and leads me outside. Nox and Wickham, Lyla, Colette and Petal have all gathered near the gate of Nox's chainlink fence.

Above us, hundreds of crows are circling, swirling into a mass, then breaking apart. Starting all over again, like they're trying to tell us something. The dove stands on Nox's rooftop, spreading his wings and stomping his feet.

Thunder bellows like a cucked god. A lash of lightning splits the storm-clouds, striking the crown of the mountain. It's late in the season for this kind of storm. A wintry wind knifes past us and heavy pellets of hail begin to fall, skittering across the ground. The rain comes slow at first—drop by drop—then suddenly, the sky opens all at once.

"Run," Nox shouts over the thunder.

35

Nox goes still in the center of his cabin, head tilted like he's listening to something the rest of us can't hear. We're all dripping from the storm—Lyla wringing out her hair, Wickham shaking the water out of his jacket. Colette and Petal are at the window watching lightning fork across Nightvale Mountain, and Martin's hand is on my back tapping lightly on my ribcage. The hail hammers the tin roof like buckshot.

But Nox isn't moving.

"Son of a bitch," he says quietly. I follow his gaze to the window above the sink.

The blessed salt he scattered along the sill this morning has started to darken. Not much. Just a shade or two, like tarnish creeping across silver.

Lyla stops wringing her hair, water still dripping. Her eyes find me across the room. "Twi—," she says.

Nox is already moving to the door, peering through the small window at the yard beyond. The incense burners hanging from the eaves are swinging wild in the wind, their chains screaming. But it's not the wind that has his attention.

It's what the wind is carrying.

The blessed salt scattered along the chainlink fence is changing color, too. Darkening in patches, like something is testing it. Tasting it. Looking for a way through.

"How long has it been raining?" Martin asks. His voice is carefully neutral, but he squeezes me closer.

Petal checks her watch. "Four minutes."

"Feels longer," Wickham says.

It does. The air in the cabin has gotten thick, harder to breathe. The lamp on Nox's table flickers once, twice, then steadies. Thunder rolls through the hollow, so deep I feel it in my chest.

"Uncle Silas?" Colette has left the window, moved closer to the center of the room. "What are we looking at?"

He lights a cigarette, taking a deep drag and letting it out slow.

"She's here," he says. "And she brought the weather with her."

The lamp flickers again. This time it doesn't steady.

"I don't feel her," I say. "I can't hear her."

The witch usually talks to me, taunts me when she comes this close. She likes my full attention.

"She's not talking to you," Martin says. "She's talking to the protections."

As if to prove his point, something above us begins battering against the roof. Wings—frantic, desperate. The sound of a bird throwing itself against an invisible barrier again and again.

A familiar torque twists inside me. That's Dad. He's trying to get through to warn us, and something won't let him.

"No," I whisper, moving toward the door. Martin holds me in place.

"Twila—"

"That's my father."

"I know." His voice is gentle but firm. "And he'd want you to stay inside."

The wings slam against the barrier again. And again. The sound of it—bones cracking, the wet thud of impact—makes me want to scream.

"We have to help him," I say.

"We can't." Martin pulls me closer. "Whatever breaks through those protections first, that's what she'll use. If we open that door—"

The sound stops.

Not gradually. Just stops, mid-flight. Then a slide down the tin roof and a thump onto the porch.

Small. Final.

My knees want to give way but Martin won't let me fall.

"He was already gone," Lyla says softly from behind me. "Twi, he was already gone. She just—she took what was left."

I know she's right. But it doesn't matter. That was Dad. Or the piece of him that stayed. And now there's nothing.

The temperature drops all at once, like someone opened a freezer door. Our breath starts to fog.

"The weapons," Wickham says. "We left them in the root cellar. Three blades. The iron we were working."

Martin's mouth sets firm. "Can't get to them now."

"She won't want the weapons anyway," Nox says.

Then we hear it. Not from outside, but *inside* the cabin. A faint scratching sound, like fingernails on wood. It's coming from the corner near Nox's bookshelf.

No. Not scratching. *Crawling.*

Black smoke, barely visible in the dim light, seeping up through the floorboards between the books. Not rising like normal smoke—creeping. Seeking.

"The pendant," Nox says. His voice is sharp as flint. "Where did I—"

He's already moving to the pantry where he keeps his dried

herbs. He pulls out the basket, kicking it down the galley kitchen, bundles and sachets of herbs spilling out all over the place, a mason jar rolling down the hardwood. Nox grabs it off the floor and opens it, throwing the lid down, then shaking the contents onto the cafe table. Something falls out with a clang, along with the dark bundles of blessed thistle, rue and white oak ash.

The herbs have turned black. Not just dark—burned through, like they'd been holding back fire.

And beneath them, ordinary as a river stone, is the pendant. It doesn't light. Doesn't pulse. It just sits there, wood and leather cord, looking exactly like the one Lyla made for me. The one at the bottom of Hallow Lake.

"Don't touch it," Martin says.

But the smoke has already found it. The black tendrils coil around the burnt up herbs, wrapping around the pendant like they're greeting an old friend.

"She made it to look like mine," Lyla whispers. "To get it past the protections. Past us."

The smoke begins to spread, flowing along the shelf, down the wall. Moving with purpose now. Looking for something.

Looking for the real protections. The ones Nox built. The blessed salt, the iron, the prayers carved into the doorframe.

Everywhere the smoke touches, the protections corrupt. The salt blackens. The iron rusts. The carved words in the wood start to smoke.

"She's turning it all against us," Petal says. "Everything blessed, she's feeding on it."

The smoke reaches the door. The wood grain darkens, spreads like rot. The hinges begin to weep rust.

Outside, something thuds against the cabin wall. Once. Twice. Not the dove this time—something heavier. The sound of it feeding.

Martin steps forward. "Nox. Destroy it. Now."

Nox grabs the pendant from the table top with his bare hand. His face contorts—it's burning him, I can smell flesh searing—but he doesn't drop it. He carries it to the stone tiles around his wood stove, slams it down on them, and brings his boot down hard.

The pendant shatters.

For a heartbeat, nothing happens.

Then smoke pours out from the fragments themselves. Silver-grey, dense as mercury, and so much of it. It floods the floor, climbing the walls, reaching for the ceiling. And every tendril, every curl of it, bends toward one person.

Lyla.

Not me. Not Martin or Colette or Nox. Just Lyla.

The wild-child me, the one at the Luna Archive. I remember what she said: *And that bitch Soma killed Daddy with her stupid covenant. Ate his brain. She'll kill Lyla, too. You just wait.*

"Martin!" I cry out.

"Get back," he says, pulling Lyla behind him. But the smoke doesn't care about his body between them. It flows around him like water around stone, wrapping around Lyla's ankles, climbing.

Colette starts speaking rapidly—a binding spell—but the smoke doesn't slow.

Martin grabs one of Nox's journals and tries to sweep the pendant fragments into the woodstove, but the smoke is too fast. It wraps around his wrist, and where it touches, the skin goes grey. He jerks back with a hiss.

That's when I feel it...a *knowing.*

It starts small—the weight of the smoke's connection to the pendant fragments, how they're bound not by proximity but by purpose. Then it expands. The pendant to the witch's will, anchored somewhere beyond the veil, threaded through time and intention.

But it doesn't stop there.

It keeps expanding. I feel the registry beneath it all—not as a book or a record, but as the living fabric of what *is*. Every binding, every covenant, every moment where magic touched this place and left its mark. Millions of years of it, compressed and singing, the mountain itself remembering when it was ocean floor, when the first moon witches walked between worlds and named the connections they found.

And then even that falls away.

I'm seeing through something vaster. Something that holds the smoke and the witch and the registry and the mountains and me—all of it—in the same eternal moment. The atoms that make up Lyla's body, the air thinning as it reaches toward space, the pull of the moon on tides and blood and magic, the slow burn of stars that died before these mountains rose. Everything connected. Everything known. Everything held in a single, incomprehensible awareness that I'm touching for one impossible heartbeat.

God's sight. God's knowing bestowed upon me.

And in that knowing, I see what can be shifted. Not the smoke itself—that's just a symptom. But what holds it here. The weight that makes it real.

Martin makes a sound. Something between pain and awe. His hand on my back goes rigid, fingers digging into my ribs like he's trying to hold me—or hold himself—in place. Through our bond, through whatever cosmic architecture makes him my anchor, he's experiencing what I'm experiencing. The vastness. The terrible, beautiful clarity.

But where I'm reaching toward it, he's *grounding* it. Keeping me tethered to my body, to this moment, to the cabin and the smoke and the people I love. Without him, I'd dissolve into that knowing. Become it. Lose myself entirely.

I don't need to speak. Just... *know it differently*.

And when I do, the smoke that was seeking Lyla seeks

something else instead. The storm. The wind outside. Back toward its own source.

The tendrils wrapped around Lyla's legs uncoil, drift toward the window and vanish.

That's when I fracture.

The cosmic knowing I was holding—it's too much for someone still broken by the covenant. The split widens, the crack running deeper through me. Like the covenant seizing its chance, using the strain to tear me further apart.

The knowing collapses back into my small, human mind. My certainty wavers. The weight I was holding slips from my grasp.

Martin's grip on me falters at the same instant. He staggers, catching himself against the wall. His breath comes ragged, like he's been running. Or drowning. His eyes when they meet mine are wild.

He's never seen me do this. Not in all the years he's known me. And he felt it. Every atom of it—felt me split wider while trying to hold power I'm not whole enough to contain.

Martin catches me as my knees buckle, but he's shaking too. "What did you just do?" His voice is rough, barely steady.

I can't answer. Don't have words for it. I only know that I held the architecture of reality itself and, for one impossible instant, was able to shift it.

And the covenant used that moment to break me further.

"The registry isn't just our history," I whisper. It's the membrane between divine knowing and material existence. And I touched it while still fractured.

The damage spreads like cracks in ice.

And the witch felt it too. I know she did.

Outside, the storm goes silent, mid-thunder. The hail ceases. The wind dies.

The worst kind of silence.

Then we hear it. From every direction at once.

Breathing.

Slow. Steady. Patient.

The witch isn't testing the protections anymore.

She's already inside.

36

T he first sign is the salt.

It's hissing, dissolving, turning the windowsill fragile as char. There's a sound like water hitting a hot pan, but there's no steam—just a kind of shimmer in the air above it, as thick as the blur of heat waves rising from summer asphalt. Until the wood is grey, crumbling, like a weeks-old corpse.

Martin pulls me away from the window. "Don't breathe it."

But it's not just the window. The salt Nox scattered this morning—along every threshold, every corner, the protective circle he laid so carefully—all of it is dissolving. Breaking down into something fine as dust, lifting into the air. The cabin fills with it, particles that catch in our throats and make our eyes burn.

Lyla starts coughing. Colette pulls her shirt up over her mouth and nose.

"The iron," Nox says. He's looking at the woodstove, at the poker Martin gave Wickham. The metal is changing color—a deep rust-brown that spreads like infection. Where Wickham grips it, his palm starts to blister. He drops it with a curse.

The hinges on the door weep the same rust. The nails in the floorboards. Every piece of blessed iron in the cabin is corrupting, turning against us.

And the words. The prayers Nox carved into the doorframe years ago—I watch them begin to char from the inside out. The wood around them warps, then sinks into darkness. One of the beams overhead groans.

"We have to get out," Petal says. She's backed toward the center of the room, away from the walls. "This whole place is—"

The beam groans again. Splinters.

Martin's already at the door, yanking it open, one arm sweeping me and the rest of the women toward it. Nox grabs his walking stick—plain wood, no blessings—and follows. Wickham shakes out his burned hand, and we spill out onto the porch, gasping in air that tastes like metal and rot.

The silence outside is worse than the dissolving salt.

No wind. No night sounds. Just our breathing and the creak of rusted chains where the incense burners used to hang. They've fallen, corroded through, lying in the dirt like broken bones.

The moon is full overhead—we should be strong, Martin and I and any moon witch blessed by this light. But I feel hollowed out, and Martin's moving like his bones ache.

The yard is dark except for moonlight on the chainlink fence. The blessed salt along it has turned to that same grey dust, drifting in small eddies though there's no breeze. And just beyond where Nox's property line ends, shapes are moving in the tree line. More solid than phantoms, but not by much.

On the porch, in a small circle of scattered white feathers, is Dad's body.

The dove. Still and broken and small.

My throat closes. That was him. The last piece that stayed. And she fed on it, consumed it, used it up like kindling.

Lyla has stopped at the edge of the porch. She's looking at the fence line, at the shapes moving just beyond it.

One of them steps forward into the moonlight.

It's tall. Almost human-shaped. But it's made of everything that was meant to protect us—the grey dust of blessed salt pulling itself into something like skin, rusted iron curving into ribs that stretch into an impossibly long spine, the ash of burned prayers making the suggestion of a face. The protections Nox built, turned inside out. Made into something that breathes.

It takes another step toward the fence. Toward us.

Toward Lyla.

And that's when the words come.

They rise up from the place Twila-the-poet and Twila-the-witch and Twila-who-touched-God's-knowing meet. From the registry itself, maybe. From love witnessed and made real.

By the old roads where we walked as children, by the sourwood bloom, the morning kitchen, by Lyla's hands that bound my wounds — by the registry's remembering— she is held.

The air around Lyla shifts—a subtle weight, as if the atmosphere itself has grown denser, more present. Like reality has decided to pay attention.

The shadow-thing stops. Its reaching arm—if that's what it is—pulls back slightly.

Martin has moved to stand beside me, close enough that I can feel the heat of him. He's watching the shadow-thing with the absolute focus of a predator, and I know he felt the words work.

But there are more shapes moving beyond the fence. And inside the cabin behind us, I hear another beam crack and fall.

The space between heartbeats stretches.

It feels like the space itself has been replaced with something that won't hold me. The porch beneath my feet loses substance and Martin's hand on my arm feels distant, as if he's reaching through fog.

A clearing appears around me without transition. Silver-white trees, smooth as bone. Air thick with sweetness that's started to turn. And at the center, something still and reflective that wants me to look.

I'm wearing the nightgown with the torn hem—a little mermaid embroidered at the top. My hands are small.

You remember this, something says. Something that lives in every cell of my body.

I do remember. Being here before. Being this young. The fractured me like a constant scream I'd learned not to hear, and this place offering silence.

I can make you whole.

The pool at the clearing's center shows my reflection—but unified. Complete. One girl with no split running through her, no missing pieces, no forgetting.

All I have to do is go to it.

My feet move without permission. Toward the pool, the promise. A melody rises—soft at first, like a lullaby remembered through water. But it isn't a lullaby. It twists mid-phrase into something raw and keening, the echo of a song my mother used to play. Sinéad O'Connor's sorrowing voice threads through the air and moves through me like a hand guiding me forward.

Behind me, someone is shouting—far away and frantic.

But I came here alone. I'm always alone when I travel. Dad doesn't know. Lyla doesn't know. I slip between worlds in my sleep and no one can follow.

Be free of the breaking.

The breaking. That's what it feels like—active breaking, day after day, the covenant working to split me until there's nothing continuous left. No memory that holds. No self that stays.

I could end it. Just kneel at the pool's edge. Just fall in and say yes.

But then a thunderclap of warmth in this cold place— hands on my shoulders, spinning me around. He's a stranger. Tall, dark-haired, eyes full of terror I don't understand. His mouth is moving, saying something, but I don't know this man. Don't know why he's touching me.

The smell of forge-smoke hits me before the sound of his voice.

"Twila," he says. "You're here. You *came back.*"

The pool behind me whispers: *He's lying. You're still there. Still small. Still broken. I can heal you. He can't.*

But the man's hands are so strong. His fear is real.

Martin.

The name unlocks something truer than memory. A recognition in my heart and soul. Of a young man who found me in the veil after I'd spent years traveling alone. Dabbling in time— a little here, a little there. He made the dangerous places safe, so that I could stay. With him.

"She's doing this," I say. "The witch. She's—"

"Using the covenant." His hands move to my face. "Weaponizing the fracture, over and over."

The clearing is still there, transparent over Nox's yard. The pool still promising wholeness. And I understand.

Someone else stood here once. Someone broken and desperate. Someone who said *yes* to the offer I refused.

It was the witch who hunts us now. Who feeds on protections and devours what's blessed. Who's been trying to pull me after her since I arrived in Sibyl Springs.

She crossed over. Traded her soul. And it didn't heal her—it hollowed her out until only hunger remained.

But I had Lyla. And Dad. I had the stubborn animal knowledge that staying fractured in the human world was better than wholeness alone in the veil.

And I had Martin, once he found me. Had a reason to keep choosing to return.

She didn't have that anchor. Or she did, once, and lost it. Lost whoever mattered enough to keep her tethered to humanity.

I close my eyes. Open them. The clearing is fading. Nox's yard solidifies under my feet.

"I'm here," I say. The sweat beats along my forehead, trickling down.

Martin's hands still hold my face. "Can you keep going?"

The shadow-things have multiplied. Four now, maybe five, pressing against the fence line. One has its attention fixed on Lyla, patient and hungry.

I look at them—at everything the witch has made from blessed things turned poison—and I think about being young and tender and saying no.

About choosing a fractured life because somewhere in it was love worth staying for.

"Yes," I say. "I can keep going."

The shapes beyond the fence are getting braver. Stepping closer. Testing the boundary where Nox's protections used to hold.

"The root cellar," Petal says. She's already moving, pulling Colette with her. "It's not blessed. Let's hope she can't corrupt what isn't sacred."

As we run, the yard feels longer than it should, the distance stretching. Behind us, that terrible breathing sound is getting louder.

The root cellar is open—left that way when the men came up for the storm. We disappear down the steps into earth-smell and darkness. The place swallows us. The forge coals burn dull red, barely enough light to see by. Above us, Wickham slams the doors shut, and for a moment there's nothing but our ragged breathing and the booming of my own pulse in my ears.

Then silence.

Real silence. The kind I haven't heard since the storm started. No breathing in the walls, no pressure against my skull. Just the smell of clay and ash and our own fear-sweat. Colette sags against the dirt wall. Petal's hands are quaking as she touches the earthen ceiling, tracing it like it can tell her something.

"I don't think they can see us," she says. "This space was never blessed. To them, it doesn't exist."

I still can't stop watching the steps. Some animal part of me expects those things to pour down any second. But the quiet holds. We're invisible here, wrapped in unholy ground.

Wickham flexes his burned hand. The blisters are already shrinking, new skin forming pink across his palm. He catches me looking and shrugs. "Heals fast," he says. "One of the perks."

Nox is at his workbench, running his hands over the three blades they were making. The metal has cooled to black, absorbing what little light the coals give off. He picks one up, tests its weight, sets it down again. Like he's already imagining what comes next.

Martin crouches near the forge, studying the arrangement of tools and half-finished weapons. After a moment, he speaks without looking up.

"My mother told me about a witch once. Eleventh century. Her anchor was killed while she was traveling beyond the veil." His voice is quiet, barely more than a whisper. "She fractured, too. Not as completely—there was no Gemini Covenant involved. But without him to ground her, she came back like a cracked mirror. Every attempt to unify her failed. Eventually she couldn't hold herself together long enough to speak her own name."

He looks up at me then. The forge-light catches in his eyes. I look away.

Lyla slides down the wall next to Colette and Petal, until

she's sitting on the packed dirt floor. Her arms are wrapped around her knees, and she's staring at the small circle of light from the forge like she can read the future in it.

I lower myself down beside her. The earth is damp through my sweats. Solid. Real.

"I keep seeing Ansel's feathers," she says. "On the porch. How small they were."

I don't know what to say to that. So I don't say anything. Just let my shoulder rest against hers.

Above us, something heavy drags across the yard. The sound is muffled through earth and wood, but it's there. Searching. We all go still, listening to it move in circles above our heads, trying to find where we went. Petal's right. It can't see the cellar. Can't perceive the space we're hiding in.

But it knows we're somewhere.

The dragging stops. Starts again. Closer this time.

Nox picks up one of the blades. Wickham moves ahead of him to stand between the steps and Lyla. Martin rises from his crouch, every line of his body coiled and ready.

The thing above us stops moving. Right over the cellar doors.

I count my heartbeats. One. Two. Three. Four. One of the doors creaks open. The cellar seems to shrink around us, the air filling with dread.

A shadow-thing tumbles down the steps—just *falling* through space it can't see. Its form is barely holding together, pieces of corrupted salt and rusted iron and ash all trying to move as one body but failing. It hits the bottom step and sprawls, formless limbs flailing.

Petal backs away. But the creature's arm—or what passes for one—sweeps out blind, catching her across the ribs. Where it touches, the fabric of her shirt goes grey and starts to crumble like burned paper.

Nox grabs Petal's shoulders, yanking her back. But the thing is still thrashing, and its other limb catches him across the collarbone. His skin goes white under the torn flannel, bloodless. The white spreads from where the creature grazed him, creeping outward.

Death spreading. Everything it touches dies.

The creature is blocking the steps. Our only way out. And it's panicking—that's what the thrashing is, I realize. It's lost and blind and lashing out at space it can't understand.

The words rise up again in the only language I have that might reach through corruption.

Iron forged in the unblessed dark, earth that holds no prayer— I name what you were before she hollowed you, before she fed.

My voice drops off, the last word slipping from my tongue and into the dark.

The corrupted protections that form the creature's body begin to separate—peeling away like bark from a lightning-struck tree. The grey dust falls in drifts. The rusted iron ribs crack and drop, clattering against dirt.

And underneath—

God help us.

Underneath is what the witch made.

Human proportions, barely. Limbs and torso and the shape of a skull. But the skin is translucent as wet silk, stretched too tight over bones that curve wrong, almost like the bones of a jackal. I can see *through* it—can see the organs moving inside, dark and pulsing, threaded with something black that flows like oil through the veins.

The face has been worn down to essentials. Eyes that still work. A mouth that still moves.

It reaches toward us with hands that are more bone than flesh, fingers curling and uncurling in a rhythm that speaks of a perverted hymn.

Its mouth forms the words around no tongue at all, *Help me.*

It remembers how to beg, that's the worst part. This thing

that was hunting us, that's spreading death through Nox's body right now—it wants our help.

Nox turns away, one hand pressed to his mouth. Petal gasps with horror, pulling him closer.

The creature takes another step forward on legs that barely hold it, those translucent hands still reaching. Sounds that are infant and animal guttering from its throat.

Martin moves past me, swiping one of the black blades from Nox's workbench. He crosses to where the creature stands, and in one fluid motion pins it to the earthen wall.

The blade goes through its chest—through the filmy skin, between the visible ribs, straight into the dark pulsing thing that might be a heart. I can see the metal pierce through, watch it embed in the packed dirt behind.

The creature's mouth opens. Relief crosses what's left of its face.

It goes still, and the black threads running through its veins stop moving. As we watch, the skin begins to dissolve—into something finer than dust.

In seconds, there's nothing left but the blade stuck in the wall and a faint shimmer in the air where the body was.

Then the scream comes.

From everywhere—from the air itself, from the earthen walls, clattering inside our skeletons. The sound a soul makes when it finally breaks free. It's beautiful in the way lightning is beautiful, in the way anything that fierce and pure and *final* is beautiful.

The scream rises and rises—then cuts off.

The silence after is worse. Because now we can hear what's above us.

Scraping. Dragging. The weight of bodies pressing against wood. Converging on the cellar from every direction. The things have found us—the scream called them here like a bell rung in a cemetery.

The doors burst open.

They pour down the steps—five, six, seven of them—their forms more solid now, purposeful. The unblessed space doesn't hide us anymore. There's death in here, fresh death, and they can sense it.

Martin pulls the blade from the wall, and turns to face the stairs. Wickham has one of the other blades. Colette is pulling Lyla behind her. Petal is on her knees next to Nox, whose collarbone has gone white, the death creeping down toward his heart like frost over glass.

The first shadow reaches the bottom step. Then another and another. They know exactly where we are.

Martin puts himself between them and me, but there are too many. They're surrounding us, cutting off any path to the stairs, and the cellar is too small, too tight—

And that's when the breathing starts again.

From something bigger than the creatures. Something vast and cut from evil.

The earth walls of the cellar grow true black, swallowing any light. And through that darkness, a shape begins to form.

Made of the witch's will itself.

The darkness inhales.

And breathes my name.

37

F or a moment, nothing.

Just that voice made of breath and darkness, my name hanging in the cellar like the last note of a funeral hymn.

Then the blackness seeping through the walls begins to recede. Not all at once—slowly, like ink being drawn back into a pen.

The creatures blocking the stairs shift. They pull back, one by one—unspooling, flowing back through the cellar doors in a formless stream, drawn by something outside we can't see.

One by one they retreat. The stairs empty.

Martin's hand is still on my arm, his grip tight enough to bruise. Neither of us moves. Above us, through the open cellar doors, I can see a slice of night sky. The fat curve of the moon is swollen and alert.

"She's toying with us," Wickham says.

Petal is pressed against the far wall, one hand splayed on Nox's chest. The white spreading through his collarbone has stopped—thank God—frozen at the base of his throat. He's still breathing. Colette goes to them and kneels at her uncle's side.

Lyla stands near the forge, staring at the stairs.

"She left," Petal whispers.

Martin shakes his head once. Sharp. "Or she wants us to think she did."

But the breathing is gone. The witch's presence—that suffocating weight of her will pressing down on everything—it's lifted. We're alone in the cellar with nothing but the dying forge coals and our own fear.

I look at Lyla. Her face is grey in the emberlight, but when our eyes meet, I see my own dread reflected back: Why pull away when she had us cornered?

"We need to see what's out there," I say.

Martin's fingers tighten on my arm. For a moment I think he's going to argue, tell me to stay put, that it's too dangerous. But he just looks at me—really looks, like he's weighing something—then lets go.

I climb the stairs with Martin a half-step behind me. Wickham follows. The night air hits my face as I emerge, cool and clean after the earthy closeness of the cellar. The moon hangs low, full to bursting, drenching everything in that silver brightness that makes beauty feel like a warning.

"There," Martin says quietly.

At the tree line, where Nox's property meets the forest, the creatures are gathered. A dozen of them, maybe more, their forms barely holding together—pieces of corrupted salt and rust and ash rippling in the moonlight.

They're standing there at the forest's edge.

Lingering.

And beyond them, in the darkness between trees, I see other shapes. The Others, still half-caught between worlds, pressing against the veil like faces behind warped glass.

As we watch, the first creature drifts toward them.

Martin's hand finds mine. I squeeze it so hard I fear my

fingers might seize. Wickham moves ahead of us, his steps measured, heavy with grace and misgiving.

Colette—she emerges from the cellar, then stumbles backward with a gasp. "I'll be damned," she says. "They weren't just stories."

The shadow-creatures drift toward the tree line. Barely holding form—corrupted salt and rust and ash flowing like spilled oil across dark water. At the forest's edge, the Others wait.

They're just like they were in my dream. Floating in black water at Hallow Lake, pale shapes moving beneath the surface like fluttering moths. Tonight there's no lake between us. The veil has torn wide open and they're standing at the tree line with flesh I can see in moonlight.

Their mouths are sewn shut. Silver thread catches the moon's bone-white chill, pulled so tight through their lips that some have split at the corners. Black blood seeps from where the stitches tear flesh. Their eyes are worse than haunted. Open and aware, they track our movement with the patience of things that are damned for eternity anyway. No need to rush.

But it's that slow movement of their bodies that makes my gut twist. Brings bile up to the back of my throat. Their limbs taper in ways no living bone ever did, and their skin is the color you only see on things kept too long in the dark. The white of absence. Misremembered. As if someone tried to rebuild a person from memory and got it wrong.

And there's an almost-lovely familiarity threaded through their ruin. It's in the slight bow of my grandfather's lip—just like the picture I found of him in the 1970s retrospective of The Montague Hotel. The Bramwell eyes, the delicate shoulders of our women. Broken echoes of people who should have been left in peace.

The first shadow-creature touches the nearest Other, and

something like reverence moves through them—an instinctive stillness, terrible in its acceptance.

The Other's sternum loosens, unwinding like a secret finally told. Its chest opens in a soft, dreadful bloom—thin layers spreading to reveal an inner darkness with weight and grain. A darkness that listens.

The shadow-creature leans close, almost tender, and pours itself in.

The sound is unbearable, a low harmonic of anguish vibrating through marrow. Its sewn mouth strains as if trying to sing or pray or warn, silver stitches trembling, the threads catching the moonlight like thin, shaking stars.

I grip Martin's hand tighter and he pulls me in close. I can hear his breath swell with a desire to do something—anything —but there's nothing to do but watch.

And the merging—God. It looks like worship. Violation. Two wounds choosing each other.

The Other's skin ripples, then begins to absorb the thing the way wet earth drinks a storm—slow at first, then all at once. The flesh shimmers, stretched too thin, lit from within by something frantic. You can see the creature's darkness unfurling through the body like sorrow finding its way home through blood.

When the wound finally seals, the skin is slick, glistening, as if the world has just birthed something it regrets.

Something meant to be lost, yet here it stands—reborn in grief, sealed in hunger, eyes blank as unlit moons.

Another creature merges—that wet, grinding, almost-human sound of two bodies becoming one.

Then another.

The Others thicken with each joining, taking on weight, gravity, consequence.

I can see the architecture of their bones now—the ridge of a collarbone, the careful curve of ribs shifting beneath the quiet machinery of tendons working as they swallow what has taken them.

The last shadow-creature merges. The final Other solidifies. And then—they step into the yard.

They move with a hideous elegance, as if they've studied us from a distance—memorized the cadence of joints, the hush of a footfall—and then imitated it with too much care. Every step is smooth, unhindered by doubt or breath. They advance in a quiet formation, their stitched mouths working against their own silence, twitching against their bindings, threads catching the moon's cold gleam like jewelry worn for burial.

The one nearest has borrowed the suggestion of a girl's face. The pieces almost reconcile—cheeks, lips, the graceful slope of a nose—but the proportions hover just beyond human.

She looks at me. Eyes black to the rim, and beneath the surface something moves, slow and viscous, a fresh wound bleeding beneath luminous scars.

When she speaks, her stitched mouth doesn't open. The silver threads hold. But I hear her voice anyway—coming from somewhere deeper than her throat. From the place where the shadow-creature merged.

"*Belov'd.*"

The consonants clipped by the stitches, the word leaking through in broken pieces.

I reach for my voice, my magic—where the moon's language makes words my blood taught me to shape. It's there, coiled and waiting, but unreliable. It surges when the moon is full on my skin and recedes when I need it most. Right now, I can't summon it.

"Back up," Martin says quietly. His voice has changed—rougher, his wolfen self coming through to the surface. "Slowly."

But Wickham is already going forward, and the Others are spreading across the yard like a slow flood.

The one with the girl's face reaches for him, to touch his cheek, trace the bones beneath his skin to see if she remembers them.

"Wickham," Martin says, low. Warning.

Wickham leans back, but it's too late. Her hand finds his wrist and he stiffens.

"Son of the mountain," she says. "You smell of old forest."

He keeps listening, and it's like she's saying something only he can hear.

"Stop," he says. Quiet and sad.

But she keeps touching him, her fingers spread across his pulse point. Dark threads crawl up his forearm, toward his shoulder.

"All these centuries," she says, her sewn mouth barely moving. "Alpha instincts in a runt's bones."

Wickham tries to pull away and can't. So, he leans forward, closer.

"At least I'm alive," he whispers to her. "I have a soul. A face that's my own and not stolen from corpses."

She squeezes his wrist and I hear the bone break into pieces. Wickham's breath hitches from pain but he won't give that thing the satisfaction of crying out. In fact, he smiles. But the corruption is spreading faster, reaching his shoulder. I can see it beneath his shirt—black veins climbing like roots through his chest.

Martin reaches for him but another one steps between them. A man, or the echo of one. He stops close enough their chests almost touch.

Martin goes rigid. Like he can't move. The thing's chest splits open the way the shadow-creatures merged—that vertical seam parting, darkness inside with depth and motion, something circling in there.

He wants to take Martin inside. And no—that's not going to happen.

I shove myself between them, my hands connecting with its chest. The cold hits me like something awful. Punches through my ribs, floods my lungs. And beneath that—it's like touching a well that goes down forever, pulling at something deep inside me that wants to fall.

But the thing, the Other, stumbles back. I must've done something.

Martin yanks me behind him. "Don't touch them."

The Other rights himself. Tilts his head. His stitched mouth strains, gleaming at the corners where the threads have cut through.

Now he reaches for me, but Martin drags me with him toward the cellar. He throws me down next to the open doors, from which Petal emerges. She's got a knife and a sickle. She ducks back inside, then comes up again with one of the rifles.

Martin takes the sickle and hurls it at the Other. It sinks into its chest, dark fluid streaming, but absorbs into it.

Behind him, two more drift closer. One veers toward Colette. They're surrounding us—patient, methodical figures moving like water finding its level.

I try to shape words, find the poem that will unmake them.

"You who were—"

The words splinter into pieces that don't fit together.

"Beloved of—stitched from—"

Nothing. I can't even name what they are. Can't find the metaphor that holds. They're too distorted, too profoundly wrong—assembled from pieces that shouldn't exist in the same body, the same world, the same breath of air.

My words recoil from my tongue, and I'm speechless. The full moon glares down at me. But all I feel is a wild, useless panic.

An Other approaches me, his hand reaching for my throat. I grab the knife Petal dropped—still lying by the cellar entrance —and thrust it into the creature's black eye.

"Something pure," I say, and I don't even know to whom. Martin, Colette, God maybe.

Something they can't twist or poison.

I grab the rough edge of the cellar doorframe and drag my forearm across it. Hard. The wood splinters and my skin tears —a gash that opens deep and immediate. Blood wells up, running hot down to my wrist.

The Other stops moving toward me as I raise my arm. I fling the blood at it and finally, the thing recoils. I begin to walk the perimeter.

"The Lord is my shepherd," I say. "I shall not want."

The creatures stop and Martin turns around.

Colette holds out her arm to him without a word. He immediately drags his thumbnail across her forearm with sharp precision. Her skin parts and blood flows.

She joins me, dripping her blood, pressing her wound to her chest, walking the other direction to complete the circle.

"He maketh me to lie down in green pastures."

Our blood hits the earth, knitting into the soil, creating a sacred seal. I feel it in my bones—a boundary forming, a line being drawn between here and not-here.

"He leadeth me beside the still waters."

Wickham tears free from the girl's grip. He stumbles, clutching his shattered wrist, but he joins us inside the circle.

"He restoreth my soul."

The Others follow our movement but they don't cross the blood-line. They just watch with those patient black eyes.

"Yea, though I walk through the valley of the shadow of death, I will fear no evil."

Colette and I meet where we started. We press our bleeding forearms together, sealing the circle.

"For thou art with me."

The air thickens—pressure building behind my eardrums.

"Thy rod and thy staff, they comfort me."

The Others keep outside. All of them. Silent at the edge of our blood boundary. The man-thing's chest slowly closes, sealing the darkness inside.

"Surely goodness and mercy shall follow me all the days of my life."

Their sewn mouths work soundlessly. Threads catching moonlight.

"And I will dwell in the house of the Lord forever."

Silence. The Others stand at the boundary. Barely moving.

Wickham sinks to his knees, cradling his wounded arm. The black veins are already receding—moonlight pulling the corruption back out through his skin. Colette kneels beside him, keeping vigil while the moon does its work.

Martin's hand finds the space between my shoulder blades. He presses his palm there—solid, warm, real. Anchoring me to something that isn't corrupted or distorted or sewn together wrong. I lean back into that touch and feel his fingers spread, taking more of my weight.

We stand like that. My blood still dripping from the gash on my forearm. We're protected by blood and scripture—the simplest, purest defense. The only thing they can't unmake.

But we can't leave.

And they're not going anywhere.

The man-thing that tried to open its chest for Martin angles its head. Its eyes drag over us leisurely, before it looks past our shoulders—toward the cellar entrance.

Its stitched mouth strains against the threads.

Not trying to speak.

Smiling.

38

"Where's Lyla?"

Martin's voice cuts through the moment like a razor. We all freeze—me with Martin's palm pressed to my back, Petal carrying blankets down the cellar stairs, Wickham rotating his newly-healed wrist with Colette kneeling at his side. Nox leans against the doorframe. The white corruption spreading through his collarbone hasn't pulled back the way Wickham's did. He's human. The moonlight can't heal him.

Our eyes dart around the boundary, past the Others standing at the blood-line. At the cellar entrance. At the absence of the one person who should be there.

"Sweet St. Romedio," I say, and I swear my heart stops.

I push past Nox and take the cellar steps two at a time. The forge coals are dying, casting long specters against the walls. The air smells of cooling metal and old dirt.

Empty.

The word echoes in my skull but it doesn't make sense. Lyla was here. She was standing right by the forge, watching me climb those stairs to face the Others. I saw her. I looked at her and she looked back and there was fear in her eyes but also that steady thing that's always been there, that thing that says *I'm here, I've got you, you're not alone.*

"Lyla?" My voice sounds like it could break glass. "LYLA?"

The others crowd in behind me. I feel Martin's presence at my back, Colette moving to check the far wall, Wickham scanning the corners like there might be somewhere she could have gone.

But there's nowhere to go. The cellar is earth and stone and one way in.

"When—" I start, but I can't complete the question.

"Last I saw she was by the forge." Petal's voice is small. Frightened. "When I came back up with the weapons, she was—"

She doesn't finish. Doesn't need to. We were all just trying to survive.

I touch the wall where Lyla must have been standing. The dirt is cool and ordinary under my palm. Compressed, settled, and solid. The kind of wall that's been here since before Sibyl Springs had a name.

Except the witch walked through it.

Through unblessed ground. Through the one place we thought was safe because it had no protections to corrupt, no sanctified earth to turn against us. We hid here because this cellar was just dirt and stone and nothing that called on the Holy.

And that's exactly what made it perfect.

The witch didn't need to corrupt blessings. She just needed to walk through ground that had never been sealed against her.

"Oh God." The words come out barely a whisper.

But why Lyla?

The question sits in my chest like a word I'm afraid to speak. Lyla—she carried a magic so thin you could breathe right through it. My thoughts scatter like crumbs and I can't hold them together. Can't think past the raw panic of *she's gone she's gone she's gone.*

Martin's hand finds my shoulder. His grip is a tether through the dread pressing in from the cellar doorway. I glance around us. Wickham has moved to the far edge of our circle, as far from the Others as the boundary allows. His back to the cellar wall. Watching.

Outside, the Others are moving. Circling, but their steps make no sound on the earth. They're close enough that I can see the silver threads of their mouths twitching, straining against their stitched skin.

And the air turns as a whisper curls in my ear—Lyla's voice, high and trembling, calling from just beyond the line.

"Don't touch me...don't...no!"

My blood rushes through my veins so hard I can hear it. I lunge, starting to climb the stairs, and Martin grabs me, lifting me off them like I'm light as air. He presses me against the wall, his arm firm against my chest as I thrash against him.

"Didn't you hear that? It's Lyla!"

"No," he says.

I can still hear Lyla calling for help, her voice getting more distant, as if they're dragging her away. Martin presses hard against me, making it difficult for me to move at all. Then it starts. My ribcage feels too small as my heart knocks against it. My breath goes shallow, each inhale too short, each exhale a gasp that doesn't relieve. The world blurs, edges of walls and voids folding in on themselves. My fingers curl and uncurl like they have a will of their own and a cold sweat beads everywhere, slick and clammy. Every noise is too loud, every moment too long. I want to run and scream. I want it to stop. Oh, God, not now. Not when Lyla needs me.

"It's ok," Martin says, pressing harder, trying to keep my body from going full-on haywire. "Just breathe. One, two, three..."

I try to focus on the numbers, his voice, my breath. Anything but the vertigo of being trapped in a body that won't obey.

"Five, six, seven." He kisses my forehead. "Eight, nine."

"Nine," I say, and take my first real breath in what feels like an hour.

I start to slide down the wall and Martin goes with me, guiding me onto the ground, where I can sit, get a hold of myself again. Across from me, Nox is sitting, too. His hand is pressed to his throat. The white is at his jaw. I give him a faint smile, for hope I guess, and he nods, his eyes blinking so slowly it's like he's dragging himself up from some distant, dark place just to meet mine.

Colette shuffles past us. "Shh, listen," she says.

Outside, the Others' mimicry swells. Lyla's voice again, terrified, but twisted now, as if something beneath it hisses through the syllables. Then a thrum in time with Martin's heartbeat, but distorted. My own voice comes in frayed and broken—mocking me calling out for Lyla, for counting, saying the number nine.

My thoughts shift back to Lyla—her absence. And then the thought lands, terrible and precise.

"Corbin," I whisper. "Lyla's a Corbin."

Martin's eyes meet mine and I see the understanding dawn there too.

The panic has loosened enough now for anger to slip in, and my head spins with the cruel, elegant logic of it.

The witch didn't want me. Didn't need uncorrupted Bramwell blood to open the vault—any Bramwell could have done that. She needed the archivist line. The one family that's kept our secrets, chronicled our history.

Beulah Corbin put the registry in that vault before she died. And only Corbin blood can take it out again.

Lyla, who never wanted to be an archivist, who mangled the

registry and ran from Sibyl Springs swearing she'd never come back. Lyla's, whose blood is the only key that matters. And she's the last of her line.

Outside our boundary, the Others have gone quiet. Their mimicry has stopped. They just stand there in their circle, hovering.

Knowing they don't have to break the boundary, or chase us out of our safe haven. That's just for sport.

Because the witch already has what she came for.

And we're trapped in a circle of our own making with nowhere to go and no way to follow.

39

The moon hangs above the open cellar doors—white, swollen, unblinking. It hasn't moved in what feels like forever, just watching with that cold celestial judgment while the creatures press against our blood-boundary. Patient as saints. Hungry as wolves. Waiting for us to make one more mistake.

We're trapped by our own hands. By the blessing we whispered into the earth with scripture and blood, believing it would save us.

And Nox is dying.

My back rests against Martin's chest, his arms loose around me, like he's keeping my pieces from scattering. No more shaking. No more skeleton-teeth chatter. No more sweats. I hate that I broke like that—hate how it made him worry about me when we're running out of time and all hell could peel back our skins any second.

Across the cellar, Petal and Colette tend to Nox like they're nursing the last ember of a fire that's given up burning. They've tucked a blanket around him and drizzle water down his cheeks from the bottles the men brought when they forged our weapons. Good weapons. Terrible plan.

The white corruption has frozen at the base of his throat in delicate, dew-lit threads. Spiderwebs spun to eat him alive. Beautiful, if I were cruel enough to admire it. His breaths come uneven and expensive—each one costing him something he doesn't have much left of.

Petal leans close and murmurs jokes, movie lines, scraps of comfort meant to keep someone tethered to this world. It's the sort of kindness that breaks your heart because it changes nothing.

I start to push myself out of Martin's arms. "We can't stay here," I say. My voice steadier than my insides. "Every minute is another minute the witch has Lyla. Another minute she's closer to getting her hands on that registry."

The implications are too big to consider. She could erase me entirely. Build herself up into anything. Reshape the mountains if she wanted to.

Colette looks up from where she's been kneeling beside Nox, her face a smudge of fear and soil. "We can't just go out there and get swallowed by those ghouls."

"If I could do something else, I would've already done it!" The words come out mean. I'm so tired of feeling like a failed storm.

It's that same amber-trapped feeling I knew when Dad was dying and the doctors lowered their voices and said there was nothing left to try. When Beckett drowned and I spent years haunting his last moments, trying to imagine what it feels like to sink and sink, lungs screaming, world narrowing to cold and pressure and the gruesome clarity that this is how it ends.

My hands are fists. My nails cutting half-moons into my palms. That powerless rage—at the universe, at fate, at myself—for standing still while everything I love gets taken.

I'm not standing still anymore.

I turn away from the stairs to face them. Nox is slumped against the wall. His half-lidded eyes flutter open when I cross to him and take his hand.

"Jesus, Nox," I say. I want to promise we'll get him out of here, but I don't want to lie.

His grip surprises me—strong and urgent. He huffs a broken laugh, then pulls me down face to face. His breath is stale, vaguely fecal. The breath of a dying man. "Be dangerous," he says.

"You think I'm a kitty-cat?"

"I think you're too careful." His voice is barely a rasp. "You're not a kitten. You're the thing that eats kittens."

"You'll be quotable even on your deathbed, you know that?" I squeeze his hand, then stand. Kiss Colette's forehead, nod to Petal and Wickham.

Wickham's been sitting at the bottom of the stairs, watching the Others with an eerie, careful deliberation. He speaks without looking away. "I'll stay. If they breach the boundary, I can get at least one of you out."

Martin is already at the top step, waiting. Something passes between them—centuries compressed into a single nod.

I climb to him. We stand together looking out at the Others in their formation. Corrupted ancestors made of stolen pieces, waiting to see what we'll do.

"Climb onto my back," Martin says.

And I do.

His back is hot and steadier than anything in this godforsaken place. As he crouches, I lean forward, reaching toward the ground, toward that invisible seam where our blood sank into the dirt. The moment my fingers make contact I feel the resistance. The air has weight and opinion.

It resists me like a hand braced against my chest.

I say the first damned thing that comes to mind. It's a command. "Boundary of bone and light, bend once for me. Let the gate remember grace—that water flows before it freezes— and let us through."

I hope it worked. Martin's not waiting to find out. He rises beneath me and steps forward. Steps through. I feel a faint shudder. Now there's nothing between us and them.

The figures drift and sway—close enough to rewrite nightmares. Their faces shift with every blink, molding to the cankered bones beneath. They have the fragile beauty of a dying girl—too pale, too perfect, already fading. Worse. Because beneath their skin, things move—slow and purposeful, like smoke dragging its claws through water.

Martin adjusts his hold on my legs. "Stay with me," he whispers.

I tighten my arms around him. "Always."

The Others tilt their heads in perfect unison—same angle, same terrible synchronization.

Then they begin to weep.

Black fluid wells up in their eyes. Too thick for tears. Viscous like oil bleeding from a wound. It pools in the hollows beneath their eyes, gathering, swelling, until it spills over and runs down their stolen faces in slow, intentional streams.

"St. Romedio's ghost," I breathe.

The fluid is too dark and reflective. It's liquid despair— suffering made visible and physical. It drips from their chins in fat drops that hang in the air a beat too long before falling.

Where it hits the ground, the earth darkens.

Their stitched mouths begin to work—that gross, metrical sound intensifying into something manic. Desperate. The silver threads cut deeper into their lips with each movement, opening fresh wounds that leak the same black fluid. It mixes with what's pouring from their eyes, running down their throats, dripping from their chins.

They're drenched in it, staring right at us the entire time.

All of their eyes are locked on mine. Weeping and weeping.

Their gazes never wavering even as the black ruins the grotesque beauty of their features, turning them into masks of grief.

On the ground, the fluid hasn't just pooled—it's spread. Seeking. The dark stains reach outward like fingers, finding specific points in the earth. Making a pattern I can't quite see but can feel in my bones.

It's a pull. Deeper than physical. Like something reaching through my chest and wrapping around my spine. Martin goes rigid beneath me.

"Martin—"

The ground between us and them begins to bulge. Something is pressing up from underneath, testing the surface. Looking for a way through.

Then it splits.

A crack opens where the black fluid pooled deepest. Narrow at first, widening with a sound like tearing fabric. And from that crack comes a smell that punches straight through my gag reflex—opened graves and mineral rot, the specific stench of meat left in damp darkness. A funk so strong that it feels physical.

A hand pushes through the earth.

White. Fingers too long, joints bending backward. It presses flat against the ground for leverage, and then an arm follows—dragging something up from below.

Another crack splits open nearer to us. Another hand. This one so close I can see the dirt caked under its fingernails, see the waterlogged flesh, the way the bones show through in places where the skin has worn thin.

The Others keep weeping. Bleeding that black fluid onto ground that's opening like mouths. Every place the fluid touched is splitting open, and from each split—hands. Arms. Faces pushing up through the earth like corpses being birthed from the mountain itself.

"They're calling them from the bone hollows," Martin says. His voice has gone flat. Deadly.

One pulls itself fully from the ground maybe ten feet from us. It stands on legs that almost remember how to hold weight. Its head tilts—listening, adjusting, finding orientation. Then its sewn mouth begins moving in that same synchronized rhythm.

Joining the pulse. Adding its breath to the collective.

Two more emerge. Then three. Then I lose count because they're coming up everywhere now—dozens of pale figures dragging themselves through the cracks, shaking loose soil from their borrowed skins, tilting their heads at the same angle.

All of them staring at us with eyes that start to weep that same black fluid.

I'm hypnotized, can't tear my eyes away—but Martin waits no longer.

He takes off with me on his back, my arms locked around his neck, legs wrapped around his ribs. Moving as liquid and powerful as I've ever seen him. Devouring ground like prey.

Behind us, the earth keeps splitting. I chance a look back and wish I hadn't.

Dozens now. Maybe more. All following us with the kind of purposeful coordination that makes my stomach drop. The original Others remain standing where we left them. Still bleeding, calling more through.

They're not trying to catch us.

They're trying to *keep* us. Here. Running. Fighting an enemy designed to multiply faster than we can handle while the witch does her actual work unopposed. Every second we spend outrunning these things is another second she has Lyla alone in that vault.

St. Romedio's blood.

We're not escaping.

We're exactly where she wants us.

40

Martin and I are airborne.

He launches us over a ravine and suddenly there's nothing beneath us—just a sickening jolt of weightlessness, the wind whipping my face, water rushing black as pitch thirty feet below. The world drops out from under us. My arms clamp around his neck to keep our balance, and then the far bank rears up and hits. Hard. Martin absorbs the impact in one, brutal, unstoppable stride—his body already moving again before my lungs even remember how to breathe.

The forest streaks past in a smear of sourwood and oak, pepper-red leaves shivering loose in our wake. Mountain laurel tightens around the trail so thick it feels like the woods are trying to fold shut behind us. Martin's breath is ruthless economy—every exhale a clipped burst of effort.

I should drop down. Run with him. The moon is full and I can feel its pull in my bones, the old strength that let me chase him through these mountains when I traveled beyond the veil. But my magic could stutter mid-stride. Those things could separate us. Martin would have to choose between wherever he's taking us and coming back for me.

He'd come back. Of course he would.

And they'd take us both.

So I stay on him and watch our backs.

On our tails comes the slithering percussion of their pursuit. The sound of the earth opening and closing.

I twist to look. Figures weave between the trees maybe thirty feet back, faces catching moonlight, black fluid dripping from their mouths in steady, obscene streams. They pass through laurel and branch without disturbing either—sliding through the world like it's loosely held together.

Too many of them.

"Martin—"

He vaults a fallen hemlock, hits the downslope hard enough that the shock rattles my teeth. My arms cinch tighter around his neck as he steadies us, his hands shifting to lock across my thighs.

The terrain is getting worse. Steeper. Rocky outcroppings jut from the hillside like the antlered crown of a fallen forest king. Martin weighs speed against safety with every stride. He chooses speed.

The storm's aftermath opens up ahead—a chaos of wind-toppled giants, massive trunks lying across our path in a dead-fall maze. Martin doesn't slow. He jumps the first, lands on a second that shifts under his weight, then launches from it before it can roll. Branches snag and tear at us. Dead wood snaps and splinters beneath his feet.

We're through one section and into another, worse than the first. A hemlock lies shattered across our path, its root ball torn from the earth, leaving a crater of exposed stone and soil. Martin leaps it, lands hard on the far side.

His left foot catches on a hidden branch and for one breath —one split-second breath—we're going down.

Then he catches us, drives forward and keeps running.

Behind us, we hear the tearing sound of something crossing the deadfall. Reaching. Pulling itself through the tangle with arms that stretch too far.

"They're gaining," I say.

Martin's breathing is fraying, like there's a cost building in every one he takes. Even he has his limits, and carrying me up a mountain while being chased by things that don't tire is pushing him toward them.

Moonlight blades through the canopy in jagged stripes, and the forest stinks of leaf rot. But underneath is something else— the scent of opened earth and bone dust.

A branch snaps across my shoulder and I duck just in time.

One of the Others breaks from the group, closing the distance with movements that shouldn't be possible. The corrupted protections it absorbed have made it denser—I can see traces of ash and rust woven through its flesh. It's maybe fifteen feet behind us now. Close enough that I can see the silver threads cutting through its lips, the inky fluid on its face dried to a crust.

It lunges.

Then stops. Raises a single hand to its own throat and drags its fingers across the flesh there, opening itself. Fresh black fluid wells up, streaming down its chest and dripping onto the ground. Wherever it falls, the earth splits. Another hand begins to push through.

No. Not more.

I bring my wrist to my mouth and tear into the skin with my teeth—ripping through flesh—tasting copper and salt as blood swamps my tongue. I bend back in Martin's grip and spit it at the creature, then fling my torn wrist forward, blood spraying hot across the gap between us.

Where it strikes, the Other recoils. Jerking and clawing at

itself, its sewn mouth working frantically. My blood hisses and burns against its chest, creating a barrier it can't cross.

Martin doesn't waste the seconds I've bought us. He surges forward with everything he has. The ground levels out. Not much, but enough that Martin can increase his pace, eating up the remaining distance in long, powerful strides. He knows these mountains, has run them for centuries, has hunted and survived here long before there were towns or roads or names for anything.

I start to recognize the shape of the ridge, the way the rocks shoulder their way out of the slope. The sourwood thins, giving way to scrub pine and wind-flayed stone. The land feels barer here, stripped back to its true face. The outcropping. Our place.

Martin's muscles tremble beneath me. His breath is wrenching from him. But he doesn't slow.

A steep rock face rises ahead, nearly vertical. Martin attacks it, fingers finding cracks and ledges, pulling us both upward with strength that's pure will now. I press myself flat against his back, making myself as small as possible, feeling each muscle strain as he hauls our combined weight hand over hand.

His breath comes in harsh bursts against the stone. One handhold crumbles and for a terrible second we slip, but he catches us, drives upward, keeps climbing.

Behind us, more of that horrible synchronized sound. The wet working of stitched mouths. The cracks of branches below as they reach the base of the rock face.

Martin finds the top and hauls us over the edge onto the outcropping—age-old stone beneath a natural overhang. The place we came to not so long ago, when everything felt less desperate.

He sets me down, gripping my elbow until my balance steadies. Then he turns toward the darkness below.

The Others are there. At the base of the outcropping. Seven of them forming a loose semicircle, and behind them—dozens more emerging from the trees. All of them staring up at us like mourners at a hanging.

They just stand there, empty. Like they've shed everything but purpose.

Martin's breathing is harsh beside me. His shirt soaked through with sweat, his hands still shaking from exertion. But we're here. We made it.

And they can't follow.

Martin's been blessing this place for centuries. We both have, even if I don't remember doing it. Five hundred years of prayers and protection soaked into the rock. The Others can feel it—I can see it in the way they sway at the boundary, not even attempting the climb.

Martin straightens slowly, watching the figures below. His face unreadable.

"They'll wait," he says, voice scraped raw. "They have nothing but time."

I look at him—really look. See the exhaustion in the set of his shoulders, the flush high on his cheekbones, the way his chest still heaves with each breath.

And I know what comes next.

What I have to ask him to do.

What might be the last thing we ever do together.

41

Martin's eyes drop to my mouth, my chin, the blood I can taste drying on my lips. The wrist I tore open is already healing—moon witch flesh knitting itself back together—but the evidence is everywhere. On my face. My throat. Smeared across the front of my shirt.

He takes my wrist in his hand, turns it over. Studies the new skin, still red and inflamed. His thumb traces the line where I tore into myself.

Then he reaches up and wipes his thumb across my bottom lip. Slow. Gentle. Brings it to his own mouth and tastes it. His eyes don't leave mine.

"I figured if they can use their blood, I can use mine."

Something crosses his face. Pride, maybe. Or just an old understanding of what it means to survive by any means necessary. He wipes more blood from my chin, then my throat, using the cleanest part of his shirt.

"Dangerous," he says quietly.

"If only I had some kittens to eat."

His mouth threatens to smile. Then he gathers my hair back with both hands and presses his lips to the crown of my head with a tenderness that just about kills me. The kind of kiss someone gives you when they're trusting you with the last good thing they have.

When he pulls back, his hands linger.

My hand drops to my side—exhaustion pulling it down—and my fingers brush against a slight bulge in my pocket. The sachet. I'd forgotten it was there.

I pull it out. It's crumpled now, stained with sweat and dirt and my blood, but the herbs inside are still potent. I can smell them—rowan and vervain and iron, bound with prayers and the work of women's hands just hours ago.

"I kept thinking of that Hughes poem as I made it," I say. "About rivers. About knowing something ancient and deep."

Martin's quiet for a moment. Then: "I've known rivers ancient as the world and older than the flow of human blood in human veins. My soul has grown deep like the rivers.'"

He takes the sachet. Holds it in his palm—like it's a human heart, still beating. His thumb traces the rough stitching where Lyla closed it.

Then he tucks it inside his shirt, against his heart, and the gesture breaks something in me.

"Martin." My voice comes out barely above a whisper. "I need to go."

His hand stays against his chest where the sachet rests. For a moment he just looks at me, and I watch understanding settle into his features—the realization of what I'm asking, where I mean to go, what it will cost.

"Twila, we can find our way out of this. We've come this far—"

"The witch is already near the cave, with Lyla. We both know it." The words tumble out urgent, reckless. "I could go see your mother. The registry—it hasn't been hidden yet. It's still accessible, with one of Lyla's grandmothers. If I can talk to your mother, we can figure something out." I pause. "And then there's Grace."

He closes his eyes.

"I think the eclipse can act like a beacon," I continue. "And you were there when it happened. You can anchor me and help guide me—at least roughly to that time."

"Twila." He opens his eyes and the look in them stops my breath. "I'm there and here. And you—you're there, too."

The words hang between us. Then, from below, something shifts in the darkness—a sound like wind through dead leaves, but there is no wind. Martin's head turns toward the edge in that wolfen way that means he's listening to something I can't hear yet.

It's then that I do hear it. Voices rising—dozens of them calling up to me.

"Little moon, you always come home."

Cutting. Intimate. Like a lover's whisper turned threat. The words skitter at the edge of my memory—familiar, almost mine —but when I reach for them, there's nothing.

Martin's hand finds my wrist. "Don't look."

But I'm already moving to the edge. The Others wait at the base of the rock face. The one that slit its own throat stands apart from the rest, face tilted up toward me. Watching.

Martin pulls me back, holding me against his chest.

"I have to try," I say.

"You're fractured. What happens when the two versions of you meet? Do you think you can just—" He stops. "There's no precedent for this. Before you, the covenant hadn't been used in a thousand years, and it worked then. Worked the way it was supposed to. But you—you broke it somehow. You've been traveling beyond the veil most of your life and no one knows why. What happens when someone like you meets herself across time?"

"I guess I'll just have to avoid myself. I avoided myself for years before Sibyl Springs. Before you."

"Twila—"

I slide my hand inside his shirt, palm flat against the sachet and his heartbeat beneath.

"I lost you to the future once," he says. "And now you're asking me to lose you to the past."

"Ye of little faith," I say, tapping the sachet against his chest.

I lean in, press my mouth to where his heart pounds through skin and bone. He smells like smoke and dirt and us, and I take it in—all of it.

When I pull back, his hand comes up to my hair. Slides through it slowly, fingers catching on tangles. The moon bleeds white light over everything. My blood has gone tacky between us, drying into something permanent.

I tilt my face up to the moon. Its light pours into me—igniting. My body hums with it, an angel's choir in my veins, burning with the fire of divinity.

"Just talk to me," I whisper.

I touch his jaw, my thumb brushing a faint bruise of moonlight along his cheek. His eyes drop to my mouth.

"Don't," I say. "Save your kiss for when I come back—muddy, triumphant, and actually able to enjoy it."

Martin gives the smallest shake of his head. "No."

He lifts my hand and presses his mouth to that blue-veined place on the inside of my wrist. My heart gives one sharp, disloyal leap, almost making me rethink things. Then he leans in, and the kiss he gives me is barely a kiss at all—just a ghost of softness against my lips, feather-light, like he's afraid the wind might carry it off before I can feel it.

Sweet. Fully human. Something I'll be able to hold onto when the dark closes in.

He starts to speak. "The mountains were young then," he says.

"Not in the way geologists use the word, but in the way a man feels youth in his bones—when the ridges still held their breath between storms and the nights came down like a curtain, sudden and absolute."

He inhales, deep with memory. His eyes hold mine, dark and depthless.

"I remember those hills as my mother knew them," he says. "Before roads were cut into the shale and before the county men named every hollow as if they'd dug them from the earth. Back then the land carried its own names, the kind spoken by women who drank of the moon and spoke to the trees as if they were prophets. And the trees answered.

My mother was one of them. You are one of them. A moon witch. A nameless thing that can't be bound or summoned or claimed."

As he speaks, the present loosens. Colors run spare before they remake themselves. The mountains shift beneath me, shrugging off centuries, and the oaks grow younger in reverse —towering, then thinning, then becoming their ancestors. Moss brightens, even in the night. The soil darkens like the heavens.

The hollows realign into old shapes I didn't know I remembered. Stone pulls itself out of earth. Streams shrink into narrow threads, or become stronger. The moon widens, older, hung lower, closer, hungry. Then a shroud pulls across it, taking it from full to new.

The air smells green and iron-rich, wild enough to hurt. Martin's voice threads through it, steadying me.

"My mother lives where the ridge breaks into the open sky, three miles past the last spring, just below the granite outcrop that catches starlight like a blade. No one goes up there unless they are lost, desperate, or looking for her. Those three things often come together."

Stars rearrange to match an older sky. A silver haze coats the stones.

"My mother, a woman who wears the pelt of a wolf and whose skin is marked with the scratch of bramble and the burn of winter wind, until it isn't. Because each night it's made new. She walks out of the laurel thickets like she's stepped through the spine of the world.

And when you come close, you will feel the ground murmur beneath your feet. Until it speaks. The wind will carry the cold iron scent of the north-facing rock wall. Smoke from her hearth will filter through the moss chinking instead of rising. Bones on the lintel. Wolf tracks in the mud. Though she kept no animals. They kept her."

The ridge tilts into place and murmurs exactly as he says— the veil stitching the world into his memory's shape. It speaks to my bones in a language with no need of form or grammar. It speaks in the language of souls.

"The night feels sharper, because it is," he says. "Fears are buried because the mountain takes them, and sometimes spits them back out again. If you hear something moving in the dark that sounds too heavy to be wind—don't look for it. Walk steady.

The moonlight will thicken and catch in the air. It will coat the bark of the sourwoods. It will know you."

The laurel around me grows denser, a living wall. The leaves shine as if dipped in milk-light. Underfoot the mud goes hard and freezing. The air follows, biting into my skin. My breath curls out of my mouth in plumes of winter.

"Hold to my voice," Martin whispers. "Walk steady to the smoke, the ridge, through the quiet and the cold.

You'll find her by the world she shaped around herself."

I see the faint thread of smoke drifting sideways instead of up. Bones swing from a lintel that is forming even as I look. The hearth flickers through gaps between bare branches. The light clings to my skin like a coat, bracing me against the sharp, crisp air.

And when you see her, Twila—don't bow. Stand as her equal. She loved that about you."

His voice fades. The world holds.

Then a figure moves between two laurel trunks—slow, tall, wrapped in the pelt of a wolf that still seems to breathe around her shoulders.

"Daughter," she says. "You've come a long way."

EPILOGUE

To her eyes, the fire begins long before anything sparks.

It starts as a compression of the air around them —those three bodies caught in the Bramwell house like insects in amber. The man and woman in their thirties, their lives still bright in them, and an older man, white-haired, but with lightning still in his veins. She sees the heat before it forms flame, a shimmer around their ribs, an invisible hand closing.

When the blaze finally rises, it seems inevitable.

The witch watches as the fire takes them *from the inside out*. Their breath turns bright first. Each exhale blooms orange before the tongues of flame ever touch skin. The house groans —a long, wooden sob—as the walls surrender their structure. Smoke unspools in ribbons, twisting around the figures like something choosing which soul to taste first.

The younger woman folds inward, her silhouette bending like soft metal in a forge. The young man, her husband—he reaches for her like he hadn't spent their marriage scattering pieces of himself everywhere but home. His arm is already losing shape, pulling into threads of light. The old man—he burns slower, his body reluctant to give up its ghosts. His outline flickers between who he was and a charcoal sketch of himself.

And through it all, the witch sees the fire's terrible intimacy.

It licks at their faces with the tenderness of a new husband. It lifts their hair and makes it leap upward in bright, frantic strands. It paints their silhouettes huge and writhing across the collapsing walls—three figures dancing a last, unwilling reel.

The heat silences their voices before their mouths stop trying to make sound.

When they finally fall, it is not as bodies but as shapes unraveling, becoming the same drifting embers that flee upward through the beams and vanish into the night air. The house settles around them with a cracking sigh, relieved to finally give its dead back to whatever waits beyond the soot.

The witch watches until there is nothing left but the smoldering bones of the home, and the faintest echo of the lives that burned away inside it.

She should feel something, but she doesn't. The space where feeling lived is smooth now. Empty as a burned house.

She made sure they were gone before she came. The two-year-old and the grandmother—safe at the hot springs, far enough that the smoke won't reach them. Far enough that when morning comes, the child will return to find only ash.

Time isn't linear for travelers beyond the veil.

She is fifteen, standing in the tree line in 1979, watching them burn.

She is two, sleeping in Sophronia's arms miles away.

She is both. She is neither. She is the girl who will wake up tomorrow in 1992 to a life where her parents died in a fire when she was small. That she's the orphan, the tragic victim, the girl everyone pities instead of suspects.

In the original timeline, they lived. Neglectful and beautiful and utterly indifferent to the daughter they handed off like an unwanted inheritance. In that version, she grew up watching them through windows, wondering what she'd have to become for them to see her.

But the veil taught her something: the past can be rewritten. A girl can become the victim of a better tragedy. Trade the slow death of neglect for the clean grief of loss.

The murders don't create the witch. They just make the story simpler.

The last beam collapses. Sparks fountain upward, briefly illuminating her face. For just a moment, she looks exactly like the daughter she'll have someday. Honey hair, ghost-lit eyes, the same constellation of freckles.

Twila.

The name rises unbidden. She'll have a daughter. She'll love that daughter with a fierceness that scares her. And when that daughter is eight years old and sees what her mother has become, she'll make this same choice again.

Not with fire. With forgetting. She'll unmake the child's power, strip away her memories, split her from everything she was meant to be. Leave her small and mortal, a tiny flower growing in some unremarkable town, never knowing what she could have been.

The hunger is always stronger than the love.

But that's years away.

In a few hours, she'll awaken to a life where she's always been the orphaned girl, raised by Sophronia until she died, then shuffled to Lyla's family. Only now, she'll be the girl whose tragedy happened years ago, whose grief is old and settled and respectable.

Rewriting herself as a victim of fire instead of unwanted would quiet the gnawing hunger, would make her whole.

But when she wakes in her timeline, the hunger is still there. Deeper now. Colder.

Being the orphan means wearing the orphan's grief. Means

letting neighbors pat her hand and whisper about poor Lavinia while the truth of what she did sits in her belly, growing heavier with each sympathetic smile.

The ruins settle into coals. Behind her, the veil winks.

Spring 1979 fades.

And Lavinia—orphan, witch, mother-to-be—carries three deaths she'll never mourn and more waiting in the dark. One of those won't kill a body, but split a soul instead. Her daughter's.

That death is still waiting. But it's already inevitable.

The fire has already started.

It just hasn't reached the kindling yet.

THE END

COMING SOON...
NIGHT OF THE OTHERS

To retrieve the registry and save those she loves, Twila must travel to the past. There, she will become whole for the first time—and live the life with Martin that the fracturing stole from her. But the journey back may cost her that wholeness forever, and as an army of the undead rises from the bone hollows, she must face the witch who started it all.

Pre-order your copy on Amazon: Night of the Others

A HUMBLE REQUEST...

If you enjoyed *Night of the Mother*, please consider leaving a starred review on Amazon or the platform of your choice.

JOIN THE SPEAKEASY!

Speakeasy Editions is an independent publisher and purveyor of art and merch. We are your hosts to a party filled with dazzling secrets, yesterday's magic, and tomorrow's promise.

JOIN OUR COMMUNITY:

https://speakeasyeditions.com/pages/newsletter

Get exclusive offers, and be the first to know when new books and products become available.

SPEAKEASY
EDITIONS

ABOUT THE AUTHOR

Victoria Dougherty is the author of three acclaimed Cold War historical thrillers, THE BONE CHURCH, THE HUNGARIAN, and WELCOME TO THE HOTEL YALTA. Readers have called her epic historical fantasy series, including the novels BREATH, OF SAND AND BONE, and SAVAGE ISLAND, "breathtaking," "mesmerizing," and "genre-defying."

NIGHT OF THE MOON WITCH and NIGHT OF THE MOTHER are her latest works of fiction and her first foray into the world of witches and werewolves. But not her last.

Ms. Dougherty's blog—COLD (www.victoriadougherty. wordpress.com)—features her short essays on faith, family, love, and writing. WordPress, the blogging platform that hosts some 70 million blogs worldwide, has singled out COLD as one of the Top 50 Recommended Blogs by writers or about writing. For more personal essays and original short stories in the *Moon Witch* universe, follow Victoria on Substack: vdougherty.sub-stack.com

www.ingramcontent.com/pod-product-compliance
Lightning Source LLC
Chambersburg PA
CBHW021406110726
47901CB00008B/2073